Meg took her te [] [] half of it, standing up by the table. And then and there, as she was still swallowing it, she knew that there was something in the cup. She hadn't outwitted the Millers after all. There was something in the tea, and she had drunk about half of it.

At that moment when she knew herself to be standing on the very edge of disaster, the fear went out of her. She came upon something which she did not know she possessed—a hard, stubborn vein of courage which meant to go on, and to fight, and to go down fighting if it came to going down. There was no anger about it. It was cool, and tough, and strong.

Half—she had only had half the tea—and she must get rid of the other half—they must think she had drunk it—she mustn't faint. She bit her lip hard on the inside. Then she lifted the cup to her lips. Her hand felt heavy. She said, "This is a good cup of tea—"

DEAD
OR ALIVE

Also by Patricia Wentworth

THE CASE IS CLOSED
THE CLOCK STRIKES TWELVE
THE FINGERPRINT
GREY MASK
LONESOME ROAD
PILGRIM'S REST
THE WATERSPLASH
WICKED UNCLE
NOTHING VENTURE
BEGGAR'S CHOICE
OUTRAGEOUS FORTUNE
RUN!
MR. ZERO
THE LISTENING EYE

Published by
WARNER BOOKS

PATRICIA WENTWORTH

DEAD OR ALIVE

WARNER BOOKS

A Warner Communications Company

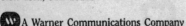

I

IT WAS THE MIDDLE OF OCTOBER WHEN BILL COVERDALE came back. One year in South America looking for a big engineering contract for his firm, and now home again. England felt very good after Chile. London felt good. The astonishingly fine summer still held. There was a blue sky, a clear sun, and a light breeze. He was going to see Meg O'Hara. Everything was very good indeed.

He was walking, because in town you had to get your exercise when you could, and also because now that he was really going to see Meg again, he wanted to get himself in hand and be sure of just how he was going to meet her. You can't be away for a year without a change in every relationship. Sometimes absence makes the heart grow fonder, and sometimes it doesn't. Mostly it doesn't. Growth, change, and development go on. If two people are in constant touch with one another, they adjust themselves to these changes instinctively, and often without realizing that there are any adjustments to be made. But a year is a long time to be away.

Bill Coverdale told himself all these things. He had loved Meg for so long that he did not believe that he would ever stop loving her, but when he left England Robin O'Hara was still alive. Now that Meg was a widow, there was change between them whether she herself had changed or not.

Change between them. . . . But just what sort of change? What was he going to be? Just the old friend of the next-door days in the country, when she was fifteen and he was twenty, and he had begun to love her? Or was there going to be a chance for him at last? He had stayed her friend because he would rather have Meg's friendship than any other woman's love. He had stayed her friend for ten years, and then she had married Robin O'Hara. That meant she was going to want a friend very badly some day. He wondered whether she had broken her heart when Robin died, or whether it had been broken before. Meg wouldn't let anyone know. She'd keep her head up whatever happened.

He walked up fifty stone steps and rang the bell of Meg's flat. He felt a kind of triumphant excitement because the year was over, and he was here, and Meg was free, and then a sudden black stab of fear lest, in the night since he had telephoned, something, anything, should have happened to set them apart again. And with that Meg opened the door.

All the things he had been thinking about went out of his head—change, fear, triumph, and Robin O'Hara—leaving just Meg, the most dearly familiar thing in all his world, the most settled, the most stable.

They came through a square yard of passage into the little sitting-room of the flat. The sun slanted in at the one window and showed how shabby everything was, but if the furniture and chintzes had been falling to bits, Bill wouldn't have noticed them, because he was looking at Meg. The trouble was that Meg was shabby too. He saw that. He had seen her pale often enough—far, far too often in the six months before he had gone away—and he had seen her tired, and had hated Robin O'Hara very fiercely, but he had never seen Meg shabby before. She had on a washed-out cotton frock. She was much thinner. There were dark shadows under her eyes. She was pale and she was tired. He loved her quite unbearably, but all he did was to hold her hand as if he had forgotten to let it go, and say,

"What have you been doing to yourself?"

It was Meg who pulled her hand away. She hadn't any intention of telling Bill what she had been doing. The last two years had been a nightmare, but when Bill was there she could wake up—not for long, not altogether, but just whilst he was there. Solid, darling old Bill. It was just as if he came crashing into the very middle of the bad dream and broke it round her. She took a long breath and said,

"Oh, Bill! Lovely to see you! And you're going to stay—you're not going out again?"

"No—I'm going to be here. My uncle's retiring, and I'm getting his place on the board."

"Oh Bill—how nice! And you're looking splendid. Did you like it out there?"

"Hated it like poison."

"Why?"

"I just did. England's good enough."

Meg laughed, her own old laugh. It made him love her terribly.

"Bill—how insular! I'd love to travel."

Bill put that away for future reference. He had an orderly mind. If Meg wanted to travel, she should. It was going to be his business to see that she got what she wanted. Always. He looked at her with a frown and said,

"You didn't answer my question. What have you been doing to yourself?"

It wasn't only his question. It is every man's question, and Meg gave him every woman's answer.

"Nothing."

She thought, quickly and bitterly, "Why do people always say that? You don't do these things to yourself."

Bill was frowning at her.

"You're pale."

"It's been very hot."

"You've got thin."

"It's the fashion to be thin."

Bill went on frowning.

"I don't like it."

Meg leaned back in the corner of the sofa. Her dark blue eyes held a sudden sparkle and there was a little colour in the cheeks that had been too pale for Bill's taste. What, after all, had it got to do with Bill? She said in her sweetest voice—and Meg's voice could be very sweet—

"I know, darling, I'm looking hideous. But need you rub it in?"

Bill relaxed into a grin.

"Now you're angry."

"Well, you *were* rubbing it in—weren't you?"

He was grave again, but not frowning now.

"Meg—won't you tell me what's the matter?"

Her colour died. The sparkle left her eyes.

"It's hot—I'm hard up—I've had to stay in town. I'm all right, Bill."

"You don't look all right. Why are you so hard up?"

"Nothing coming in. I had a job for a bit, but it petered out in July."

"I thought you'd come in for some money—you wrote and told me you had."

Meg laughed a little.

"Bill, that was really funny. It was old Cousin Felicia, and she left quite a lot to be divided up amongst her female cousins, but when they came to hunt them up, how many do you suppose there were? Fifty-six. So what I got wasn't worth writing out to you about, and anyhow I haven't got it yet." (And now he'll want to lend me money, and if I don't take it he'll be miserable, and if I do—)

The sparkle came back into Meg's eyes. You can borrow money when you've got it yourself, but if you haven't any—and no one but Meg knew just how little she had— why then you begin to lose things that money can't buy— pride, courage, and self-respect. Before Bill's tentative "Meg—" was well across his lips, she had shaken her head.

"Nothing doing, darling. But I'll lap up a job if you can find me one. I can type. I suppose your firm does have typists?"

Mr Coverdale was sharply revolted.

"But look here, Meg, what about the Professor? He can't know. Have you told him?"

"Darling Uncle Henry? Have you ever tried to talk to him

about money? Robin did when we were first married. He said it was perfectly ridiculous Uncle Henry having no relations but me and a flourishing banking account, and the two things being so to speak insulated. He thought it would be an awfully good idea for Uncle Henry to give me an allowance, and when I said I couldn't ask him he said he'd do it himself. Well, he did it quite beautifully. We were having tea in the garden, and honestly, Bill, I thought he was going to pull it off. He led up to it in his most charming manner, and Uncle Henry sat there beaming and drinking his tea. He liked Robin when he noticed him, and he is fond of me—he really is. But just when Robin thought it was all over except the 'Henry Postlethwaite' on the banker's order, Uncle Henry put his cup down three inches off the edge of the table and said, still with that pleased sort of smile and without noticing the crash, 'Yes, yes, my dear—and I think if you don't mind I will leave you to make a note of it. These trains of thought are very elusive, but Hoppenglocker will be bound to admit the force of this.' I took hold of his arm and I said, 'What are you doing to make a note of, darling?' He looked over the edge of his spectacles at me and said, "My reply to Hoppenglocker,—but I'm afraid you wouldn't understand it, my dear.' So then I said, 'Did you hear what Robin was saying just now?' and he shook his head and said, 'No—no—I'm afraid not. Some other time, Margaret,' and off he went. And Robin said he did it on purpose, but he didn't, you know—he's like that."

Bill sat large and immovable. Meg was trying to put him off, but it wasn't any use, he wasn't going to be put off. He would much rather help Meg himself, but the Professor was the proper person to do it. He was glad she had mentioned Robin, because Robin had got to be mentioned, but he wanted to straighten out this business about the Professor first. He just waited till she had finished and then asked what he had planned to ask.

"Have you written and told him you're hard up?"

Meg nodded.

"Yes, I did. He didn't answer the letter. Bill darling, what's the good of looking like that? He doesn't answer letters—he just doesn't—and he's in the middle of another book."

"Have you seen him?"

She shook her head.

"No. He's on his island. I told you he'd bought an island to write this book on, so that he could get right away and be quiet—no dogs, no motor horns, no nieces, no anything except a bird or two. You can't get away from birds."

The Professor appeared to be a wash-out, for the moment at any rate. But Bill was not prepared just to leave it at that. Even the most absent-minded professor on the most secluded island can be made to realize his responsibilities. Perseverance would probably be necessary, but perseverance was one of Bill's strong suits. The snag was that perseverance takes time, and meanwhile here was Meg looking as if she was living on buns and or whatever it was that women did live on when they were hard up. Something had got to be done about that here and now. He said abruptly,

"Meg, how much money have you got? Didn't Robin leave anything? His affairs must be settled up by now."

He thought Meg looked at him oddly. Then she looked away. Then she said,

"No—they're not settled."

"But the lawyers would advance you something."

She got up and went to the window. When she moved you could see how thin she was. The blue dress that had lost most of its colour made her look like a ghost. Meg used to look so pretty in blue. It wasn't only the dress that had lost its colour. She stood with her back to him, and the sun touched the ends of her dark hair with gold. She looked at the ugly houses opposite and felt her heart knock against her side. It would be better if Bill went away, but she couldn't make him go. She said with an effort,

"Bill—who told you about Robin?"

Bill Coverdale had turned in his chair and was watching her. He was wondering if she was broken-hearted about Robin O'Hara. It didn't seem possible, but you never could tell. She had married the fellow. He answered her with a puzzled note in his voice.

"Garratt wrote and told me."

"What did Colonel Garratt say?"

Quite impossible to tell Meg what Garratt had really said. Garratt didn't mince his words, and he didn't like O'Hara. A free translation was necessary.

"He said Robin had taken on a dangerous job, and when he didn't turn up, they were afraid something had happened. And then—"

"Go on."

Bill didn't go on.

"Please, Bill—I want to know what he said."

"Well, he said that a body had been found in the river, and that there wasn't any doubt—"

"And then you wrote to me. It was a very nice letter."

"You didn't answer it," said Bill Coverdale.

"And so you wrote again!"

"And you didn't answer that."

"I don't think Robin's dead," said Meg O'Hara.

II

AS SOON AS SHE HAD SPOKEN, MEG TURNED ROUND. SHE had said it, and saying it had broken something. It had been terribly hard to say. It had taken every bit of her strength, and now that it was said she felt weak and shaken. She came back to the sofa and sat down on it, leaning forward with her elbows on her knees and her chin in her hands.

Bill was looking at her in a shocked, incredulous manner.

"Meg, what do you mean? Garratt said there wasn't the slightest doubt."

Her mouth twitched a little. She made no reply.

"Garratt said his wallet was found in the river."

She said, "Yes—"

Bill got up and began to walk about the room.

"But what makes you think—Garratt said—"

Meg lifted her lids as if they were heavy, looked at him for a moment, and then looked down again. It was a hurting, wounding look. It set Bill a long way off, beside Garratt who talked about things of which he had no knowledge. Colonel Garratt, the efficient head of the Foreign Office Intelligence, might have been grimly amused. Bill Coverdale was sharply hurt, and, being hurt he was angry. He said, with the warmth of that anger in his voice,

"I'd better go—you don't want me!"

And with that Meg lifted her eyes again. The wounding look had gone. They were the eyes of a child afraid in the night. The blue of the iris was almost swamped. They were black with fear. If Bill went away and didn't come back, the nightmare would close down again. She put out her hand as if she would hold him. But there was no need for that. The fear in her eyes wiped his anger away. He took her hand and kissed it gently.

"Meg—what's the matter?" And his voice was gentle too.

Meg O'Hara drew a long breath.

"I thought he was dead—"

"And why don't you think so now?"

She said, "I'll tell you, but you must sit down. I want to tell you, Bill."

He had been holding her hand, and now he let it go and came back to the shabby armchair which faced the sofa. The pattern on the chintz had been a winding stem entwined with peonies and pomegranates. There had been little blue birds amongst the branching fruits, but the peonies were drab and the birds were grey, and all the colour and the bloom was gone. Meg sat there as colourless. The hand which he had kissed was in her lap. The other hand covered it in a straining grip. She said,

"I did write to you."

"I never got it."

"No—I tore it up. I wrote three letters. I tore them all up."

"Why?"

"I'm going to tell you. It isn't easy, but I can't go on—I must tell someone." She looked at him for a moment, a quick frightened look that glanced from his and was veiled by the down-dropped lids. She said, "It's so difficult," and her voice had an exhausted sound.

Bill held himself where he was. What had been happening whilst he was away? Whatever it was, he had got to know. He said,

"Meg, do tell me. What is there that's so difficult? if you mean you weren't happy with Robin, I knew that all along."

She took this with a kind of shock of relief. Then she drew a long breath and said,

"*Happy?*"

So it had been as bad as that. . . . His little Meg—his darling little Meg. . . . He was physically incapable of speaking for the moment, and Meg went on:

"I *can't* talk about it—but if I don't, you won't understand; besides, some of it must have been my fault. If I knew whether he was dead or not, it would be easier."

Bill sat there big and solid. He said in a rough, commonsense voice,

"I don't see what that's got to do with it. If he didn't treat you properly, he didn't."

Meg looked up for a moment.

"He didn't beat me—it wasn't anything like that. It was partly my fault. I'm stupid—it's easy to hurt me—" She stopped suddenly because she couldn't go on. By some horrible illusion it wasn't Bill sitting there, with his big frame, fair hair, and rugged features, but Robin O'Hara, dark and slim, with the air of charm which had stolen her heart and the bright cruelty which had broken it. The eyes smiled behind their black lashes—beautiful grey Irish eyes, looking at her as if he loved her, whilst he stabbed with bitter words. He had known just how to strip her of her defences and strike suddenly and deep. He had known how to betray her lightly with a kiss. But how could she tell Bill these things? She couldn't. With an effort she controlled the trembling of her body, but her mind shrank and all her thoughts were quivering with pain. She said in a small quiet voice,

"No, we weren't happy. Just at first—" Just at first she had been in a fool's paradise and had taken it for the truth. Just at first Robin had been the dream lover of the most beautiful dream in the world—just at first. . . . She went on as soon as she could. "It's difficult. He thought Uncle Henry would give me an allowance. I can see his point of view. I was living in the house—like a daughter—there was lots of money. He thought it would come to me—some of it at once, the rest later. I suppose it was natural if you didn't know Uncle Henry. When I told him, Uncle Henry would leave all his money for research work, and that that was all money meant to him, research, it—I think it was a most awful shock. I'd got so used to Uncle Henry's point of view that I never thought about it. I've tried awfully hard to be fair, and I think some of it was my fault because I didn't explain, and some of it was his because he took too much for granted."

Bill clenched his hands. Meg wouldn't talk if he let fly. If she didn't talk, he couldn't help her. But to sit there and hear her blame herself because that swine O'Hara had been a disappointed fortune-hunter took every bit of his self-control. He said,

"Go on."

If Meg looked at him—But she didn't. She looked down at her own clasped hands.

"It got worse and worse. I was stupid—I minded—too much. I hadn't anyone to talk to. Uncle Henry went off to his island. You went to South America. Then I told Robin I couldn't go on. I said I would divorce him—" Her voice just left off.

"When was that?" said Bill.

"This time last year, just before—Bill, it was the day before—"

"How did he take it?"

"I don't know."

He laughed.

She stopped, because Robin's laughter rang in her ears. He had seemed amused, and then there had been a sudden flare of anger—"You'll do nothing of the sort! Do you hear? When I want a divorce I'll let you know!" And then he had laughed again, and tipped up her chin and kissed her with a sort of hard mockery. Then, just at the door, he had turned and flung her his farewell. "Perhaps you'll be saved the trouble," he had said, and was gone. And that was the last touch and the last word she had had from Robin O'Hara.

She left the touch alone, but she told Bill about the words, her voice halting on the syllables and ceasing when she had said "trouble." It was trouble he had brought her, and it was the last of all the words that he had had for her.

After a time she said suddenly, "Letters kept coming for him. Then Colonel Garratt rang up. I said I didn't know where he was, and he said they didn't know either. I went to see him, and he asked me if Robin had told me what he was doing. I said no, he never talked about his work. Then Colonel Garratt said Robin's job wasn't a dangerous one, but he thought he'd been working a line of his own, and that it might have taken him up against very dangerous people. He said they would make inquiries. A week later they found his wallet in the river. It was quite empty. Colonel Garratt said I ought to be prepared—they thought something had happened to Robin. In December—there was a body—they thought—was his. I thought he was dead."

"Garratt wrote to me in December."

Grim details about an unrecognizable corpse had been Garratt's idea of a Christmas letter.

"I thought he was dead," said Meg again.

"And what made you think he wasn't?"

She lifted her hand to her cheek and leaned on it. The worst part was over.

"Colonel Garratt said I ought to see a lawyer and get leave to presume death. There wasn't any will. There was a little money in the bank, but there was a packet of some sort labelled 'To be opened by my wife in case of my death.'"

Bill exclaimed.

"I think it's only papers. They wouldn't let me see it or anything. He had only brought it in the week before. The manager said he must have legal proof that Robin was dead before he could hand it over. I don't suppose it's anything that matters. It can't be money, because he was always saying how hard up he was."

It sounded off to Bill. But then O'Hara was just the sort of fellow to do an odd thing like that. He said with a frown,

"Did you see a lawyer?"

Meg's hand went down again. She said,

"No."

"Why didn't you?"

"Because that's when I began to think Robin wasn't dead."

"Why?"

"Things began to happen."

"What things?"

"Little things—they frightened me. It's so dreadful not to be sure. It's so dreadful to think that there's someone who wants to keep you like that—not sure—never knowing."

Her hands were twisting in her lap, fingers interlocked and knuckles white. Bill leaned forward and put his own hand over them, a big, warm hand.

"Steady, Meg. Just go on telling me what happened."

She didn't speak at once. A minute dragged by. He wondered what she was going to say. He took his hand away and leaned back, and as if that had been a signal, Meg said,

"The first thing was a newspaper. Someone must have put it in the letter-box. I found it on the floor when I got up."

The bitter cold of that January morning came back as she spoke. Her feet were as cold as they had been bare on the linoleum and she had stopped to pick the paper up. It wasn't a paper she had ever taken. She told Bill that, and was glad to have something that was easy to say.

"It wasn't a paper I'd ever had before. It hadn't come through the post. I thought it had been left by mistake. It was folded inside out. I thought that was funny. Then I saw some of the letters were underlined. No, that's wrong—they weren't underlined—they had lines drawn round them. I couldn't help putting the marked letters together. The first one was an I. After that an A and an M, and then A L I V E.''

The giddiness that had come over her then just touched her now. She heard Bill say:

"What paper was it?"

"The *Daily Sketch*."

"What did you do?"

"I went to Colonel Garratt. He said he thought it was a hoax. He said he was quite sure Robin was dead. He looked—odd. Afterwards I thought—Bill, it was rather0 horrid, but I thought he believed I'd done it myself."

"Why?"

"I don't know. He said he'd go into it, but I believe that's what he thought. I didn't know what to think. I couldn't believe anyone would do a thing like that—as a joke, but if it was really Robin there didn't seem to be any point in it. I mean he could have written or telephoned. Someone must have put the paper in at my letter-box. The person who did that could have put in a note. Colonel Garratt said all those things, and they were true—" She stopped suddenly. Impossible to say what had been in her mind all through, but it might have been Robin, for Robin was cruel enough to play a trick like that. She didn't know anyone else who would be so cruel. But she couldn't say that to Bill.

"Did you keep the paper?"

She nodded.

"Yes—but—" She looked at him suddenly with a steady mournful look. "That was the first thing that happened. I didn't tell Colonel Garratt about the other things—I didn't tell anyone—I couldn't. I was afraid they would think I was mad."

"You had better tell me," said Bill Coverdale.

"In February I wrote to Uncle Henry. His secretary wrote back and said he wouldn't be attending to any personal letters until he had finished his book."

"Has he got the same secretary? She was a Miss Wallace, wasn't she?"

"No—she got ill. It was before you went, I think. It's a new woman—sandy hair and spectacles, and a sort of fussy white mouse manner. I shouldn't have thought he'd have stood her for a month, but she seems to have dug herself in. I expect she's efficient. Her name's Cannock. Well, after that I knew Uncle Henry was a wash-out, so I thought I'd better go and see the lawyer. He was Uncle Henry's lawyer, Mr Pincott. I rang up to make an appointment. I'd got a job then, so I was out all day. When I got home someone had been in the flat. Nothing was missing, and everything was quite tidy, but—Bill, you won't think me mad, will you? —someone had taken my scissors and a sheet of writing-paper, and they'd cut the paper in strips and laid them out on the floor to make letters. They were all across the hearth-rug—A—L—I—V—E, in capital letters about two inches high."

"You ought to have told Garratt."

"I couldn't—I was frightened. It frightened me in a queer sort of way, because how could anyone have got into the flat? It frightened me dreadfully. You see, Robin had a key and I had a key. Someone had put those letters out like that. If it wasn't Robin, it was I."

"Don't talk nonsense," said Bill Coverdale.

She looked down and said in a quick fluttering voice,

"It mightn't be—nonsense. People do things—like that—and forget. I might have done it."

"I'm quite sure you didn't."

"Then it was Robin."

Bill shook his head.

"That doesn't follow. Someone might have pinched his key."

Meg looked up for a moment. He had a glimpse of her fear.

"It wouldn't matter to anyone except Robin whether I thought he was alive or not."

Bill shook his head again.

"It might. You don't know what's behind all this. Until you do you can't say what matters and what doesn't. Well, that was in February. You said—other things. What else happened?''

''There wasn't anything else for a long time. Then I lost my job, and—I thought I had better go and see Mr Pincott after all.''

''You hadn't been?''

''No.''

''Not at all? You said you had an appointment.''

She was very pale. She shook her head.

''No—I didn't go. I wrote and said my plans were changed.''

''Why? You ought to have gone.''

''I thought Robin was alive,'' said Meg.

''If he was alive, what was he living on?''

''I don't know. He had money. I don't know where it came from.''

Bill groaned.

''Go on.''

''I lost my job in July. I wrote to Uncle Henry again. Miss Cannock wrote back and said he sent me his love, and he was very busy and he hoped to finish the book within the year, and that then he would look forward to seeing me. I felt desperate, so I screwed myself up to go and see Mr Pincott. I didn't make an appointment—I just thought I'd go. And then something happened. When I took the post in—the first morning delivery—there was an envelope without any address on it. It was in the letter-box with the other letters. There was a letter from you, and two bills, and this envelope. It was Hieratica Bond, like I use myself, and there wasn't anything on it, but it was stuck down. I opened it, and at first I thought it was empty, and then I saw it wasn't. There was a leaf inside, a maple leaf, and there was something pricked on it—little holes pricked right through in a pattern. I held it up to the light, and it wasn't a pattern, it was letters—the same letters as before, A—L—I—V—E.''

Bill sat forward with a jerk.

''*A leaf?*''

Meg struck her hands together sharply. A faint flush came into her face. Her eyes were afraid.

"There—you don't believe me! And you want to know why I didn't go to Colonel Garratt!"

"Meg, I didn't say—"

"No, you didn't *say* I was making it up!" She was angry for a moment, but she couldn't go on being angry. She had been unhappy too long.

"Oh, Bill darling, I don't blame you a bit. I couldn't believe it myself if it hadn't happened. I don't always believe it now. It's too like the horrid sort of thing that happens in a dream, and sometimes I think I must have dreamt it all."

Bill hesitated and then plunged.

"Are you quite sure you didn't?"

She turned her head away.

"I—don't—know." Then all at once she turned back again. "No, Bill, that's not true. When it's really *me* thinking, I do know. I know that these things happened. Someone put that marked paper in at the door, and someone came in here and put those letters on the hearth-rug, and someone slipped that blank envelope in among my letters. But when I'm tired, or I've been looking for a job all day, or when I wake up at about four in the morning, it's like other people talking in my head, and then I'm not sure about anything."

Bill had been wanting to put his arms round her for ten years. At this moment the longing to comfort her became almost unendurable. Yet if he was to help Meg, he had got to endure it. If he failed her, she would have no one to help her at all.

It was a pity that feelings of such a chivalrous nature should have made him look so cross. Instead of kissing Meg he frowned at her and said in a very abrupt voice,

"Have you got the envelope?"

It appeared that she hadn't.

"I didn't keep it. There wasn't anything to keep it for. It might have been one of my own envelopes—I use that sort. It might have been anybody's envelope. It didn't prove a thing."

"And the leaf?" said Bill.

Meg threw out a hand.

"It shrivelled right up. What was the good of keeping it?"

"You didn't?"

"No."

It made it easier—to feel really exasperated with Meg. Bill felt genuinely exasperated. Ten thousand to one she'd got drawers full of hoarded rubbish. But she hadn't kept the envelope with what might or might not have been a message from Robin O'Hara!

He said in a patient voice, "I'd like to look at that *Daily Sketch*—the one with the first message, the marked letters."

Meg grew a shade paler.

"You can't. I was going to tell you—it's gone."

"You said you kept it."

"Yes, I kept it. I put it in my writing-table drawer. It's gone."

"Where did it go?"

"The day I found the letters on the hearth-rug. I opened the drawer, and it was gone."

"You're sure?"

"Quite sure."

"Do you mind if I have a look? Papers get caught up at the back of a drawer sometimes."

"This one didn't. But look if you like."

Bill looked very thoroughly. He took the drawer out of the table and examined the grooves in which it ran, and then he took everything out of the drawer itself. The dozen letters he had written to Meg from Chile were there. She had kept them, even if she hadn't answered them.

There were a great many other things, like stray ends of string, old theatre programmes, bills, notes, and half sheets of paper. There were three fountain-pen fillers. There was about an inch of yellow pencil which looked as if it had been gnawed by a mouse. Meg always bit her pencils to the bone.

Bill dropped the horrid little end into the waste-paper basket, from which she at once rescued it.

"Bill, I'm not a millionaire—I can't afford to throw away perfectly good pencils!"

"I'll give you another." He produced one from his pocket as he spoke, brand new, with a shining tin protector and an india-rubber cap. "Chuck that beastly gnawed thing away! And what about these bills?"

Meg smiled a little bitterly.

"You might as well chuck them away too."

"They're not paid?"

"Darling Bill!"

He put them in a neat pile. Most of the notes got torn up. He put everything in neat piles. Just before he pushed the drawer home he picked up one of the half sheets of paper.

"Was this what was used for the letters?"

Meg nodded.

"Then whoever did it opened this drawer, and when it was open he saw the *Daily Sketch* and pinched it."

"Or he might have been looking for it. If it was Robin, he would know where to look."

Bill shut the drawer with a bang.

"If it was Robin, what was he playing at?"

Meg winced. She said,

"I don't know. Thanks for tidying my drawer. I just wait till it bulges, and then have an awful clearance, and generally find I've thrown away my stamps, or a letter that has simply got to be answered, or a postal order or something."

"Why should anyone take that paper?" said Bill.

"Perhaps someone thought it was safer not to leave it here. Perhaps Robin thought so."

"It can't be Robin!" said Bill violently.

"It might be," said Meg O'Hara.

III

BILL COVERDALE STRETCHED HIS LONG LEGS AND LAID his head back against the shabby back of a large and shapeless chair. A spring bulged under the splayed seat and the stuffing was coming through on the arms. There was a loose spiral of horsehair quite close to the large left hand which lay spread out, mahogany brown, on what had once been crimson leather. Bill had rather an out-size in hands, not a bad shape, but large and decidedly battered. He looked at the window and saw a narrow strip of blue sky—a good colour English blue sky—and then all the rest of the pane a glare of new concrete patched with innumerable blank even windows, all very modern, light, and airy, and a great improvement on the low dingy houses which this great block of flats had replaced since last Bill Coverdale had stretched himself out in Colonel Garratt's shabby chair and stared out of that window.

Garratt jerked into the picture with an arm thrust between him and the concrete.

"Admiring my view?" he said, and laughed his short barking laugh.

"Very soothing," said Mr William Coverdale. "You can put yourself to sleep counting windows instead of sheep."

Garratt walked to the window and stood looking out. His little steely eyes dwelt upon the block of flats with malignant dislike. His short grizzled hair stood up all over his head like a ten days' beard. He wore, as usual, the sort of clothes that make you wonder why any tailor capable of perpetrating them should have escaped being lynched. No one knew the man's name. He remained anonymous, and under the shelter of this anonymity he had for twenty-five years abetted Garratt in every kind of sartorial outrage. A mustard tweed and a pink-checked suiting are still remembered at the Foreign Office. This afternoon the crime was a purplish West of England tweed with a green line in it. The pockets bulged—Garratt's pockets always bulged. The invariable red bandanna trailed a flaming four inches or so from the most crowded pocket of all, which had to accommodate, beside the handkerchief, matches and a pipe, a tobacco-pouch, and a bunch of keys. The colour scheme thus brightening the view was completed by a school or club tie of unknown origin combining a cheerful royal blue with orange zigzags and a device suggestive of squashed earwigs.

Bill Coverdale looked, wondered, and averted his eyes.

Garratt turned back to the room with a jerk.

"First you pull everything down. Then you build it up. Then you pull it down again." He grimaced. "Makes a bit of mess. Dangerous when the bricks begin to fall."

Bill did not say anything for about half a minute. What he said then might or might not have been irrelevant. He was twisting the spiral of horsehair between the finger with the white slashed scar across the knuckle and the thumb which still wore a strip of sticking-plaster. He said, looking at the black stubborn twist of the horsehair,

"What about O'Hara? Did you ever find out what happened?"

Garratt frowned. When he frowned, he was quite hideous.

"O'Hara? They got him. Dead. A year ago."

Bill wound the horsehair slowly round the finger with the scar. When the black had crossed the white three times, he said,

"Is he dead? Are you sure?"

"Sure? Of course I'm sure! Why? What's eating you?"

"Mrs O'Hara doesn't seem sure," said Bill slowly.

Garratt's voice became furious.

"You been seeing her? What does she say?"

Bill pulled the horsehair tight over the scar. By pulling it very tight he could make it go round a fourth time. He said,

"Yes, I've seen her. We've known each other a long time. She isn't sure." The horsehair broke and he shook it off on to the floor. "Look here, Garratt—what happened?"

Garratt shrugged—not the neat French lift of the shoulders, but a sideways jerk which was all his own.

"Knife in the back. Sandbag." He shrugged again. "I wasn't there. They got him somehow."

"He was on a job?"

Garratt nodded.

"What job? Where?"

"What's the good of digging it up?"

"I want to know. I *want* to know, Garratt."

Garratt sat down on the arm of a chair, thrust his hands into his pockets, and swung a restless leg.

"Some people want to know everything!"

Bill nodded. Except for the play of finger and thumb he had not moved till now. His attitude was one of repose, but to those steel-pointed eyes of Garratt's the stillness of the long frame was the immobility of control and not of relaxation. He wasn't moving, because he wasn't letting himself move. He was holding his muscles from movement, and he was holding his voice from expression. Only when he had said, "I *want* to know," there was a sudden heavy weight upon the word.

Garratt stared at him and said, "Why?"

"Because I do."

There was a short pause. Then Garratt laughed.

"All right, you can have it! It's damn little. You know what O'Hara was like. Brilliant in spots. Erratic all the time. Close as a clam." He shrugged. "You can't run intelligence work by rule of thumb, but O'Hara—" He shrugged again with that jerking movement of the shoulder. "I can do with a man being a law to himself, but O'Hara wasn't that. He was a series of revolutionary outbreaks. Bound to come to grief sooner or later."

"What was he doing when he came to grief? How did he come to grief? And how do you know he came to grief?"

There was a little break between each of the three questions, but there was no break in the pertinacity of Bill Coverdale's manner.

"I told you he was on a job," growled Garratt. "And if you want to know what the job was, you'll have to want, because I don't know myself. Here's the whole bag of tricks, and you can make what you like of it. The Foreign Office Intelligence don't touch crime *qua* crime, but when crime slops over into politics, or politics slops over into crime, it's our job. International crime is always on the look-out for a chance to exploit international politics. That was the Vulture's* stunt. We got him, but we didn't get the people who worked the show under him. One of them's a damned clever woman, and she slipped through our hands. We got one of the men the other day, but the show's still running. O'Hara picked up the trail of the people who are running it in this country. At least that's what I think. Officially he was doing something else, but last time I saw him he dropped a hint and then shut up. Noting more out of him but 'Wait and see.' But he was on to something. Something big. Bit too big. It smashed him. If he'd had the sense to tell me what he'd got on to, we might have made a haul. As it was, they got him, and they got away with it."

"Mrs O'Hara doesn't think he's dead."

Garratt kicked the leg of his chair.

"She doesn't, doesn't she?"

"She came to see you?"

"She came to see me," said Garratt. "And she told me a cock and bull story about someone having put a marked newspaper in at her letter-box—letters with ink circles round them, spelling 'I am alive' or some flapdoodle of that sort!"

"Why should it be flapdoodle?"

"The answer to why is because," said Garratt. He laughed rudely. "My good Bill, what would be the point of O'Hara sending his wife that sort of tripe?"

Bill kept his temper. Garratt was an offensive brute, but

*See *Danger Calling*.

he was used to him. He was a cousin in some seventeenth or eighteenth degree. He was an old friend and a good friend, but he had never had any manners.

"She says that herself," he remarked.

"Then it's the first sensible thing I've ever heard her say. There couldn't possibly be any point about it. It was either a hoax, or she'd had a go of hysterics and done it herself."

Bill shook his head.

"I don't think so. I've known Meg a long time—she's not like that. Now look here, Garratt, you won't believe what I'm going to tell you, but I'm going to say it all the same. You shan't say afterwards that you were kept in the dark."

"All right, go ahead." Colonel Garratt's little eyes were intent.

Bill told him about the letters on Meg's hearth-rug—chopped up pieces of writing-paper to make the word "Alive."

Garratt said nothing. He jingled the contents of his pocket and lifted his eyebrows, but he said nothing.

Bill told him about the blank envelope which had contained a maple leaf with the word "Alive" pricked out on it.

Garratt's eyebrows came down and he stopped jingling. He said,

"The girl's batty!"

Bill wasn't angry. It wasn't any good being angry with Garratt. He said,

"No, she isn't,"' and left it at that.

"All right," said Garratt, "trot out the exhibits—*Daily Sketch*, bits of notepaper, blank envelope, dead leaf. I suppose the leaf's dead if O'Hara isn't."

Bill smiled quite cheerfully. There had been a certain amount of thin ice about. Now that Garratt had smashed it, things felt more comfortable.

"There aren't any exhibits. Meg put the *Daily Sketch* in a drawer—her writing-table drawer—but it went missing the day she found the letters on the hearth-rug. The paper that had been used for them was in the same drawer."

"And someone broke in and burgled the leaf, I suppose!" Garratt made a face. "This what you call evidence? It's sheer lunacy!"

"O'Hara was an odd chap," said Bill slowly.

Garratt got there in a flash.

"You mean he might be playing cat-and-mouse with her. What terms were they on?"

Bill didn't answer that at once. Then he said,

"You'd better know just where we are. I've cared for Meg for ten years. She's never cared for me. She married O'Hara. He made her damned unhappy. Now she doesn't know whether she's free or not. He was a cruel devil—it would be like him to keep her like that, not knowing."

Garratt jingled his keys. "It might be. . . . O'Hara was like that."

Bill went on speaking.

"It's an abominable position. She can't even get probate."

There was something sticking in his mind about those papers in the bank. No, it was a packet of some sort. Meg didn't know if there were papers in it, she only thought there might be. He didn't know why they stuck in his mind, but they did.

Garratt grinned.

"Do you expect me to believe that O'Hara had anything to leave? I suppose she wants to be sure she's a widow. She was a fool to marry him—but women are fools, especially girls. Now look here, Bill—O'Hara's dead. I told her so when she came to see me. He's dead, and he'll stay dead. The body they got out of the river in December was his all right. Stripped—and ordinary identification impossible, but there had been an old break of the right leg. I happen to know O'Hara broke that leg about five years ago. We didn't identify him at the inquest because it didn't suit our book. We were still hoping to pick up the trail he was on. We most particularly didn't want any headlines in the papers. What Mrs O'Hara wants to do is to go and see her lawyer and get leave to presume death. We'll back her up—now. There needn't be any publicity. Tell her to see her lawyer at once. All this about letters, and leaves, and snips of paper is either a hoax, or it's hysterics. O'Hara's as dead as Julius Caesar—she needn't worry."

He got up, went over to the other side of the room,

clattered at a drawer, and came back with an untidy note-book in his hand. He sat down again on the arm of the chair and flicked at the crumpled pages.

"Here you are—October '33. First entry about O'Hara on the 3rd. He was due to report, and he didn't report. . . . October 4th—rang up Mrs O'Hara. O'Hara missing. She wanted to know where he was. So did we. We gave it another forty-eight hours, and then we began to make enquiries. Nobody had seen O'Hara since eight o'clock on the evening of the 1st, when he walked out of his flat. Nobody'd seen him. Nobody'd heard from him. He never turned up, and he never will." He shut the note-book with a snap. "You tell Mrs O'Hara to see her lawyer and get on with it!"

Bill Coverdale was sitting up.

"You say nobody saw O'Hara after the first of October?"

"One Oct: thirty-three," said Garratt laconically.

"Well—I saw him."

"You?"

"I. And I can fix the date, because I sailed for South America next day, and I sailed on the fifth."

"You're sure of that?"

"Dead sure. But you can verify it if you want to."

Garratt fished a pencil out of his pocket and sucked the end of it.

"All right, if you're sure. You saw O'Hara on the fourth. That's four days after anyone else did. Where did you see him? What was he doing? Who was he with?"

"He was in a taxi," said Bill Coverdale. "It was some-where short of midnight, because my train was a bit late, and it was due at eleven."

"Where were you coming from?"

"King's Cross. I'd been up north, and I'd run it fine, so I was in a hurry. I was sailing the next day. I was held up at a crossing, and I saw O'Hara go by in a taxi. I didn't think anything about it at the time, and barring that it was somewhere between King's Cross and Piccadilly Circus I can't say where the hold-up was. I just didn't think anything about it."

Garratt scribbled in his note-book.

"You're sure it was O'Hara?"

Bill nodded.

"Oh, yes, it was O'Hara."

"And it was a taxi, not a private car?"

Bill shut his eyes for a moment.

"Yes, it was a taxi—one of those green ones."

Garratt scribbled again.

"You're twelve months after the fair. We might have got on to the taxi if we'd known at the time. Was he alone?"

Bill Coverdale got up and walked to the window. Like Garratt he frowned at the hygienic flats, but unlike Garratt he did not see the bright blank windows or the staring concrete. He saw O'Hara in a taxi at midnight—O'Hara with every feature clear and distinct, and beyond him, close at his shoulder, a woman. The anger which he had felt then swept over him again. To have Meg for his wife, and to go chasing off with that sort of girl! He tried to visualize her and failed. . . . Yet he had had the impression that she *was* that sort of girl. There must have been something to give him that impression.

Garratt repeated his question impatiently.

"Was he alone?"

And with that Bill turned back to the room again.

"No, he wasn't. There was a girl with him."

"See her face?"

"I suppose I did. I can't describe her."

"You're being damn useful!" said Garratt with a growl in his voice. "All this is about as much use as a sick headache. You're sure there was a girl?"

"Yes, I'm sure of that."

"You wouldn't know her again, or anything like that?"

Bill was half turned away. He was frowning deeply. Behind that impression of his there must be something if he could only get hold of it. He said without knowing what he was going to say,

"I never said I wouldn't know her again."

IV

BILL COVERDALE WALKED BACK TO HIS HOTEL. IT SEEMED pretty fairly certain that O'Hara had been dead for the best part of a year. That being the case, the next thing to do was to follow Garratt's advice and take any steps that were necessary to get O'Hara pronounced dead legally. Garratt seemed to think there wouldn't be any trouble about it.

He began to wonder how soon he could ask Meg to marry him. He wanted to take care of her. He wanted to give her things. He wanted to take her out of London. He had a picture in his mind of an open car, and himself and Meg, and the luggage in behind, and nothing to stop them going anywhere they chose. October could do some pretty good weather for touring when it gave its mind to it, and the weather this year seemed to have got into the habit of being fine. They could go to Scotland. They could go to Wales. They could go to Cornwall. They could go anywhere they chose.

Bill indulged this dream for a little, and then woke coldly. He hadn't had the faintest reason to suppose that Meg would marry him. Why should she? "She wants looking after. She's never wanted you to look after her. If she had, she wouldn't have married O'Hara. If she had, she'd have married you five years ago." That was when he had first asked her—on her twentieth birthday. He hadn't asked her before because she was so young and it didn't seem fair, but lots of girls married at twenty. Meg had just laughed at him.

"Bill darling—how silly! I know you much, much, *much* too well, and I'm much, much, *much* too fond of you. I don't want to marry for ages and ages, but when I do, I expect it'll be someone I don't know a bit, so that I'll have all the thrill of being an explorer—you know, the 'I was the first that ever burst into that silent sea' sort of feeling.''

"You wouldn't be," Bill had said with sturdy common sense.

"I don't suppose anyone ever is, but it's a most thrilling romantic feeling."

"And I'm not romantic."

"Darling angel, how could you be? I've known you since I was fifteen."

That had always been the burden of it—she knew him too well, and she liked him too much. And she married Robin O'Hara whom she did not know at all.

Bill walked, frowning, into a telephone-box and dialled in. Presently Meg's voice came along the wire.

"Yes—who is it?"

"Bill," said Bill Coverdale.

"Oh—hullo, Bill!" Her voice, which had been a little breathless, sounded pleased.

"I want you to dine with me."

"I don't think—"

"You don't need to think—I'm doing the thinking. Where would you like to go? I thought about the Luxe."

"Bill, I *really* don't think—"

"I thought we might do a theatre. What have you seen?"

"Nothing."

"All right, I'll call for you at a quarter to seven."

"Bill, I haven't got any clothes."

"Well, the best people don't seem to be wearing them much."

"You don't mind if I'm terribly out of date?"

"I'll bear up, I expect. Quarter to seven, Meg." He rang off.

He was rather pleased with himself because he had resisted the temptation to tell her that it didn't matter what she wore, because she always looked nicer than anyone else anyhow. It didn't do to say that sort of thing if you could help it. You might feel like a door-mat, but so sure as you let a girl know it, she started walking all over you. Meg would be much more likely to marry him if he kept his end up. From which it will be perceived that that devout lover Mr William Coverdale was not without a spice of the serpent's wisdom.

Meg hung up the receiver. She ought to have said no, but it was such ages since she had been out anywhere—such ages, and ages, and ages. It would be nice to dine with Bill, nice to get out of the flat, and very, very nice not to have bread and margarine for supper. Last week there had been cheese, but now there was so little money left that it was bread and margarine, and scraps at that, with the tea-leaves saved from breakfast to make something you could pretend was a cup of tea. Of course she ought to have given up her telephone the minute she lost her job, but it seemed like the last link with her friends. Only everyone had been away holiday making, so it hadn't really been much good after all, and now that people were coming back again, the telephone would have to go, and she would have to sell something to pay the quarter's rent and the calls she had had.

She pushed all that away. She was going to dine at the Luxe and go to a theatre. The question was, what was she going to wear? She hadn't anything that was less than two years old. It was two years and a month since she had married Robin O'Hara, and it hadn't run to any new clothes since then.

She went into her bedroom, opened the wardrobe door, and stood there considering. . . . Not her wedding dress. She had worn it many times since, but looking at it now, all those other times faded away. . . .

For better, for worse—for richer, for poorer. . . .

The better and the richer had faded out in the first month, leaving her only the worse and the poorer part.

No, not her wedding dress.

There wasn't much choice really. She had never liked the pink lace. Pink wasn't her colour, but Robin had said he thought he would like her in pink. And then when she wore it, he had stared at her coldly and told her she was losing her looks. No, she certainly wasn't going to wear the pink.

It would have to be the black georgette. She put it on, and thought it didn't look so bad. Uncle Henry had given her a cheque, and it had cost a lot two years ago. Meg looked at herself in the glass, and thought she was too thin for black, and too pale. She could put on some colour, but the little knobs on her spine showed all the way down the open back. She shifted the hand-mirror this way and that, and thought what ugly things bones were, and what a pity the dress was cut so low, and then slid off into thinking what a lot it had cost, and how out of sight was out of mind. There was Uncle Henry with lots of money, and she'd lived with him from the time she was fifteen to the time she married, and he had paid all her bills without a murmur and given her nice fat cheques for her birthday and Christmas, and things like that, and then the very minute she married Robin he didn't seem to mind what happened to her any more—just vague and affectionate when they met, but no more cheques. It was a whole year since she had seen him now, and he hadn't even bothered to answer her letters. He had just faded out, and Bill might say what he liked, she wasn't going to write again and have that Cannock woman sending one of her white mouse letters and saying how busy Mr Postlethwaite was, and how important it was that he shouldn't be disturbed.

Meg was quite ready at a quarter to seven. She wore the black georgette, and she had fastened one of the long scarf-ends on the left shoulder with the brooch which Bill had given her for her twenty-first birthday—two diamond daisies and a leaf. She had been in two minds whether to wear it or not, but in the end she put it on. Other people faded, but Bill didn't—Robin, Uncle Henry, people you thought were your friends, but never Bill. So why shouldn't she wear his brooch? She didn't look pale any longer. She had tinted her cheeks and brightened her lips, and to Bill she was the old pretty Margaret of two years ago, only she was too thin. It went to his heart to see her so thin.

They dined at the Luxe and then went on to the theatre. The two years might never have been at all. It was just like one of their old times together. Meg was young. She had been unhappy for a long time, and now quite suddenly the burden of that unhappiness seemed to have lifted. She felt as if she had had an illness and it was over, and the tides of health were flowing in again. She felt a consciousness of strength and of renewing. The flat had been full of tired, sick, frightened thoughts, and she had come away from it and left them behind her. The music pleased her, and the lights—the laughing voices, and the new queer frocks. Hers must be frightfully out of date, but it didn't matter—Bill had always had a way of making you feel better dressed and better looking that you really were. Darling old Bill—she was very glad she was wearing his brooch.

They talked about the old times down at Way's End—Meg's procession of governesses—the one who thought her such a tomboy and wanted her to wear gloves in the village—the one who used cheap scent—the one who tried so hard to marry the Professor that even he became aware of it in the end and ran away to Vienna to a congress—

"I ought to have gone to school," said Meg. "If you're an only child you ought always to go to school, because otherwise you don't make any friends. Of course I should have screamed with rage if Uncle Henry had tried to send me, because there were you and Jerry Holland, and I didn't want anyone else. But when Jerry went to India and you went to Chile, there didn't seem to be anyone at all."

"Well, I've come back," said Bill cheerfully. "Meg, why did the Professor leave Way's End? I thought he was dug in there for life."

Meg nodded.

"So did I. I was most awfully surprised. I—I hadn't been seeing him much, and then in September—September last year—I wrote and said could I go down for a bit. I felt as if I must get away, but he wrote back to say he was going to move. Of course I wanted to know why, and all about it. This time Miss Cannock wrote, and she said the village was getting so noisy with motor horns and dogs, and Uncle Henry felt he must have perfect quiet because he was going to start the book he'd been collecting notes for ever since I was born. I can't remember what it was going to be called, because I never can remember the names of any of Uncle Henry's things, but it was 'Meta—something-or-other'—or perhaps I'm mixing it up with something else. Is there such a word as metabolism?''

''I believe so.''

''Do you know what it means?''

''Not an idea.''

Meg sighed.

''I haven't either, but it doesn't really matter. Anyway the Cannock said Uncle Henry had bought an island, and he was going there so that he could write his book without being disturbed. Well, I was feeling awfully desperate, so I went down to Way's End without saying I was coming.''

''Good for you!'' said Bill. ''Did you see the Professor?''

''Why did you say that?'' said Meg. And then, ''Yes, I did. But it didn't look as if I was going to—not at first. I saw the Cannock, and she was in the most awful fuss about the move, and Uncle Henry not being disturbed, and the precious book, and everything. I don't know how he stands her. She gives me the pip.''

''But you did see him?''

''Only because I sat there, and every time she stopped to take breath I just said, 'I'm afraid I can't go away without seeing my uncle.' I just kept on saying it, and after about the hundred-and-first time she got all pink about the eyes and the tip of the nose—she really is exactly like a white mouse—and she flapped her hands and said, 'Oh dear, oh dear!' and went away, and after about ten minutes Uncle Henry came drifting in, awfully vague, but quite pleased to see me, so I was glad I had stuck it out.''

Bill was frowning over something in his own mind. What the Professor wanted was a good sharp jolt, and it wasn't going to be Bill's fault if he didn't get one.

''Where's this island of his?'' he said shortly.

''Well, it's not a proper island—not a sea one, you know. He told me all about it. It's just an island in a lake.''

''Where's the lake?''

''Seven miles from Ledlington—a place called Ledstow. There's a lake, and a house, and an island. Uncle Henry was as pleased as Punch about the island. The house is on the bank, but there's a sort of covered bridge that goes over to the island. It was built by an eccentric old lady who thought people were trying to murder her, so she had her own rooms on the island. She used to sleep there and just come over to the house in the daytime. Uncle Henry was most frightfully bucked. The bridge had a door at each end, and once he'd locked those doors behind him it was going to be as good as being on a desert island—nobody could get at him, nobody could disturb him. He was so full of it that after all I didn't tell him the things I'd gone down there to tell him."

"Oh, my dear!" said Bill involuntarily.

Meg looked at him, half rueful, half smiling.

"Darling Bill, I couldn't. He was all pleased and happy. What was the good of upsetting him? It wasn't as if he could do anything about it really. So I came away, and after that he just faded out."

"Well, he's got to fade in again," said Bill grimly. He was having some tolerably harsh thoughts about Henry Postlethwaite. You can't stand in the place of a girl's parents for years and then go off casually to an island and leave her with a disappearing husband and no money. The Professor was a vague old boy, but Bill felt perfectly competent to get through the vagueness and make him sit up and take notice. He restrained the feelings with which he was seething and said,

"I'm going down to see him—probably tomorrow."

"Oh, you mustn't!" said Meg quickly.

"I'm going to."

Meg sighed. Bill was most dreadfully obstinate. If he had made up his mind to go, he would go. And quite suddenly she didn't want to go on talking about Uncle Henry. She said so before she knew that she was going to say anything at all.

"Oh, Bill, don't let's talk about it any more. I—oh, Bill, *please*—"

She didn't finish her sentence—she didn't need to finish it. Her sudden flush and the distressed look in her eyes spoke for her. She wanted to leave all those things which had hurt her. She wanted to get away from them, to forget for an hour, to stop thinking, to take this evening as a respite from endurance, and in that respite to give herself up to all the gay and pleasant surface impressions with which she was surrounded—lights, flowers, music; the sort of food she hadn't tasted for months; Bill looking at her as if he found her good to look at. . . . She wanted to draw a charmed circle round this hour and keep it happy. She had been unhappy for two whole years. She wanted her hour.

They had their coffee and rose to go. It was just then that an odd thing happened. A couple who were sitting at the table behind them got up, the man of a flushed amplitude with a hanging jowl and bright greedy eyes, the woman a platinum blonde in a backless dress of silver gauze, hair, dress and skin all pale, all shimmering under the many lights. Bill, at a cursory glance, took her for the next thing to an albino and felt vaguely repelled. Before he got any farther than that, Meg, a pace in front of him, checked suddenly. She turned, and as she turned, he saw her hand go up to the neck of her dress and come down again with a little crumpled handkerchief just showing between her fingers. The handkerchief fell to the floor. Bill picked it up, but when Meg had thanked him and moved on again the couple were still beside their table. The woman was lighting a cigarette. Her eyes were a pale, hard grey. She used an odd shade of lipstick, the colour of—now what in mischief's name was it the colour of?

Meg went past without a glance, and Bill followed her. Then, when they had almost reached the door, he looked round again.

The woman was holding her cigarette between the first and second fingers of her left hand. The very pointed nails matched the lipstick to a hair. She was looking at Meg, her lips wide in a smile, and all at once Bill knew what her lipstick reminded him of. He knew that, and he knew something else. The two things collided violently in his mind. The lipstick was exactly the colour of a pink zinnia, of all flowers and of all colours the most artificial, and it was those zinnia-coloured lips which he had seen in a taxi beyond Robin O'Hara on that October midnight more than a year ago.

V

Bill did not speak until they were clear of the dining-room. The voices, the laughter, the music seemed suddenly to have become unnaturally loud. The whole big echoing room throbbed and vibrated with sound. He and Meg walked through it silently. They came to an archway lined with mirrors, and as he drew abreast of her, each threw a quick involuntary glance at the other. Their eyes met. Bill's sense of shock was intensified. They came out into the wide corridor, and he said quickly,

"Do you know who she is?"

Meg drew a little away from his. Her eyebrows made a faint, fine arch over the deep blue of her eyes. She said in a small, cool voice,

"Who?"

What was the sense of pretending like that? Whether she liked it or not, he was bound to get at what she knew. And she did know something. There wasn't a shadow of doubt about that.

"Meg, I'm sorry, but it's important. That woman at the table behind ours—I've seen her before, and so have you. Tell me who she is."

"I don't know her."

"Do you know who she is?"

"It's quite obvious, I should think."

"Meg!" Bill could have shaken her. "I'm asking if you know her name."

"I believe she calls herself Della Delorne."

There was a most curious sense of strain between them—anger, resentment, pride. Meg's voice was low and hard. Her hour's respite was over. Couldn't Bill let her have just this one evening, that he must question her about Della Delorne? Did he admire her so much that he had to know her name—now, all in a hurry, in the middle of this one hour?

Bill, on his part, was astonished and a little angry. She was the beloved woman, but Lord—the fundamental unreasonableness of women! She had known him for ten years, and she could use that tone to him! It was as if she accused him. His anger rose. Meg of all women in the world to think that he would be caught at a glance by a simpering platinum blonde with a gold-digging eye! He said stiffly,

"Do you happen to know where she lives?"

Meg said "Yes," in a stiffer tone than his own. Her colour had ebbed right away, leaving the clear, faint artificial tint in pathetic relief. She turned from him and moved quickly in the direction of the cloak-room. The evening was spoiled, but they would have to see it through. She must get her coat, and then she and Bill would sit side by side for a couple of hours hating one another and thinking about Della Delorne.

When they were in the taxi, Bill put his hand on hers.

"Meg—don't be angry."

Meg looked away from him at a whirling sky-sign all scarlet and blue.

"I'm not in the least angry."

Bill's hand pressed hers. He said,

"Liar!" And then, "Why does Della Delorne make you angry?"

"I'm not angry—I told you I wasn't."

Bill pulled her round to face him.

"Look here, Meg, come off it! I want the woman's name and address for Garratt, not for myself. You're behaving as if I'd insulted you. If you hadn't known who she was, I should have had to find out some other way."

"Let me go!" said Meg. And then all of a sudden she melted. "Bill, you don't know—"

"No, but you can tell me, my dear."

It was she who was holding him now, one hand on his arm, the other on his wrist. Where her fingers touched his skin he could feel how cold they were.

"Bill, I'm sorry—I was a beast—but it came over me. That woman—I saw her—with Robin—twice. He wouldn't tell me who she was, but other people did. She calls herself an actress. I believe she's sometimes been in the chorus of a revue—I don't know. I told you I was going to divorce Robin. That was what I wanted to see Uncle Henry about. Why do you want to know about her?"

He hesitated. The hand on his wrist tightened.

"Was it because you'd seen her with Robin too?" Her eyes implored him. In the half light of the taxi they looked larger and darker than they were. "Did you see her with Robin, Bill—*did* you?"

Bill nodded, and at once her grasp relaxed. There was a feeling of relief from strain. It was only the old trouble, not a new one. She leaned back in her corner with a sigh. The taxi had come to a stop. There was a block of cars in front of them. Neither spoke until the block broke up. Then Meg said,

"When did you see them?"

"*Please*, Meg."

"I want to know."

Well, it was better to tell her. No good letting her imagine things. He said,

"Well, that's the whole point, my dear—I saw Robin in a taxi with a woman at midnight on the fourth of October last year."

"The fourth!" said Meg in a startled voice. And then, "But, Bill—that was after—he disappeared—"

"Yes, I know."

"He was with Della Delorne?"

"Well, that's what I don't know, but I think so. When I told Garratt—"

"You told Colonel Garratt?"

"Yes, of course I did. Well, when I told him, I said I wouldn't know her again, but just now in the dining-room as soon as I saw that woman, something went click in my brain. I couldn't have sworn to her features, or her face, or anything. I only just had an impression of her beyond Robin in the taxi, but there was something that made me put her down for—well, for the sort of woman she is. I couldn't get hold of it when I was talking to Garratt, and I told him I wouldn't know her again, but when I saw her at the Luxe it came back and I remembered what it was."

They were held up again at a cross road. The traffic streamed by in a blur of sound. Against this blur Meg said clearly,

"What was it?"

"Her lipstick. Did you notice it? A beastly sort of unnatural pink."

"Yes, it is, isn't it?" Her voice was warm and eager.

"Well, that was what did the trick. So I had to find out who it was, because of course I must let Garratt know."

The traffic ceased to flow past them. They moved again.

"You saw her with Robin four days after he—disappeared!" Meg leaned forward suddenly. There was a note of terror in her voice. *"Bill—where—is—Robin?"*

The taxi drew up smoothly at the kerb. Bill put his hand on her shoulder for a moment.

"Robin's dead," he said. "Garratt is quite sure he's dead."

The driver got down from his seat and opened the door.

VI

THE PLAY FLOWED BY VERY MUCH AS THE TRAFFIC HAD flowed by, in a blur of sound. The people who went about the stage and spoke their words made as little impression on

Meg O'Hara; the inner current of her thoughts moved in too full and bitter a tide. Once she looked at a woman who wept on the stage, and wondered what it was all about, and once it came to her that the play must have been going on for hours, and then she found that it was only nine o'clock. She had thought that she and Bill would have to sit there side by side in a hating, angry silence, but it wasn't like that at all. Bill didn't hate her. She had been horrid to him, and he had been kind and patient. But it all felt a long way off—the play, and Bill, and everything. It was a horrid, strange feeling, and it frightened her.

She made a great effort in the first interval, and Bill helped her. They talked about safe, comfortable things like the weather, and the new pedestrians' crossings, and Chile. Meg found Chile a most reassuring place to talk about. It was such a long way off, so remote from the closing circle of her fears.

After that she was able to follow the play—a little vaguely, a little hazily, rather as if she were watching it through an unfocussed glass, but still to follow it.

When it was over, Bill took her home. They went up to the third floor together in the little lift that you worked yourself. They had been rather silent in the taxi, and they were quite silent now.

When Meg took out her key and fitted it into the lock and the door opened upon the small dark hall, she felt a momentary chill. She had been coming back to this empty flat for a year, but tonight it seemed emptier than usual. A thought looked into her mind like a stranger looking in through the window. If Bill and she were coming home together, the flat would not be cold and empty, but welcoming and warm. That was the thought; but it wasn't her own thought, it was a stranger looking in. She stepped over the threshold and switched on the light—a bright light in the little closed-in space which was the hall. To her surprise and consternation she felt the colour come burning to her face. She said good-night quickly and shut the door.

Bill took himself down in the lift. He had seen that sudden startled colour, and it had sent his spirits soaring. He hadn't the slightest idea why she should have blushed, but he did know that she had never blushed for him before. It seemed to him that it was a very encouraging sign. But he did wonder what it was that had made her fly that scarlet flag. It wasn't as if she could possibly have known what he was thinking, or how hard it was to leave her and come away. Well, perhaps some day they would come home together and he wouldn't have to leave her. That was what he had been thinking, but of course she couldn't have known.

He came out on to the pavement and turned to the right. It was a dark night with a feel of rain in the air. He meant to walk to the hotel, and presently he crossed over and took a shortcut down a narrow side street. It was when he was about half way down this street that it occurred to him that there had been someone behind him ever since he had left the flat. It would be a good deal of a coincidence if someone else should at this hour be taking just his way through these unfrequented streets.

He turned at right angles into a paved alley with a row of posts across the mouth of it. When he came out at the other end, he knew beyond a doubt that someone was following him. It interested him a good deal. Did he look sufficiently opulent to tempt a thief to follow him on the chance of getting away with his wallet? But he was sure that the footsteps had been behind him all the way from the flat. Why should a thief have picked him up at the flat? It didn't seem very likely. O'Hara's name flared through his mind like a squib. O'Hara, tormenting Meg, spying on her. . . . No, it wasn't reasonable. There wasn't any motive. O'Hara was either dead or alive. Garratt said he was dead, and Garratt didn't say things unless he meant them. O'Hara was dead. But, for the sake of argument, if O'Hara was alive, he had deserted his wife. And then why should he spy on her. She had been his, and he had chucked her away. He had left her for a year without help, or comfort, or money. All this supposing him to be alive. But he wasn't alive—he couldn't be. Garratt said that he was dead. All the same, Bill turned out of the alley and made two quick strides of it to the nearest doorway, where he stood pressed up against the door to see who would come out after him.

There were posts at this end of the alley too. It was very dark. He could only just see them, but he thought if O'Hara came out, that he would recognize him. There was a way he had of walking, an impudent confidence, a turn of the head.

The place into which he had come was a narrow street of poor houses, crowding one upon another. He had come up three steps to the doorway where he was sheltering. There was no light in this house, nor in the half dozen houses that were nearest, whether on his own side of the street or on the other. There was nobody afoot the whole length of the street. He began to wonder whether he had been mistaken. If someone were really following him, where was he, and why didn't he emerge? And then he heard the footstep again, quite near, in a faint stumble as if the foot had slipped on a worn place or stubbed itself against one of the posts. Another moment and someone came cautiously out into the street.

Bill had said that he would know O'Hara, but here there wasn't anything to know—a shadow standing motionless just clear of the black alley-way, with the darkness confusing height, shape, and outline. There wasn't any outline. The shadow was one with the other shadows. When he stared at it, he was no longer sure that he could see it at all, but when he looked away and looked back again, it was there, quite motionless, just not merged in the blackness out of which it had come.

He made one step of it to the street level and spoke. "Who are you—and what do you want?"

The shadow receded a little. There was no answer.

Bill Coverdale came on, but even as he came, there was a flash in the dark, and a report that was deafeningly loud in the narrow place. The wind of the explosion came against his face, acrid with the smell of burnt powder. The top of his left ear stung, and as he clapped his hand to it, the blood ran hot between his fingers. The shadow was gone, and Bill went pelting down the alley after it in a fury of anger. The fellow had tried to kill him. He had the blanketing dark and a sideways stumble over a pot-hole to thank for his life. The pistol had been fired from not more than a yard away.

He came to the posts at the far end, and saw by the light of a distant lamp that the street was empty. He had enough sense not to emerge upon the pavement, faintly though it was lit. Instead he flattened himself against the wall of the right-hand house and looked back, listening. There was nothing either to see or hear. Nobody moved, threw up a window, or concerned himself with the shot which had come within half an inch of achieving a murder.

Bill began to feel that he was uncommonly lucky to be alive. He also began to wonder whether he was going to be able to stay alive, or whether the shadow would have a second shot at him as soon as he came out into the light. He didn't think the fellow had got away in front of him. No—most likely he had stood against the wall, let Bill charge past him, and then made his get-away up at the other end. Of course he might not have been bothering about getting away. A really persevering assassin would be all out for that second shot. On the other hand, he couldn't have banked on the neighbourhood having absolutely no reactions to midnight murder. Personally he thought the swab would have cleared out.

He waited five minutes, heard nothing, saw nothing, slipped out of the alley between the end post and the wall, and walked home to his hotel without further incident.

VII

When Meg had shut the door on Bill Coverdale she went into the sitting-room and put on the light there.

That is to say, she pulled down the switch, and the light *should* have come in, but it didn't. She remained standing just inside the door, frowning at the dark room, with the one bright shaft slanting in from the hall to a spot about a yard in front of her. She pushed the switch up, and then down again. There were two little clicks, but nothing happened.

She went back into the hall, opened her bedroom door, and tried the switch there. Again nothing happened except the click. Her frown deepened. It seemed odd that both these lights would go wrong together, when the hall light was all right. She tried the bathroom and the kitchen and found both light were gone. Well, she hadn't got a spare bulb, and she hadn't got any candles, so she would just have to make the best of it and feel her way to bed in the dark. Of course she might take the hall bulb and see if it would work in her room, but if she did that, she would have to make the change in the dark. A little cold shiver ran over her. She didn't like the idea. If there was anything wrong with the fuse, it might spoil the new bulb and leave her without any light at all. That was a definitely unpleasant thought.

She left her door open, and found that she could see well enough. Besides she didn't want to see. She wanted to undress as quickly as she could and get to bed and sleep, a long, long, dreamless sleep. She didn't need a light for that.

She kept all her thoughts on the surface as she undressed. Her dress hadn't looked too bad—she must find the right hanger—she could do that by feeling for it—it was a little colder tonight—the wind was this way—she couldn't be bothered to fill her hot water bottle— nice to slip into bed and lie down—nice to feel sleep waiting for you— Nice to stop thinking and go down into forgetfulness. . . .

But after all she dreamed. Sleep betrayed her and she dreamed. At first it was pleasant enough—a mere hazy sense of being amongst trees, and the sound of a stream flowing somewhere out of sight. She was walking on pine-needles. That was her first really clear impression—thick, soft pine-needles which gave out an aromatic smell when her feet bruised them. She must be walking under pine-trees, but she couldn't see them, only the smooth drifted needles at her feet. And then she knew that she wasn't alone in the wood. There was someone walking behind her with a step that kept pace with her own, so that she could not hear when it fell. She began to run, and the thing that followed her ran too, faster and faster, faster and faster, until with a little click the dream broke off short and she was awake in the dark. Her heart was racing, her mouth was dry. She pushed the bed-clothes away from her shoulders and got up on her elbow to listen. The click which she had heard—had it been in her dream, or here? It had broken the dream, but had it broken it from within or from without? She stared into the even darkness. It was everywhere.

But she had left her door open. She had left the hall light burning, a piece of the most shocking extravagance and one for which she was now being punished, because if she hadn't left it burning it would have been just natural and ordinary to wake up in the dark instead of most unnatural and alarming. She had left the light on, and she had left the door open about a foot. There should have been a lighted patch on the floor, and a long bright panel between the door edge and the jamb. The click that had waked her might very easily have been the click of the closing door. . . .

The draught from the open window stirred her hair. She drew a long breath of relief. The door had blown to, and that was what had broken her dream.

But she ought to have been able to see a bright gleam from under the door. There was always that line of light at the sill when this room was dark and the hall was lit.

The bulb in the hall must have gone wrong. Stupid of her not to have thought of that before—very stupid. Well, there wasn't anything she could do about it now. She had better turn over and go to sleep again—much better—much, much better.

She remained leaning on her elbow—listening. If you listen in the night, there are always things to hear—faint almost inaudible rustling, creaking sounds. If you listen long enough, you can hear your own pulses, the beating of your heart. If you listen longer still, you can hear your own thoughts, your own sick fears. Meg heard all these things. She said to herself, "Get up and go to the door. Open it and strike a match. Go into the sitting-room and see for yourself that there isn't anybody there." *See?* When the minute you struck a match it went out again? Meg said, "I *won't!*" and went on listening. The arm on which she was leaning had gone to sleep. She sat right up and began to move it to and fro to get the feeling back into it again. This was better than listening.

And then all at once there was a sound she did not have to listen for. It came from the sitting-room, and it was a sound which she knew as well as the sound of her own voice. The second drawer of her writing-table squeaked when it was drawn fully out. The sound went right away back into her childhood, because the writing-table was her mother's and that drawer had always squeaked it if was pulled more than half way. Someone must be in the sitting-room at this moment pulling out the drawer. She threw off the bed-clothes and jumped out of bed. The spurt of anger which had taken her as far as this took her for the moment no farther. She stood bare-foot on the linoleum and felt her anger die down into a sort of cold horror.

It was then that the stranger thought looked in again at one of the defenceless windows of her mind—if Bill were here, she wouldn't be frightened and alone like this. This time she was much too cold and afraid to blush. The thought would even have been company if it hadn't been for the sharp realization that Bill was at least three miles away, and that somebody else was in the next room.

With a most frightful effort Meg lifted first one cold foot and then the other, and so took herself to the door. She leaned against it for a moment and then turned the handle and pulled it a bare half inch towards her.

There wasn't any light in the hall. She knew that already, so it was perfectly idiotic for her heart to bang like this. She had known there was no light in the hall from the moment she had looked at the door and seen only even gloom, with no prick of light at the key-hole, no line of light at the sill.

There wasn't any light in the hall, but there was a light in the sitting-room. . . . Was there? She thought so. The door stood half-way open now, and she was sure she had left it wide. It stood half-way open, and the room beyond was not as dark as the hall. There was some light there, and as she stared, one hand on the door and one on the jamb, a sudden shifting ray told her what that light was. Only an electric torch casts a narrow ray like that. The anger that had got her out of bed flared up again. It was very heartening, but it didn't last. If she had been sure it was a burglar in there pulling out the drawers of her writing-table, nothing would have been easier than to run out on to the stair and scream for help. The burglar would be certain to run away, and with any luck he might run into trouble and be caught before he could reach the street. Meg had a very good scream, and she thought she could bank on rousing the block. But she wasn't sure it was a burglar. Suppose it was Robin. Horrible to feel that you would be more frightened if it was your husband than if it was a burglar. Impossible to risk screaming the house down if it was Robin in there with the torch.

Robin was dead.

She stared into the darkness. How could it be Robin, if Robin was dead? A faintness that was not physical came over her. It was her will, her courage, that was near to fainting. If it was Robin who was there and Robin was alive, what was he doing? What darkness and cruelty was this in which he hid himself? What darkness and suspicion was there in her that she should think him capable of such a thing? She felt an agony of self-abasement. Robin was dead. Whatever had been wrong between them should be blotted out. How vile, *how vile*, to accuse a dead man in her thought—to bring him back from the grave in order to accuse him.

She straightened herself suddenly and stood clear of the door. It was no good. If it was vile to think Robin capable of this, then she was vile. But it was he who had taught her to believe the unbelievable. There was no cruelty and no betrayal which she could not believe of Robin O'Hara.

A calmness came over her. She would rather know whatever there was to be known. She caught the edge of the door and pulled it wide. The two open doorways faced one another now with the hall between. She had only to cross the hall and she would know whether it was Robin who was there in the sitting-room. She took a step forward, and all at once that small bright ray leapt out of the darkness and struck her in the face. It dazzled and went out. She shut her eyes involuntarily, and she made some sound that was not quite a scream. Then, before she could move or open her eyes, someone went past within a yard of her and the outer door swung in without a sound and closed again with no more than the click of the latch.

Meg went and stood against it. It was shut. She was alone in the flat. The outer door was shut. No one could come in without a key. No one could have come in without a key. Her own key was in her bag. She had used it to let herself in when she came home with Bill. It seemed as if it was hours, and hours, and hours ago. No one else had a key except Robin. No one could get in without a key. Tomorrow, she thought, she would have a bolt put on the door. No, it was today—today, as soon as the shops were open. She would go to the ironmonger round the corner and get a really efficient bolt.

She left the door and went to the sitting-room. She wasn't afraid any longer. The flat was empty of anyone but herself. But there had been someone here, and she couldn't wait for daylight to know what he had been doing. There ought to be matches on the mantelpiece. She found them and struck one.

The first thing she saw, quite close to her beside the matchbox, was an electric bulb. She wondered if it were the one from the hall. She wondered if the bulb in her bedroom had been taken out too. If it had, then he must have been in the flat before she came home. The match burnt her fingers and she dropped it into the fireplace. A second one showed her the drawer of her writing-table pulled out. She came nearer, but the match went out before she could see whether the papers had been disturbed or not.

She was just going to light a third match, when her mind suddenly woke up. There she was, striking matches like a dazed idiot, with a perfectly good electric bulb only waiting to be put in.

She had to climb on a chair and feel for the socket inside the cloudy bowl which hung from the ceiling. When she moved the chair it knocked against something, and when she put out her hand she found that a small walnut table had been moved out of its place. She wondered why it had been moved.

She went back to the door, but with her hand on the switch, she felt an acute stab of fear. If it didn't work, if the light didn't come— She had the feeling that she wouldn't be able to bear it. Stupid, because you always have to bear things, whether you feel as if you can or not. Her fingers moved with a jerk and the light came on. With a most blessed sense of relief she looked about the familiar room. There was the writing-table with the drawer pulled out, but she had seen that already and her glance went past it. The writing-chair had been moved to one side. She passed that too.

It was the small walnut table which arrested her. As a rule it held books and papers, but they were all gone, cleared off it and thrown upon the couch. The light came from the bowl in the ceiling, and the table stood under the light. It had been moved so that it might stand there. Its surface was broken by a small rectangular card, white against the warm polished brown.

Meg came slowly to the table and looked down at it. The card lay there right in the middle, an ordinary calling card. It had neatly printed across it in the conventional manner:

Mr Robin O'Hara.

VIII

"IT SOUNDS TO ME LIKE A PACK OF NONSENSE!" SAID Garratt. He glared resentfully at Bill Coverdale and went on cramming tobacco into his pipe.

Bill leaned against the mantelpiece and waited. It wasn't the slightest use arguing with Garratt, but when he had told you what a damned fool you were he would as a rule give you a fair innings. He waited therefore quite amiably until the pipe was alight.

Garratt tossed the match in the direction of the fireplace and missed it.

"A pack of twaddle-bosh!" he said rudely. "First you say you wouldn't recognize the woman you saw with O'Hara, and then you come here and tell me you've recognized her."

Bill nodded.

"I recognized her all right."

"Then why did you tell me you wouldn't be able to?"

"I never said I wouldn't know her. And when I saw this Delorne girl at the Luxe last night I recognized her at once—that is to say I recognized her lipstick."

"You recognized her *what?*"

"Lipstick," said Bill. "You know—the stuff girls put on their mouths."

He got a baleful glance.

"How do you mean you recognized it? Every woman in London plasters herself with the stuff!"

"Oh—you've noticed that? Then perhaps you've noticed that the stuff isn't all the same colour. This particular brand wasn't. It was pink, a sort of flannelette pink, and the minute I saw it I knew that I'd seen it before. And I knew when—and where."

"Well?"

"The night before I sailed last year—that's when. And just beyond Robin O'Hara in a taxi—that's where."

Garratt pulled at his pipe.

"You're sure?"

"Yes, I am."

"You can't be!"

Bill picked up the spent match and dropped it amongst the wood and coal of the unlighted fire.

"Well, there's some corroborative evidence—"

"Why didn't you say so?" snapped Garratt.

Bill laughed a little.

"Just waiting for you to say your piece," he said.

"Well, what is it? I suppose you know I've got a job to get on with. What's your evidence? Trot it out!"

"Well, Meg O'Hara obviously recognized the girl—saw her, and didn't want to see her—dropped her handkerchief and turned away to pick it up just as we were passing Miss Delorne. Then when I pressed her she said she knew who she was. She gave me her name—Della Delorne—and when I went on pressing her she told me she'd seen her with Robin O'Hara." He hesitated, and then went on with some change of voice. "It's no good trying to keep things back in an affair of this kind, so you'd better know that she was going to sue for a divorce. O'Hara was a rotten husband. He was a cruel devil, you know, and she'd have been well quit of him. I gathered that Della Delorne would have been the co-respondent."

Garratt blew out another cloud of smoke. He looked through it sharply at Bill Coverdale and said,

"How much did you know of this when you—recognized her?"

"I didn't know any of it."

"Sure of that?"

"Oh, quite sure."

"And after you recognized this girl's lipstick Mrs O'Hara gave you to understand that she was going to have cited her as co-respondent—if O'Hara hadn't disappeared?"

"That's what it amounted to."

"All right," said Garratt, "we'll get on to her. You've probably made a mistake, and we shan't get anything out of it, but we'll try a cast or two. Good-bye—I'm going out."

Bill laughed again.

"I'd hate to keep you, but it might interest you to know that I was shot at last night."

On his way to the door Garratt stopped and came about with a jerk.

"You were *what?*"

"Oh, just shot at—on my way home—in a nice convenient backwater where the local inhabitant is warranted to sleep through anything from an air raid to the day of judgment.''

Garratt came back with a scowl on his face.

"Are you fooling?"

Bill looked mildly innocent.

"Certainly not.''

"Then tell me in plain English what happened."

Bill told him. Before he got very far Garratt produced a map, and he had to start again and trace the way he had taken step by step.

"Minnett's Row—" Garratt jabbed with his thumbnail at the thin black line which represented the lane of crowding houses where Bill had stood to see who would come out of the darkness of the alley-way. "Morton's Alley, and Minnett's Row." Garratt jabbed again.

"It hadn't anything to do with the street," said Bill. "I cut up the alley because I thought I was being followed, and I wanted to know who was after me. As a matter of fact, I'm pretty sure I'd been followed all the way from the flat."

Garratt snapped out a single word—"Why?"

"Well, I was about here"—it was Bill's turn to put a finger on the map—"when I began to think someone was trailing me, and the minute I began to think about it I felt pretty sure I'd been hearing him behind me all the time."

"And the footstep came after you through the alley into the row, and then fired a pistol at you point blank and missed you clean? You weren't drunk, I suppose?" Garratt's tone was in the last degree offensive.

"I was not—I hadn't even taken a drink. And you've got it all wrong. He didn't miss me clean—he took the skin of the top of my ear, and I walked home bleeding like a pig."

Garratt cast an unsympathetic eye upon the wound.

"The fellow must be a damn bad shot. Sure you didn't cut yourself shaving?"

Bill Coverdale straightened up and went back to the hearth.

"Have it your own way," he said. "I thought I'd just tell you—that's all.''

Garratt glared at the map for a moment, and then gave it a shove which sent it off on to the floor.

"Any idea who it could have been?" he said.

"None."

"No one with a grudge against you?"

Bill shook his head.

"Not that sort of grudge."

"You didn't get into a mess in Chile?"

Bill laughed.

"No good trying to drag Chile in."

Garratt walked round the table, picked up the map, folded it with a ruthless disregard for the way in which it was meant to be folded, and banged it down upon his blotting-pad. Then he came over to Bill and prodded him in the chest with a nubbly forefinger which felt exactly like a piece of an iron gas-pipe.

"Who was it? Who do you think it was? You were thinking of someone when you were telling me. Who was it?"

Bill made a slight movement of the shoulders which could not have been called a shrug.

"I thought about O'Hara, but it couldn't have been O'Hara."

"*O'Hara?*" said Garratt explosively. "Damned nonsense!" He went over to where he had left the map, took it across to a book-case at the far side of the room, and jammed it in between a *Who's Who* and a *Burke's Peerage*. Then he looked over his shoulder with a scowl and said sharply, "*Damned* nonsense! O'Hara's dead!"

IX

BILL HAD A DAY BEFORE HIM. WHEN HE HAD INTERVIEWED Garratt he walked round to the dealer from whom he was getting a car, paid for it, collected it, and drove away. He drove to Ledlington, and having in mind that the car was not yet run in, he did not allow himself to exceed thirty-five miles an hour, though he would have liked to have gone a great deal faster. He wanted to see Henry Postlethwaite with the least possible delay, and he wanted to see him before he saw Meg again. Owing to the rather emotional turn which the evening had taken, the Professor had faded into the background. Meg had been too much startled by her encounter with Della Delorne, and too much upset by his questions, to remember that he was going down to see her uncle today. If she had remembered, she would have tried to cramp his style. He knew his Meg, and she would certainly have tried to make him promise not to worry Uncle Henry, not to tell him that she hadn't got any money, and above all things not to suggest that it was his business to provide her with some— all of which things Bill had every intention of doing. He was fond of the Professor, and he meant to be kind, but he also meant to be firm, and he was quite definitely of the opinion that his immediate job in life was to see that the Professor did worry about Meg. It was therefore going to save a lot of wear and tear if he kept out of her way until after he had seen her uncle.

It was a very nice morning for a drive—blue sky, rippled over with small fleecy clouds, some wind, and a sun so warm as to seem more like June than October. There had been rain overnight, and bright drops still beaded the brambles on the shady side of the hedgerow here and there—a wonderful blackberry crop, and the thorn trees loaded down with crimson haws.

He lunched in Ledlington, parking his car in the Square watched over by the statue of Sir Albert Dawnish, whose Quick Cash Stores, now so beneficently universal, had their origin in a humble establishment not twenty yards from this very spot. Ledlington is justly proud of her great man. She has set him aloft in the rigid trousers and all the other distressing garments peculiar to statuary in these islands.

After lunch Bill drove out to Ledstow. The road first crossed an open heath and then, coming on to a lower level, wound amongst trees. Ledstow village consists of a church, a public house, a row of petrol-pumps, and a single street of cottages varying from the timbered Elizabethan hovel to the converted railway-carriage of the post-war period. They all appeared to be equally unsanitary, but alas not equally picturesque. The village pond, thickly blanketed with green slime, gave out an archaic odour which seemed to be holding its own against the twentieth-century smell of petrol. The church, ancient and beautiful, was surrounded by a very large, damp graveyard set about with yews.

On inquiry Bill discovered that Ledstow Place, the property recently bought by Henry Postlethwaite, was known locally as The Place without any further qualification. It was about a quarter of a mile from the village, and was approached by a dark lane which turned at right angles by the pond and skirted the churchyard, the farther end of which marched with its boundary wall. There was a wall all round it—a very sizeable wall.

Bill came to a locked gate, with a lodge beyond it crouching amongst evergreens. He had to sound his horn half a dozen times before anyone came, and then it was an old woman, very slow and deaf, who looked through the gate and asked him his business. He began to think he ought to have wired to say he was coming. He produced a card, passed it through the bars, and shouted,

"I want to see Mr Postlethwaite! I'm an old friend!"

"He don't live here," said the old woman, shaking her head.

"Who doesn't?" said Bill at the top of his voice.

"There's never been any Smiths here that I know of," said the old woman.

"Postlethwaite," said Bill—"not Smith! Professor Postlethwaite!"

"Not that I ever heard tell about," said the old woman dolefully.

It occurred to Bill bitterly that from the point of view of complete security from interruption the Professor had certainly found an ideal retreat, but if anyone thought he, Bill, had come down here just for the pleasure of going away again, they were badly mistaken. He printed the name Postlethwaite on the back of another card, and was rewarded by a fleeting gleam of intelligence.

"Then why did you go asking after Smiths?" said the old woman crossly. "Never none here so far as I know of, and you can't get from it."

"*Post*lethwaite," said Bill with fearful intensity.

The old woman shook her head.

"He don't see no one except by appointment. Very busy gentleman, Mr Postlethwaite."

He certainly ought to have wired, but he had had the oddest, most insistent desire to arrive without warning.

He produced a third card, and wrote on it under his name—"Just back from Chile. Very anxious to see you. Bill."

Five shillings accompanied this through the bars.

"I want to see Mr Postlethwaite. Can you send this up to the house?"

The old woman pocketed the money, read the card with interest, and lifted up her voice in an eldritch scream.

"John-*ee!*"

Round the corner of the lodge there came a slouching lout of eighteen or so. From the state of his boots and hands, he had been digging. He took the card between a grimy thumb and forefinger and set off up the drive at a very leisurely pace. The old woman went back into the lodge.

Bill looked about him. He thought the Professor had taken on a white elephant. The place seemed very large, overgrown, and neglected. The drive had certainly not been gravelled since the war, and there was twenty years of unpruned growth on the shrubs and evergreens which darkened it. The property had probably gone for a song, but it would cost a lot to put it in order. Of course the Professor wouldn't bother. Very likely the lout was all the gardener there was. He was very glad that he had not brought Meg down with him. He had thought of it, but he had wanted a free hand with Henry Postlethwaite. He would have hated it for Meg to sit and wait at her uncle's gate as he was waiting now. It didn't matter for him, but he would have hated it for Meg. There was something depressing about this mouldering old place.

The best of the day was over, though it was not much after half past two. The small fleecy clouds of the morning had spread into an even grey. There was a palpable damp in the air, and a chilly wind which rustled the yellowing leaves of the horse-chestnuts on the other side of the wall. The fruit was falling early because of the drought. Lord—what a melancholy place for old Postlethwaite to bury himself in! He thought of Way's End with its beautiful Georgian front looking, at a dignified distance, upon the village street. . . . Oh well, the Professor had wanted quiet, and he had got it with a vengeance.

The lout came down the drive, and disappeared round the lodge without taking the slightest notice of Bill.

Bill sounded his horn.

Nothing happened. No one came. Three chestnuts dropped. He sounded it again, and went on sounding it.

Presently the old woman came slowly out with a key. She fitted it into the lock, and then stood back and said with sudden loudness, "You can go along up to the house." After which she took two hands to turn the key and opened the gate only just far enough to let him through.

Garratt by this time would have been gibbering, but Bill was the fortunate possessor of a very equable temperament. He meant to see the Professor, and in pursuit of that aim he was prepared to exercise any amount of patience, perseverance, and push.

He walked up the untidy drive at a good swinging pace. It turned almost at once, so that he was out of sight of the lodge. There were weeds everywhere. The shrubbery on either side was choked with untended growth. Beech and chestnut sent out their branches so low across the drive that it would have been dangerous to come up it at night.

There was a second turn, and he came suddenly in sight of the lake. It was quite a considerable body of water, with a belt of woodland coming right to the edge on this side of it, whilst beyond on the farther side, flat down by the water, stood a square barrack of a house with the rough, unkempt grass-land of the park right up to the very walls. The water might have been beautiful, but the house was frankly hideous. There wasn't a tree anywhere near it. There was no attempt at a garden. There wasn't a creeper on its blank grey walls. It had rows of windows looking upon the lake. But its most noticeable feature was, of course, the bridge which ran out to the island.

Bill stood and looked at it. The island was perhaps fifty yards out—a medium-sized island, with a high stone wall all round it. The bridge pierced the wall, and at the shore end entered the house on the ground-floor level at the extreme right of the building. It was a covered bridge on wooden piles, solid, clumsy, and altogether a blot on the landscape.

He began to walk round the lake. The drive skirted it, rising a little and then dipping again, until in the end it landed him upon what had been a large gravel sweep with the front of the house looking down upon it. The gravel had disappeared under weeds and a sort of scumlike moss which was very slippery to walk on.

The house itself was not quite so ugly on this side, but it seemed desolate and uncared for. Some half dozen steps led up to the front door, and they looked as if they had not been cleaned for years. The bell was of the old-fashioned hanging type with a wrought-iron handle like a stirrup. Bill pulled it, and heard the wire squeak faintly in its slot. He had no means of knowing whether the bell had rung or not. In a place like this anything that could get out of order was almost certain to be out of order. Or if it rang, it would ring in some remote sepulchral kitchen where no one would hear it. The house had an extremely uninhabited look.

After a decent interval he rang again. Almost at once footsteps approached and the door was opened. An elderly man-servant stood there looking up at him from under bushy grey eyebrows. He looked up because he was of medium stature and Bill was on the large side. He had the harassed air that any servant might have had in a house so large and so unkempt. Bill looked past him and saw in the hall the familiar furnishings which he had known at Way's End—the carved and twisted Victorian chairs which went so oddly with the panelled oak chest and the great Flemish cupboard with its polished bosses in high relief. He wondered what had happened to Evans. He must have buttled for the Professor for at least twenty years, and it seemed odd that the cupboard, and the chairs, and the chest should be here and not old Evans. All this was in his mind as he said,

"I'm Mr Coverdale. I think Mr Postlethwaite is expecting me. I sent my card up."

Without answering, the man held the door wide open, and when Bill had passed through and he had shut it again, he led the way to the back of the hall. A door stood open there, and Bill came into a small room which was familiar in everything except the outlook from its windows, which gave upon the lake. There were two of them, and they were framed in blue curtains which had hung in Meg's own little room at Way's End. Her old blue carpet was under his feet. Her mother's picture looked down at him with the eyes that were so like Meg's. The chairs in their faded chintz covers were the chairs in which he and Meg had been sitting when he asked her to marry him and she said no. The only things missing were her writing-table and herself.

He wondered why she had left her mother's picture behind her when she went to the flat. He was looking at it, when the door opened and a woman came in. He recognized her at once from Meg's description as Miss Wallace's successor—the white mouse—Miss Cannock. The description was apt enough—the forward stoop of the shoulders and poke of the head, the light greying hair done in some archaic fashion of a fringe frizzed low on the forehead under a hair-net, and fastened up behind in a knob from which faint clinging strands came down upon a bright blue collar and a batik scarf patterned in heliotrope, purple, and grey. It was not only the collar that was blue. The whole dress was of that eye-splitting shade known as royal. It made the sallow face about it a good deal more sallow than it need have been. The scarf, which was long and wide, kept slipping off and sliding down. Bill felt an extraordinary irritation. The woman couldn't help being plain, but she could help wearing clothes like this—and in Meg's room too, where that horrible blue shrieked at the curtains.

Miss Cannock advanced with a timid hand outstretched. She wore large horn-rimmed spectacles with smoky-coloured lenses, behind which her eyes had a vague and peering look. She wore black Cashmere stockings, and shoes with beaded toes. She smiled, showing yellowish teeth, and said in a very high-pitched lisping voice,

"Oh, how do you *do*, Mr Coverdale!"

"Miss Cannock?" said Bill.

X

MISS CANNOCK SMILED AGAIN.

"Oh yes!" she said, and Bill found himself holding a limp hand which weighed heavily in his for the briefest possible moment and then withdrew.

He was astonished at his own relief when she moved away from him and, going over to the window, sat down in a small hard chair with her back to the light. Some ridiculous vein of sentiment made him feel glad that she had chosen this chair which was a stranger, and not one of the blue chairs which belonged to his memories of Meg.

She said, "Won't you please sit down?" and Bill had actually taken his seat before it occurred to him that this was rather ominous. The feeling added a touch of firmness to his manner as he said,

"I'm hoping to see Mr Postlethwaite. I don't know if he has spoken of me, but I am an old friend. Does he know that I am here?"

Miss Cannock was pleating one end of her old-maidish scarf. She didn't look old, but she looked like an old maid. She said,

"Ah yes—that is just the point, Mr Coverdale—that is just the question I was going to raise with you." She smiled in a deprecating manner, and as she did so, he noticed with distaste what seemed to be a slight distortion on the left side of her face. Her smile ran up crookedly and emphasized this twist or whatever it was. He wished she wouldn't smile.

He said, "Yes—but I am very anxious to see him, Miss Cannock."

She continued to smile. Now that she had her back to the light, he couldn't see her eyes at all, only the solemn smoky circles behind which they were looking at him.

"Oh yes, Mr Coverdale—and I'm sure it would give him great pleasure, but if you are an old friend, you will know how difficult it is to interrupt him when he is working— very, very difficult indeed—and I don't know—"

Bill interrupted *her* rather brusquely.

"Does he know I'm here?" he asked.

She fidgeted with her scarf.

"That was the point I was going to raise, Mr Coverdale. It is most natural that you should want to see him—such an old friend, I'm sure, though he doesn't talk about people, at least not when he's working. But just at the moment he is so very much taken up with the book—I should perhaps say *immersed*. He hardly seems to notice the outside world at all. You see, this is his answer to Professor Hoppenglocker,

and he expects it to dispose once and for all of Ottorini's
theory, which he has always considered to be unsound in
principle and—er—fundamentally unscientific."

Bill had not the slightest interest in Ottorini's theory,
which he now heard of for the first time, but he intended to
see the Professor. He said,

"Yes, I know—but he can't work all day and all night, and
I shan't keep him very long. Has he been told that I'm here?"

"Well, as a matter of fact, Mr Coverdale—"

"He hasn't?" He got up. "I wonder if you would kindly
let him know, Miss Cannock. I am afraid I must see him."

Miss Cannock got up too. Her scarf slipped from her
shoulders and she made an awkward flustered movement to
pick it up.

"So very difficult, Mr Coverdale—such strict orders—I
hope you realize. I'll see what I can do, but he is, as I said
before, so *immersed*."

Bill went to the door and opened it.

"Will you tell him that I want to speak to him about his
niece—about Mrs O'Hara," he said.

Miss Cannock clutched at her scarf.

"Oh certainly, Mr Coverdale. You may rely on me to do
my best, but these very clever men are all alike—a world of
their own—no interruptions—and, I am afraid, sadly vague
about family affairs. I have had to urge, positively to urge
him to answer Mrs O'Hara's letters, and very often without
success, but you may rely on me to do my best—oh yes."

She went out, smiling her crooked smile. As if half
unconsciously, she turned to shut the door, but more because
of some inward antagonism than for any real reason Bill
kept his hold of it and watched her, after a moment's
hesitation, cross the hall and pass out of sight down a
passage of which he could see only the nearer end. He
thought he would keep the door open. If there were to be
any comings and goings, he might as well be aware of
them. He disliked that Cannock woman a good deal, and
remembered stout, placid Miss Wallace with regret.

Time went by. A clock struck three. That would be the
old wall-clock which had faced the barometer across the hall

at Way's End. It wheezed a little between the strokes, and unless it had set up new habits in the last year, the time was now half past three. The hands would be all right, but for some reason which no one had ever fathomed, the strike was always half an hour behind. It must be nearly twenty minutes since Miss Cannock had gone away. He wondered what she was doing and whether she wouldn't just come back presently and say, with that smiling lisp, that the Professor was too "*immersed*" to see him.

He walked to the left-hand window and stood looking out upon the lake. It was dark and leaden with the reflection of the low cloud overhead. A slight drizzle had begun, and already there was a suggestion of mist on the ground beyond the water's edge. He was prepared to bet that there would be fog here five nights out of seven in the winter. He could see the bridge going over to the island—all of it, that is, except the bit nearest the house, which was hidden by what he guessed to be the drawing-room bay. The island looked like some ridiculous toy, with its high walls and two chimney-pots sticking up like ears from the sloping roof of the house inside. He remembered that the bridge had a door at either end, and he wondered whether the Professor had locked himself in on his island and was refusing to answer Miss Cannock's not very insistent knock. He had the feeling that she would not try unduly hard to make him hear.

He turned back to the room and went over to the hearth. There was no fire. He wondered how long it was since there had been one. Everything smelt damp—and that after the driest summer on record. What the place would be like in a wet winter beggared imagination. What a mutt Henry Postlethwaite was!

He stood frowning at the mantelpiece, a depressing piece of work executed in a marble which looked exactly like jellied brawn. The little blue and gold enamelled clock which had belonged to Meg's grandmother ticked softly between the blue candlesticks which she had been so fond of. These three things had been at Way's End, but not the horrible family of wooden bears, or the olive-wood box, or the really dreadful photograph frame—silver filagree upon red plush. These bespoke Miss Cannock, and he found himself most savagely resenting them. The frame contained a photograph of the Professor, a badly taken snapshot several times enlarged. From the resulting blur he gathered that Henry Postlethwaite had taken to a beard.

His frown deepened. What was Miss Cannock doing taking snapshots of the Professor, having them enlarged, and framing them? It seemed to him that the old man wanted looking after. True, he had managed to remain a bachelor for seventy years or so, but he was so vague that a determined woman might almost marry him before he woke up sufficiently to resist. He thought Meg had better take the matter in hand. The prospect of having the Cannock as an aunt was most unnerving.

He had another look at the hall, and found it dark and empty. Even considering the afternoon, no house ought to be as dark as this.

He emerged and looked about him. The door immediately opposite would lead into the drawing-room. The staircase went up on the right between him and the front door, and rose to a gallery which ran round three sides of the hall. The passage down which Miss Cannock had disappeared divided the rooms at the front of the house from those at the back. He strolled across to have a look at it, and found it even darker than the hall. It had no window of any kind, and when the doors which gave upon it were shut, as they were at present, it resembled one of those gloomy corridors in an old-fashioned country hotel. Bill wondered whether it was all one one level, or whether, after the manner of such passages, it concealed an unexpected step or two in its shadows.

He was just thinking that he had never been in any house that he liked so little, when a door at the far end of the passage opened, letting in a grey light, and against that light he saw Henry Postlethwaite.

With the cheerful feeling that at last something was going to happen, Bill advanced along the passage. There was a sudden step down which nearly cost his his balance, and as he recovered himself he heard behind him the voice of the man-servant saying,

"This way, sir, if you please."

This presumably meant the way he was going, so he held on with a "Hullo, Professor!"

The door at the end of the passage remained open and afforded enough light for him to see that Henry Postlethwaite was coming to meet him. There was another step, up this time. He stubbed his toe, and then they were shaking hands and he was saying,

"Very nice to see you again, Professor."

"Yes—yes—" said Henry Postlethwaite vaguely. He stood where he was, a stooping shadow with the leonine head and shaggy mane of hair which were so effective in a photograph. The new beard showed as a grey blur against his dark coat.

Bill came straight to the point. You always had to if you wanted to talk to the Professor.

"I know you're most awfully busy, sir, so I won't keep you, but I want to speak to you about Meg."

"Ah—yes—Meg—" said Henry Postlethwaite in his gentle voice. "Ah yes—Meg—how is she? Is's a long time since I've seen her."

"If there is somewhere we can talk, sir—"

The Professor patted his shoulder.

"Yes—yes. Are you in London—are you making any stay?"

"I'm home for good, sir. The firm is giving me my uncle's place on the board. But I wanted to talk to you about Meg."

It was exactly like the Professor to prop the wall, and to remain impervious to any attempts to shift him. Well, if he had got to talk about Meg's affairs in a passage, he had got to, and that was all about it. He wasn't going away without talking about them, and at least Miss Cannock had made herself scarce.

"Yes—yes—" said Henry Postlethwaite—"in town, you say. Then I wonder if you would find it troublesome to go to Malverey's in the Strand and ask them whether they have been able to trace that early pamphlet of Hoppenglocker's that I have been inquiring about. If I could show over his own signature—"

Bill repressed a groan.

"All right," he said. "But about Meg, Professor—I

wonder if you've had all her letters. She's in a very difficult position, and I think she's more than hard up—I believe she's starving herself. I don't know what O'Hara had to leave, but she can't touch any of it until his death has been proved. I'm trying to make her see her solicitor—she ought to have done it long ago, but—"

The Professor laid a hand upon his arm.

"Yes, yes, my dear boy—but just now I haven't time. Of course if Meg wants money—she'd better write to me and tell me how she stands. Did you say she had written? These country post offices are not always very efficient, which is why I should be grateful if you would look in at Malverey's for me about that pamphlet. The early Hoppenglockers are scarce—very scarce—and before I've done with him Hoppenglocker will be wishing they were scarcer still, because if my memory serves me right—and I think it does—in fact I'm sure it does—he has committed himself to a statement—I believe it is on page four—which I can use with really pulverising effect. Hoppenglocker may have forgotten what he wrote in 1903, but I have not." He finished on a triumphant note, patted Bill on the shoulder, and said, "You won't forget—Malverey's in the Strand," and, turning, began to walk back along the passage.

Bill hurried after him.

"But, sir—one moment—" Then, in desperation, "I don't know the name of the pamphlet you want."

Henry Postlethwaite checked that drifting walk of his. He half turned and spoke over his shoulder.

"Number three in the first series—*Wesensgleichheit der Wissenschaft*. I have the other two. At least—" he put his hand to his head and dragged at his hair—"at least I should have—but this move—I must ask Miss Cannock—an invaluable secretary—invaluable."

"I don't think I got that name, Professor. You'll have to write it down for me. Perhaps if we could come somewhere where there's a bit more light—"

"Yes, yes," said Henry Postlethwaite—"number three in the first series. And I'm pretty sure the passage I want is on the fourth page—rather near the top,—a right-hand page."

He produced a note-book and tore out a leaf, which he handed to Bill. "Write it down—write it down. I'll give you a pencil. Ah, here you are! Now write it down carefully, so that there's no mistake—*Wesensgleichheit der Wissenschaft*." He spelt the words out letter by letter.

Bill put the paper in his pocket.

"Professor, I really do want to have a talk with you."

Henry Postlethwaite began to walk away from him again.

"Another day, my dear boy, another day."

"But Meg, Professor—her affairs won't wait. I wouldn't be worrying you like this if they weren't urgent. She won't take money from me, and—"

The Professor stopped by the half open door through which he had come.

"No, no—of course not," he said—"naturally not—she wouldn't care to do that. She had better come down here. Yes, yes, she had better come down here on a visit. Tell her to write to Miss Cannock. I am very busy—very busy indeed. And you won't forget to go to Malverey's, my dear boy, because that is important. And now if you will excuse me." He went through the doorway and shut the door behind him.

Bill turned with an exasperated shrug of the shoulders and made his way back to the gloomy hall. There was no one in sight, and there seemed to be nothing to wait for.

He found his hat, let himself out, and proceeded once again to skirt the lake. Quite definitely a mist was now rising off the water. There was a smell of rotting leaves. He looked back at the house and thought of Meg going to stay there, and hoped with all his heart that she wouldn't go.

He walked on, and just where the drive rose he halted again for a last look at the island. He supposed that the Professor had gone back to it by now. Very bad for him shutting himself up like that. Meg ought to try and shake him out of it. The old woman who had built the house on the island and then walled it all round like a prison must have been as mad as a hatter. You could just see one window over the top of the wall, and no more. The house had a gable, and the window showed—a bare foot of it. He was just going to turn away, when this small square of glass broke suddenly. Something came through it with violence—something with an edge to it that showed for a moment and then was gone, with the effect of having been snatched away.

Bill stared, but could see no more than a dark star-shaped splintering of the glass behind which nothing moved. No sound came from it. Only a very loud sound would have carried that distance. There was no sound at all.

Bill walked on. Someone had broken a window. It was odd, but it wasn't his business.

XI

"I DON'T WANT YOU TO GO," SAID BILL COVERDALE.

"Beggars can't be choosers," said Meg O'Hara.

They were in Meg's sitting-room. The time was about eleven o'clock in the morning, and Bill had been giving an account of his visit to Ledstow the day before. With a good deal of reluctance he passed on Henry Postlethwaite's invitation. Meg might have felt reluctant too if she had either seen Ledstow Place—or not been so hungry. Everything is comparative, and the comparison between dry bread and milkless tea for breakfast, lunch, and supper in London, with three if not four meals a day in even the dreariest of country places, is all in favour of the latter. Also, the tea was running out, and by the end of the week the money would have run out too and there wouldn't be any more bread. So Meg O'Hara said, "Beggars can't be choosers," and managed a smile as she said it.

"Come out and lunch with me," said Bill abruptly.

Meg brightened a little.

"It's too early for lunch," she said.

Bill had another timely recollection.

"Come and have an elevens. We can have lunch afterwards."

Meg hesitated for a moment. Was she going to tell him that there had been someone in the flat the night he had brought her home? She wasn't sure. If it wasn't Robin, she could tell him, but if it was—if it was—

"No good bottling things up." Bill's voice was very quiet. "You'd better tell me what's been happening."

It was no good—she must tell him. She couldn't bear it alone. If you hadn't anyone to talk to, you stopped seeing things as they really were. They got bigger and bigger until you felt as if something was going to burst.

She told Bill about the lights having gone wrong, and about waking up in the night and hearing someone in the sitting-room.

"Pity you didn't see who it was," said Bill when she had finished.

A light shudder ran over Meg. Suppose she had had a match. Suppose she had struck it and seen Robin—looking at her. He had looked at her in so many ways—lightly, appraisingly, coldly, tauntingly, cruelly, and with what she had taken for love. That hurt most to remember now. The shudder threatened to become uncontrollable. Whoever had been in her sitting-room that night has passed her so near that they might with any unreckoned movement have touched. If he had touched her, she would have known whether it was Robin O'Hara.

Bill's voice broke in upon her thought.

"Why wouldn't the lights go on?"

This at least was easily answered.

"Because the bulbs had been taken out."

"The hall light was all right when you went in."

"Yes, I know, Bill—that was clever, because if the hall light hadn't gone on, you would have come in to see what was the matter. But I didn't find out there was anything wrong till you had gone, and of course I hadn't got a candle, so I just left the hall light on and my door open. Then, after I was asleep, my door was shut and the hall bulb taken away." The shiver went over her again.

"Where were the bulbs?"

"One on the sitting-room mantelpiece—that was the one I found and put in—and the others on the kitchen table."

"What was he looking for?" said Bill.

"Do you think he as looking for something?"

"Must have been, otherwise the whole show is pointless."

Meg shook her head. She was very white. Her eyes avoided his.

"It might have been—to frighten me."

"Why should anyone want to frighten you? Who would want to frighten you?"

Her silence said the name she would not speak. If she had had any other name in her mind she would have spoken it aloud.

"It's the most preposterous nonsense!" said Bill violently.

Meg nodded. She was thinking of other preposterous things which Robin O'Hara had done.

"My dear girl, be practical!" said Bill. "Nobody took all that trouble and risk for nothing. Oh yes, it was a risk all right—I might have come in with you and caught him on the premises."

She shook her head.

"No—he wasn't here then."

"How do you know?" His voice was quick and angry.

"I don't know how I know, but I do know. There wasn't anyone here when I came in."

"You mean he came and took out the bulbs and went away again, and then came back when you were asleep?"

She nodded.

"Yes, that's how it was. I'm quite sure there wasn't anyone here when I came home."

Bill was frowning heavily.

"Have you been through the drawer? Is anything missing?"

She made a little helpless gesture.

"'I don't know. You see, the things in that drawer weren't mine—at least most of them weren't. It was Robin's drawer, and I've never really been through it. I suppose I ought to have, but—" Her voice died away on the word.

"So you've no means of knowing whether anything was taken?"

She shook her head in a hesitating way. Then she said rather breathlessly,

"The card might have come from there."

"What card?"

She got up, went over to the writing-table, and came back again. There was a small white card in her hand. She laid it on Bill's outstretched palm and went and sat down again. She was glad to sit down again, because her knees were shaking.

Bill looked at Robin O'Hara's card and said sharply,

"Where was this?"

Meg pointed at the little walnut table, now heaped with books and papers.

"*That* was out in the middle of the room. All the books and papers had been cleared off it. They were on the sofa. There wasn't anything on the table except that card."

Bill stared at the printed name—*Mr Robin O'Hara*. Then he turned the card over and sat up straight.

"Why do you think this card came out of the drawer?"

"Because there's about half a packet of Robin's cards there."

"Get them, will you? I'd like to have a look a them."

She brought him the narrow yellow box, still loosely folded in its white wrapping-paper. The lid came off and the cards ran out upon the wide arm of the chair. A single glance was enough. He said sharply,

"I thought not. That card never came out of this box—at least not this year, Meg."

"What do you mean?"

He held up the card which she had given him.

"Look! This isn't a new card out of a box—it's a card that's been knocking about in somebody's wallet. Look at the colour beside one of these. And look at the corners—worn—you see?"

Meg saw. It was impossible to help seeing what was so evident once it had been pointed out. But it didn't seem to her to make any difference, except that this worn card was more of a witness to Robin's presence than a brand new one would have been. It had been with him through these months of absence. He had touched it and handled it. She knew just where it had lain in his wallet. And with that she had a sudden stab of terror, because Robin's wallet had come empty out of the river a year ago.

The telephone bell rang, and went on ringing. Even after she had put the receiver to her ear, it went on upon a ghostly thrumming note. She shook the instrument and said, "Hullo!" She shook it, and the note went on buzzing in her ear. Then all of a sudden it stopped, and a man was speaking.

"Is that Mrs O'Hara?"

Bill heard her say "Yes," and then "Oh yes, I am." And after that, "What is it? . . . Oh yes, I could. . . . Yes, I think I'd rather. . . . Yes, twelve o'clock would be all right for me." She rang off and turned round to Bill.

"That was the bank manager—Robin's bank. He wants to see me. He won't say why." She spoke in a slow, troubled voice.

Bill laughed a little.

"I should say at a guess you're overdrawn."

She shook her head.

"I haven't got anything to overdraw. It's not my bank—it's Robin's. I've never had an account there."

"Then it can't be anything to bother you."

She said, "I don't know," letting the words fall slowly. And then, "Will you come with me, Bill? I don't want to go alone. You see, the only think I can think of—the only reason he might want to see me—is something to do with that packet I told you about. I was to open it in the manager's presence if Robin was dead. It might be something to do with that, and it if is, I would like you to be there."

Bill shook his head.

"It won't be that, Meg—he'd want legal proof before he'd let you open it. But of course I'll come."

He made her have a cup of coffee and something to eat on the way. His relief at seeing how much better she looked after the food and the hot drink was off-set by exasperation and distress. If she wasn't starving herself, a cup of coffee and a bun wouldn't bring her colour back like that. He cursed the conventions with all his heart. They permitted him to take Meg out and feed her, but forbade him to finance her so that she could feed herself at home. At least that seemed to be Meg's point of view.

They were shown into the manager's private room. He rose to greet them, shook hands, and asked them to be seated, with an air of brisk efficiency. Meg's introduction of Bill as an old friend who was helping her with her business affairs was received with a hard look which only just fell short of being a stare. Not, Bill thought, a genial person, in fact a good deal the reverse, but efficient, undoubtedly efficient. A little man with black hair and a cocksure carriage of the head. He leaned forward in his chair, facing them across the table, and rapped upon his blotting-pad with the fingers of his left hand. It was rather as if they were a class and he was calling it to order. He said,

"I have asked you to come here, Mrs O'Hara, because I was anxious to know whether you can give me any information with regard to your husband." His eyes were sharp on Meg's face. They saw her wince.

She said, "But, Mr Lane—" and then stopped. Her eyes went to Bill.

Bill leaned forward.

"Mrs O'Hara, on the advice of her friends, is about to ask leave to presume her husband's death. We believe that it will be granted. There is—evidence which has lately become available."

Mr Lane transferred that very direct gaze of his to Bill.

"Evidence of Mr O'Hara's death?"

"Yes."

"What kind of evidence?"

"I'm not at liberty to say, but the application will undoubtedly succeed."

Mr Lane looked down at his blotting-pad. There was for a moment a certain effect of rigidity. It seemed to Bill as if he had just heard something which surprised him very much, and that he did not wish to show that he had been surprised.

The effect passed. He looked up again at Meg and asked quickly,

"Then you have not seen your husband lately?"

It was Bill who said, "Of course she hasn't!" And after than Meg answered in a wavering voice,

"Oh no!"

"Or heard from him?" said Mr Lane quite unabashed.

"Mr Lane," said Bill, "Robin O'Hara disappeared over a year ago. Evidence is now available to show that he met with his death by misadventure at the time of that disappearance or a little later. Now may I ask what you are driving at?"

Mr Lane said, "Certainly." He leaned back in his chair and addressed them both. "A week before he disappeared Mr O'Hara deposited a packet with us for safe custody. He told me that it contained papers of considerable importance, and that he wished to safeguard them by imposing some very stringent and unusual conditions. He wrote those conditions down and insisted that we should both sign them. The conditions were as follows. During his lifetime the packet was only to be surrendered to him in person, he himself signing for it in my presence. In the event of his death, it was to be surrendered to his wife, who was similarly to sign for it in my presence. The packet was then to be opened, and she was to consult with me as to the disposal of the contents. I have no idea what the packet contains, except that Mr O'Hara once informed me that he was doing government work of a confidential nature, and I concluded that the papers about which he was taking such precautions had some connection with this work. When Mrs O'Hara informed me that her husband was missing, and that it was feared he was dead, I told her what I am now repeating. I added that I considered myself bound by the conditions under which I had accepted the packet, and that it would therefore be necessary for the death to be proved legally before I could consider that the second of the contingencies provided for had arisen." He spoke with an air of being pleased with his own lucidity.

Meg said "Yes?" in a faintly inquiring voice.

Bill said, "Well?"

Mr Lane went on speaking. He leaned forward. His delivery became less measured, and he tapped on his blotting-pad to emphasize a salient point.

"I will now come to my reasons for wanting to see you, Mrs O'Hara. At ten o'clock this morning, as soon as the doors were open, I received a letter asking me to deliver to the bearer the packet deposited by Mr O'Hara."

"*What?*" said Bill. Then he looked at Meg. She was very pale indeed. Her hands clasped one another tightly. Her face had a pinched and horrified look. He saw her try to speak, and he saw her fail. He asked what she had not been able to ask.

"A letter? You say you had a letter. Who wrote it?"

The manager opened a drawer on his left, drew out a thin sheet of paper, and laid it down on the blotting-pad before him.

"It was signed by Mr O'Hara," he said drily, and once again his eyes were on them both with that look which was not quite a stare.

Meg spoke then. She said,

"Robin—" in a small quivering voice.

"Robin O'Hara," said Mr Lane briskly. He lifted the sheet of paper and passed it across the table.

It was Bill who took it—an ordinary sheet of typing paper with yesterday's date and no heading—a brief typed note:

"Dear Sir,
  Kindly hand over to bearer the packet which I left in your charge just over a year ago.
                                    Yours faithfully
                                    Robin O'Hara."

The noticeable ornamental signature with its upward thrust stared from the white paper. Bill stared back at it. When Meg put out a hand he gave her the letter. Their fingers touched. Hers were very cold. He thought they were too stiff and cold to shake.

She read the letter through and put it back on the table.

Mr Lane picked it up. None of them had spoken a single word.

The silence went on until Bill said bluntly,

"What did you do?"

Mr Lane tapped the blotting-pad.

"There was only one thing I could possibly do."

"You refused?"

Mr Lane's manner became rather more reserved.

"I wrote a line to Mr O'Hara reminding him of the conditions which he had himself laid down, and asked him to call for the packet at his convenience."

Meg made a sudden movement.

"Why did you want to see me?" she said, her voice low but perfectly controlled.

"Because," said Mr Lane, "to be quite frank, Mrs O'Hara, I wanted to know whether you had any knowledge of your husband's whereabouts, and I also wished to ask you for your opinion of this signature."

Meg's eyes widened. She took up the letter, looked at it for a long time, and then gave it to Bill.

"It's Robin's signature," she said.

After one quick glance at the manager's imperturbable face Bill reversed the sheet and studied the signature upside down. Mr Lane's hand offered him a magnifying glass.

"Satisfy yourself. I see you know how the ordinary forgery is done." He turned to Meg in explanation. "Forgers usually turn a signature upside down and copy it stroke for stroke as if they were drawing. A magnifying glass will show where the pen has been lifted. But if this is a forgery, it wasn't done that way."

Bill had been looking through the magnifying glass. He put it down now and said,

"No, there's no break."

"None at all," said Mr Lane. "I naturally subjected it to a careful scrutiny. May I ask whether you were familiar with Mr O'Hara's signature?"

"Yes—we were at school and college together."

"And you would say that this—"

"I should have said that he had written it, if I didn't know that it was impossible."

"And your reason for supposing it to be impossible?"

"I have told you—I believe O'Hara to be dead."

"And you, Mrs O'Hara?"

"I—don't—know," said Meg in a faint, steady voice.

There was a pause. Then Bill said,

"The man who brought this letter—what was he like?"

"District Messenger," said Mr Lane drily. "His instructions were to take the answer back to the office. I asked him to describe the person who had commissioned him, and he gave a description which might have applied to Mr O'Hara."

"What did he say?" said Meg quickly.

"A gentleman in a blue suit and a bowler hat—not out of the way tall, but taller than some. He couldn't say whether he was dark or fair, he hadn't noticed. He supposed he might have noticed if the gentleman had been very much one way or the other. He couldn't say what colour his eyes were. The gentleman was a very pleasant gentleman. He said he'd call back at the office for the answer."

"Not a very useful description," said Bill. "It would fit a good many thousands of people."

Mr Lane nodded.

"Exactly. I did my best to check up on it by instructing one of the clerks to follow the messenger."

"You did?"

"With very disappointing results," said Mr Lane. "The clerk followed him all the way to the office and hung about there for some time. When the messenger came out again, he made some excuse and asked him about the answer. Well, the boy said the gentleman had met him outside the bank, so he had given him the answer there. It must have been just before the clerk came out. He couldn't add anything to his description except that the gentleman was a real gentleman and had tipped him five shillings."

"I see," said Bill.

XII

"WHAT DOES IT MEAN BILL?" SAID MEG AS THEY WALKED away.

"I don't know," said Bill Coverdale.

"It was Robin's signature."

"It looked like his signature. But I'm asking why the letter should have been typed, or why it should have been written at all. You see, Robin evidently considered the packet very important. He laid down those very strict conditions about its surrender, and he would know perfectly well that the manager couldn't go back on them. That packet wasn't to be handed over to anyone except Robin in person or you in person—Robin, if he was alive, or you if he was dead. Now nobody who had made those conditions would be likely to have forgotten them."

"Robin might," said Meg. "You know, Bill, he took things up for a bit and—and dropped them." That was what Robin had done with her, taken her up and—dropped her. Her breath caught for a moment, but she went on. "He ran things hard, and then—lost interest. They were everything one minute and nothing the next. He *might* have made those conditions and forgotten them—I do really think he might."

Bill frowned over that. He said,

"I doubt it. But if he'd lost interest enough to be hazy and indifferent about the packet, why should he want it at all? And if he did want it, why not write a holograph letter, which he must have known would carry a great deal more weight than a bare signature? It seems to me that there's

-77-

only one possible reason for that letter's being typed, and that is that the forger knew he could fake a perfect signature, but was afraid to risk anything more. Did you ever know Robin to type a letter?''

Quite unexpectedly, Meg said, "Yes."

"When?"

"He got a typewriter about a month before he—went. It was a new toy, and he was typing everything."

"He didn't take it with him?"

"No—I sold it the other day. But you see, he might have typed this letter. And if he didn't, who did, Bill? That's what I keep asking myself. Who sent me that paper? Who has been into the flat—twice, and each time left something to make me think Robin is alive? Who *is* it, if it isn't Robin?"

She was so pale that he put his hand on her arm.

"We're going to have lunch. We can't talk like this in the street. It's early still, so we'll get a quiet table if we come in here. Then I'll tell you what I think."

She followed him into one of those small lunch-rooms which have multiplied during the last few years. It was painted in primrose and green—green walls, green floor, green ceiling; primrose linen, primrose china; and waitresses in primrose smocked with green, pretty girls with the air of amateurs at a charity bazaar. There was a table in an alcove which promised privacy.

The prettiest waitress brought them soup in porringers and withdrew. The soup was good and hot. Meg was very glad of it. She felt shaken and bewildered. She waited for Bill to tell her what he thought, and Bill waited to see her colour come back, because just now in the street he had been afraid that she was going to faint.

When the porringers had been taken away, and a chicken and mushroom stew had been set before them in a primrose casserole, he said,

"You've got to eat before we talk, and when we've talked I'm going to put it across you, so you'd better brace up and have a good lunch, because you're going to want it. I'm feeling pretty fierce."

He got a smile which shook him a little. Meg said aloud,

"You're *frightfully* good to me, Bill."

In her heart she felt, "Why have we got to go on like this? It's been so long—I'm so tired. Why have we got to go on talking about Robin? I'm too tired to go on. He was cruel. I'm young—I want to be happy. Perhaps Bill doesn't love me any more—perhaps he does. . . ." The thoughts went to and fro in her mind while she listened to Bill talking about Ledstow, and the Professor, and Miss Cannock. She was glad that he didn't want to go on talking about Robin until she had eaten something and got rid of that muzzy feeling in her head. You ought to be able to live on dry bread, but when you are not used to it you get an uncomfortable sort of feeling of being too light. Ever since yesterday she had felt as if there wasn't anything really to prevent her floating slowly up into the air. It was difficult to think clearly when you had this sort of feeling.

She ate her stew, and the law of gravity resumed its normal action. Bill insisted on cheese, biscuits, and coffee. By the time they had come to the coffee Meg had herself in hand again. It wasn't any use being a coward and not wanting to talk about Robin, because they'd got to. And it wasn't any use saying "I can't go on," because whatever happened you had to go on, and if you had a scrap of decent feeling, you kept your head up and tried not to make things hard for other people. There was no point, for instance, in harrowing Bill. With all her professed uncertainty as to the state of his affections, Meg was sure that it would be terribly easy to harrow Bill. She must therefore be sensible, practical, and a number of other things all rather difficult. What she didn't guess was that her strained courage tried Bill Coverdale higher than her tears would have done. It was so obvious that she was holding on to it with every bit of her strength, and he wanted so terribly to take her in his arms and let her cry there.

"Perhaps we'd better talk now," he said. "Now, Meg— we've got to talk quite plainly or it's no good talking at all. Let's start with the packet. I've got a hunch about that packet—I've got a feeling that it's very important. Just listen a minute. You say, who sent you the marked newspaper with the letters spelling out 'I am alive'? You say, who's been twice in the flat and each time left something there to make you think that Robin is alive? The first time it was the word 'alive' laid out with slips of paper on the hearth-rug. The second time it was one of Robin's visiting-cards. Now I want you to cast your mind back to what was going on when those things happened. The first thing, the newspaper, was in January, wasn't it? And when you told me about it you said Garratt had been urging you to see a lawyer. I asked you if you had seen one, and you said no, because things had begun to happen, things that made you believe that Robin was alive. Garratt had been telling you he was dead, and then this marked newspaper came along and made you think what the person who put it in at your letter-box wanted you to think—that Robin wasn't dead. *And you didn't go to your lawyer.*"

Meg looked at him with startled eyes.

"You mean—"

"Wait a minute. The next thing was someone coming into your flat and laying out the word 'Alive' on your hearth-rug in slips of writing-paper. That was in February, and it happened just after you made up your mind to go and see Mr Pincott after all. You had written to the Professor and been told that he wasn't attending to his personal letters, so you got desperate and made an appointment with Mr Pincott—and right there you came home and found those letters on the hearth-rug. *And you didn't go and see the lawyer that time either.*"

"I couldn't," said Meg. "Bill, I *couldn't.*"

Bill put out a hand and drew it back again.

"That is exactly what you were meant to feel. Then in July you lost your job, had another shot at the Professor, failed, and once more screwed yourself up to seeing Mr Pincott. You didn't get as far as making an appointment with him that time—did you?"

"No—I hadn't time."

"And before you had time someone put what might have been one of your own envelopes in at your letter-box. There was nothing inside except a leaf—a maple leaf—and on this leaf someone had pricked out the word 'Alive.' *And you gave up the idea of going to see Mr Pincott.*"

"Bill—"

"Wait a minute. Now we come down to the present day. I come along, and I urge you to see Pincott. Garratt urges you to see Pincott, and says his people will back you up in an application to presume Robin's death. What's the result? Someone walks into your flat in the middle of the night and leaves Robin's visiting-card on a polished table which has been carefully cleared and put bang under the light where you can't miss it—all very melodramatic and impressive. Now, Meg, think—think hard! What's at the back of all this? Someone who doesn't want you to get proof of Robin's death. Why? What happens when you get your proof—what is the first thing you do? You go the the bank with it, and you and the manager open the packet which Robin tied up with such very strict conditions. That's where we get down to brass tacks. I don't know what's in the packet, and you don't know what's in the packet—but someone does, and that someone is prepared to go to pretty dangerous lengths to prevent its being opened."

Meg looked at him with tired, steady eyes.

"But don't you see, it all points to Robin. You say it's someone who knows what's in the packet. Robin knows. You say someone doesn't want the packet to be opened. Robin wouldn't want anyone to know his affairs as long as he was alive. The person who came into the flat had a key—Robin's key. He had Robin's card—an old card that had been carried about in a wallet. Don't you see that it points to Robin all the time?"

"Wait, Meg—I haven't finished. You've got to take today's attempt to get hold of the packet. Now it may have been a serious attempt, or it may not. That would depend on how much was known about the conditions. If the conditions of surrender were known, no one could have hoped to get away with it on the strength of a signature to a type-written letter presented by a messenger-boy. But the conditions may not have been known—I don't believe this, but I feel bound to put it in as a possibility—or there was no serious expectation of getting hold of the papers, the real object being to strengthen your belief that Robin was still alive, and to make the bank manager sit up and start thinking along the same lines. In other words, it was a try-on of the same kind as the others.''

"And doesn't that point to Robin?" said Meg. "It does—you must see that it does."

"No, it doesn't," said Bill bluntly. "If it was Robin who was nervous about the packet and wanted to make sure it wasn't handed over to anyone else while he was alive, he'd only got to walk into the manager's office and show himself. That's one absolutely solid reason why I don't believe it was Robin."

Meg said in a voice so low that the words only just reached him,

"He wanted me—not to be sure—"

"Meg, *why?*"

She leaned her head on her hand. It had not seemed possible that any words could be fainter, but what she said now had so little breath behind it that it seemed to Bill as if he were hearing her thoughts.

"He was angry—because I said—I would divorce him. He said—I wouldn't find it so easy—"

Bill looked at her. Because her eyes were hidden, he could just for that space let all his passion of love and anger have free course. Was it possible that the truth was behind Meg's whispered words? That Robin O'Hara was capable of a cruel revenge he had no doubt. There was a devilish ingenuity about the man which would have fitted him into a plot like this. Meg had threatened to divorce him, and he had told her that she would not find it so easy—and by gum, he was right. As long as his fate was uncertain, he had Meg tied to him. If she could prove that he was alive, she could divorce him. If she could prove that he was dead, she would be free. It would be most entirely like Robin O'Hara to keep her in a torturing uncertainty. He said,

"Meg, *don't!* We've got to think straight, and we've got to talk it out. If it was Robin who wanted the packet, he could have gone to the manager, and if he wanted him to keep his mouth shut he could have bound him to secrecy. I don't believe Robin was behind today's attempt. There isn't any earthly reason why he should have typed a letter that he could just as easily have written with his own hand. No—it was a try-on, and it was meant to make you and the bank manager feel shaky about assuming that Robin was dead."

Meg dropped her hand and looked at him.

"And do you think that anyone who was playing a trick like that would have dared come right up to the bank to meet the messenger-boy and take the answer from him? No—it was Robin—*it was Robin*.'"

How horrible to be afraid that it was Robin—to be afraid that Robin was alive. If anyone had said to her two years ago, "You'll be afraid to know that he is alive," it would have seemed the maddest lie in the world.

Bill shook his head.

"That's bad reasoning, Meg. Why on earth should Robin have sent a messenger-boy at all if he could come to the bank himself? It's arguable that he might have sent for the packet if for some reason he couldn't come, but if he could come right up to the bank, he could walk in and get the packet. As for its being a risk for anyone who was playing a trick, I don't see that at all. The manager took a very unusual course in having the messenger-boy followed, and supposing this man had thought of that possibility, why, the very safest place for him to meet the boy and take the answer would be just as he came out of the bank, because that's just what nobody would be expecting, and if the boy was being followed, it would be certain to be at some little distance—he would be able to count on that."

"Robin would be able to count on that," said Meg. "It's no use, Bill. I think you're right in nearly everything you say. I don't think it was a serious attempt to get hold of the packet. I think it was a try-on, but I think it was Robin's try-on. He wants to make sure that the packet won't be opened, and he wants to keep me from being sure whether he's alive or dead. It's a trick, but it's Robin's trick. It's no good going on talking about it. You'd better start scolding me—you said you were going to, but you didn't say why."

Bill's expression changed. She was right, it was no good their going on talking about it, and meanwhile he'd got to stop her starving herself. He said bluntly,

"I should think you could guess why. This starving business has got to stop. You've got to have some money to go on with. Call it a loan or anything you like, and if it makes you any happier, I'll swear to dun the Professor for it."

Meg smiled at him with a sudden bewildering sweetness.

"All right," she said in rather a shaky voice. "And don't scold me any more, because I was going to ask you—I really was. Will you lend me five pounds? And you shall get it out of Uncle Henry if you can, but I warn you that it will be a tough job. I sometimes think there's a method about Uncle Henry's vagueness, because it always comes on extra bad the minute anyone starts talking about money— especially if it's his money and they want some of it."

Bill frowned.

"Five pounds is all nonsense!"

She shook her head.

"Bill, you're a lamb, and I know you'd produce fifty without a murmur and never bother whether Uncle Henry paid you back or not. But I don't want more than five pounds, because I've made up my mind to go down to Ledstow. I wouldn't borrow at all, only to be quite honest, I'm down to my last half-crown and that wouldn't get me there, so I'll take the five pounds and say thank you kindly."

"I don't like your going to Ledstow," said Bill.

"Nor do I," said Meg.

"Then don't go."

Meg laughed a little sadly.

"Needs must when necessity drives."

XIII

"WELL, THAT'S WHERE WE ARE," SAID BILL COVERDALE. He addressed Colonel Garratt, who was sitting with his back to him rummaging in one of the drawers of his writing-table.

There was a pause, during which Garratt dragged a file from the recesses of the drawer, dumped it on the floor, and then rummaged again.

"I suppose you haven't been listening by any chance?" said Bill presently.

Garratt turned a grinning face over his shoulder. The grin was a malevolent one.

"Every word. And if you want to know what I think about it—*poppy-cock!*"

"Why?" said Bill from the depths of the least·uncomfortable chair.

Garratt spun his chair round and tipped it back at a dangerous angle against the table.

"Why? Because it *is* poppy-cock. And if you weren't in a besotted frame of mind about this young woman, you'd know it was poppy-cock. Good Lord! Marked newspapers slipped into letter-boxes and then vanishing into thin air— visiting-cards at midnight—leaves with mysterious messages pricked on 'em—letters on the hearth-rug! Your young woman wants a husband to look after her, and you'd better marry her and take her away for a change of air. I hope for your sake she'll lay off the hysteric stunt, because if she don't you'll have your work cut out."

Bill kept his temper. He said:

"Are you suggesting that she was the gentleman in the nice blue suit and bowler hat who sent the messenger-boy to the bank this morning? She's got an alibi for that, you know, because I was talking to her when the manager rang up. Or are you going to prove that she was the thug who followed me into Minnett's Row and blew off the top of my ear? I'm afraid that's no go either, because there really wasn't time for her to get into trousers and pursue me—and I'm prepared to swear to the trousers. Of course she might have had 'em on under her evening dress all the time she was dining with me and going to the theatre—there's such a lot of room under the sort of skirts girls are wearing that no one would notice a flimsy little extra like a pair of trousers!"

Garratt made the most hideous grimace.

"I thought you said it was dark?"

"So it was. But when he legged it he legged it good and proper, and I'm prepared to swear the legs were in trousers. No one could have run like that in a long flapping chiffon skirt and high-heeled shoes."

"Meaning Mrs O'Hara had a long flapping skirt and high-heeled shoes? Well, you can have all that, because I didn't think she'd been shooting at you. Why should she?" He shrugged his shoulders. "You may have annoyed someone else who was keen on her, or it may have been a playful drunk, or—" He looked maliciously at Bill, rolled his eyes, brought his chair down with a thump, and swung round again to the table.

Bill came over and sat on the corner of it facing him.

"Meaning that I'd caught a touch of Meg's complaint—hysteria being well known to be catching. All right, have it your way, but I'd like to know why it is your way. You don't really believe that I faked the top off my own ear, so I would like to know why you're stunting that you do? However, if you don't want to tell me you won't. I notice you haven't put up any theory about the bank business. To my mind that packet's the crux of the whole business."

Garratt looked up suddenly and sharply, nodded, and looked down again. After waiting for a moment to see if he would speak Bill went on.

"I don't suppose you want to know what I think, but I'm going to tell you. O'Hara deposited that packet a week before he disappeared."

Garratt looked up again.

"Sure?"

"Dead sure. According to you he thought he'd got on the track of something pretty big. He dropped hints, but he wasn't giving anything away—wanted to scoop all the honour and glory for himself, I should say. *But* I think he wrote down what he'd got hold of up to date, and I think that packet has got his notes in it, and any bits of evidence he may have come across. Now is there any way of getting that packet handed over?"

Garratt shook his head.

"Only by getting leave to presume O'Hara's death. Has she been to her lawyer?"

"She won't," said Bill.

Garratt swore, not noisily, but with concentrated bitterness.

"Why won't she?"

"She thinks O'Hara's alive. I don't and you don't, but she does. Well, if O'Hara is alive, he wouldn't want that packet to be opened."

"Damn nonsense!" snapped Garratt. "O'Hara's dead!"

"You think so—Meg doesn't. She thinks he's lying low for his own ends—to prevent her getting a divorce amongst other things. Suppose that's so, and suppose he's got other reasons for wanting to be thought dead—reasons connected with the Vulture's old gang which he was trailing—then you see he wouldn't want to have the packet opened prematurely, and he'd be quite likely to take steps to stop Meg's seeing a lawyer or doing anything to establish his death. That's what Meg believes, anyhow. If you don't believe that, then I think you've got to believe that there's someone else who is interested in the packet. Well, who would it be? The fellow O'Hara was trailing—the fellow bossing the Vulture's old show over here. You say O'Hara was trailing him, and that he knocked O'Hara out. Well, then he can't afford to have that packet opened—can he? Say he knows that it'll be handed over to O'Hara's wife as soon as

O'Hara's proved dead—what would he be likely to do? Why, just what somebody has been doing. If he can make Meg so doubtful about Robin's death that she can't bring herself to try and prove it, he's safe. Don't you see, Garratt, he's safe as long as Meg thinks Robin is alive. And that's my theory—I don't believe O'Hara is alive, but I think someone is trying to make us believe that he is.''

"Gleams of intelligence," said Garratt drily. "What you've got to do is to take that young woman of yours by the scruff of the neck and get her into her lawyer's office—galvanize her and galvanize the lawyer—make yourself damn disagreeable—ring up twenty-four times a day until he'd rather get on with it than hear your voice on the telephone again. Your name'll be mud, but you'll get a move on. We want that packet—we want it damn badly. When we've got it open we shall know who's right." He gave a short laugh. "Amusing if it's only his will! I don't suppose he had anything to leave but debts."

Bill put the flat of his hand on the table and leaned on it.

"Look here, Garratt—"

"What?"

"What *was* the Vulture's game?"

"High-class blackmail," said Garratt—"very high-class. Used it to produce strikes. Used it to produce political situations and then played the markets. That was his main line. Lots of ramifications going off into ordinary crime—dope, coining, all that sort of thing. We came into it on the political side. We broke the Vulture—he committed suicide. But the show went on. It's international, and when they've made one country too hot to hold 'em they move on. France has been having a round-up, so it'll be our turn again. We've never been able to stop all the earths.''

"You think—"

"I think O'Hara got on to something. He was a fool to try and work alone. He wouldn't have a chance against that crowd. They got him.''

"And the packet?"

"There may be something useful there—it looks like it. Get Mrs O'Hara going, and keep her going until we can get hold of it. It's up to you. And don't swallow any of that tripe about O'Hara's being alive. If he ran his head into that hornets' nest he was as good as dead before he started.''

Bill got up to go, but when he was nearly at the door Garratt called him back.

''About that Delorne girl—''

Bill turned round.

''Yes?''

''I've had a report about her. Not much in it. Not so young as she was. The sort of actress that don't act—hangs around the theatrical agents once in a while. Comes and goes a good bit. Said to have been abroad. Was in a Pierrot show at Blackpool for a few days in August—had a row and walked out. That's the only professional engagement there's any evidence of. There's always a man in tow. Small flat in Oleander Mansions—she's had it for about fifteen months, but more often away than not. No maid—daily woman when she's there—respectable person who works for several people in the block. Someone's been put on to sound her about O'Hara.'' Garratt made a grimace. ''The char may remember him—Della probably won't by now. I suppose you wouldn't like to try your luck with her?''

Bill smiled pleasantly.

''More in your line, Garratt,'' he said, and made haste to be gone before the storm broke.

XIV

MEG WENT DOWN TO LEDSTOW THAT SAME AFTERNOON. She sent a wire and caught a train, refusing Bill's offer to drive her down. She was, in fact, running away—from Bill, from the telephone to which bank managers called you, and from the flat of which someone else had a key. If Bill went on coming to see her and being a perfect lamb, she would end by crying on his shoulder, and then things would become impossible. If she had simply got to make a fool of herself and weep on anybody's shoulder, it would be much safer for it to be Uncle Henry's—much, much safer. She didn't want to go to Ledstow, but Ledstow would be safe.

She got to Ledstow in the dusk of a windy evening, and long before she arrived there she was regretting Bill and the proffered car. First there was the change at Ledlington, and three quarters of an hour to wait for the local train to Brant. At Brant there was another change, and a twenty minutes' wait, after which an even slower and more local train conveyed her and two other passengers to Deeping, which was still three and a half miles from Ledstow. There was said to be a bus, so Meg waited for it. As Ledstow was only seven miles from Ledlington, she had begun to wish that she had given the trains a miss and walked, only she had a trunk and a hat-box, and you can't walk seven miles with a trunk and a hat-box.

When the bus came it was very doubtful indeed about the trunk, but in the end they permitted it to be balanced precariously upon the wide step, where Meg and the conductor had to steady it all the way to Ledstow.

The bus stopped at the Green Man. The problem of transport had once more to be wrestled with. The landlord's wife, a large solidly built woman with a high colour and a hard eye, suggested William and the wheelbarrow, whereupon William was produced from the garden, a lanky hobble-dehoy in a bright blue pull-over which made his red hair look exactly like a newly scraped carrot.

There was an argument about the wheelbarrow, which was full of pig manure—William, covered with blushes and freckles, being understood to say that when he was garden-ing he was gardening, and if they didn't want the ground dug, well, why didn't they say so and have done with it, and as for putting the lady's box in a-top of the manure, that wasn't no way to treat a box nor a barrow neither.

Everybody in the inn had by now gathered about Meg and her luggage—the landlord, Mr Higgins, the large square pendant to his large square wife; Miss Yeoman from the post-office and general shop next door who had come in for a word with Mrs Higgins, who was her sister; and an old woman with very thin white hair and a man's cloth cap who appeared to be William's grandmother. She had a high piping voice and was full of bright ideas.

"Tip the muck out on the marrer-bed."

"What's the good of that, mother?" said the publican. "Marrers is over or next door to it."

"Not until there's a frost they ain't," said the old woman. "You tip it out like I say, William, and your mother'll give you a nice piece of newspaper to put in the barrer to keep the young lady's box from the muck."

Miss Yeoman stood on the top step and looked refined. She wore tight stays, a long skirt, and a carefully controlled fringe. Her thin nose twitched with disapproval.

William disappeared sulkily, and as sulkily returned with a large wooden barrow which reeked of pig. It was the old woman who produced the newspaper, sheet upon sheet, mostly *News of the World,* and then superintended its disposal in the most efficient manner. Miss Yeoman tittered a little, the publican and William stacked the luggage, and Meg set off, walking beside the barrow, up the lane that skirted the churchyard.

They were stopped, as Bill had been stopped, by the locked gates. It really did seem the last straw after that interminable journey. When it appeared that they would have to wait whilst a message was sent up to the house, Meg could have wept with pure rage.

"Why do they keep the gates shut?" she said to William as they waited.

William blushed scarlet.

"I couldn't say, I'm sure."

The waiting seemed endless. She tried to lure William into conversation.

"Are you fond of gardening?"

William flushed an even livelier scarlet and shook his head.

"Do they always keep these gates shut?"

"I couldn't say."

"Do you know that boy who's gone up with the message?"

William shook his head. A tuft of his thick red hair fell over his eyes and he pushed it back again.

"Don't he and the old woman belong here?"

He shook his head again, and the hair once more came down into his eyes.

Meg gave it up. She had never seen a boy who blushed so easily or who had so many freckles. Even his ears and the back of his neck were scarlet.

It was getting darker every minute. She thought regretfully of the world she had once inhabited. In that world you didn't have to wait outside a locked gate while the garden-boy went up to the house and asked if you could come in. Neither did you arrive on foot with your luggage in a smelly wheelbarrow which had been used for carting pig manure. No, you drove in, and people were waiting to welcome you and give you tea. The thought of the hot tea of which there didn't seem to be any earthly chance was dreadfully unnerving. The dusk continued to fall, the gate-woman had gone back into her cottage, William blushed silently beside her, and the barrow smelled to heaven.

Someone came into view round the turn of the drive, and Meg's heart leapt up. It was a soft and affectionate heart, and the fact that Uncle Henry had taken the trouble to come down himself and let her in had an instant and uplifting effect. She felt that it was lambish of him—but then of course he really was a lamb, except when he completely forgot that you existed.

"The old gentleman's coming," said William in an awed tone.

The figure that was advancing towards them could not even in the half light have been anyone except Henry Postlethwaite. The stooping figure with the slight limp, the broad black wide-awake, the ulster with its out-of-date shoulder-cape, were all as unmistakeable as they were characteristic.

As he came up to the gates, Meg saw the white beard

straggling across the dark muffler. She remembered with a shock that he had grown a bread—Bill had said so. But what a horrid, untidy thing to do. She would have to try and get it off again.

Henry Postlethwaite came up to the gates and opened them with a key which he took out of the ulster pocket. He threw back the right-half leaf, and in a moment Meg had run into his arms.

"Darling, why are you all locked up like this? Is it a siege? And weren't you expecting me? Didn't my wire come, or did you forget to open it? I think it's time you had me back to look after you. Aren't you pleased to see me?" She kissed a small piece of cheek and a much larger piece of muffler.

Henry Postlethwaite patted her shoulder in the vague and amiable manner of one who feels that a demonstration of affection is expected of him and is anxious to do the right thing.

"Yes, yes—just so, my dear." His voice, that very soft and gentle voice which had a trick of dying away in the middle of a sentence, now performed that trick. He seemed about to shut the gate, but Meg hung on his arm.

"There's William and my luggage, darling. Even if there is a siege, I must have my luggage. Come along in, William."

"Yes, yes," said the Professor.

The wheelbarrow appeared to surprise him. He stood aside to let it pass, and he and Meg then followed it up the overhung and gloomy drive. It was practically dark under the trees, but William seemed to know the way. The barrow squeaked along at a good pace, and Meg reflected that even in the pitch dark it would be possible to follow it by scent alone. She squeezed the Professor's arm through the folds of the ulster.

"Darling, you haven't told me why you're all locked up like this. Is it so as not to be interrupted?"

"Yes—yes—that was my reason for coming here—I told you."

"I shouldn't think there was anyone here to interrupt. The book ought to get on like lightning."

"Fairly well," said Henry Postlethwaite—"fairly well—but I mustn't be interrupted."

He was telling her that she mustn't interrupt. But he needn't tell her that. It hurt after all the years they had lived together. The feeling that she had had a long journey and no tea came over her again. She said quickly,

"Darling, you know I won't."

He said, "No—no," but not as if he really meant it.

Her hand fell from his arm. He had been shutting her out ever since she married Robin O'Hara, but somehow she had thought it was going to be different now. He had asked her to come, and she had thought it would be like going back into the old times. But you can't do that—you can't go back.

They came out from under the trees, and she saw the black glimmer of the lake, and the house on the far side of it with a bright shining window uncurtained right in the middle of its dark rectangle. She could just make out the shape of the island against the water. There was no light upon it. And as she looked, the lighted window in the house shut like a closing eye. Someone had pulled down a blind, and the even dark was over all.

They skirted the lake in silence and slowly. Henry Postlethwaite had never been active. He had been lame for years, but she thought his limp more pronounced and dragging than it used to be. She would have liked to say something, to ask him how he was, but she felt that he was far away and out of reach. A wave of homesick longing for Bill came over Meg. There was nothing new about Uncle Henry's going off into his own thoughts, but just now, just tonight, it did give you the most dreadfully isolated sort of feeling. A depressing sentiment from Matthew Arnold came into her mind:

> "Yes, in the sea of life enisled,
> We mortal millions dwell apart."

One of the gloomier classics. It finished on a really cheery note with the assertion that:

"A god, a god our severance ruled
And bade between our shores to be
And unplumbed salt estranging sea."

The tears stung sharply in her eyes. What a fool she was to think about Bill. He wasn't here, and that was an end of it. She had come here to get away from him, so what was the good of wishing he was here? The more she wanted him, the more it proved that she had been right to run away. If Robin was alive, there could be nothing but that unplumbed salt estranging sea between her and Bill. The tears stung again. What on earth had made her think of that mouldy poem? She supposed it was the island, and that horrid lapping water, and the new desperate feeling that she must, must, *must* go back to town. No, not town—Bill. . . . She had retreated as far into her thoughts as Henry Postlethwaite had into his. Neither of them spoke a single word until they reached the house.

Henry Postlethwaite walked straight in. There was a man-servant in the hall. He spoke to him as he passed, and went on and away out of sight.

The man-servant came forward—a nondescript middle-aged person in a grey house-coat. His manners were so correct that William and the pig-barrow did not ruffle them in the least. He had the luggage brought in, told William to wait, and after showing Meg into the room where Bill had interviewed Miss Cannock he returned to see William and the barrow down the drive and lock the gates after them.

XV

MEG WAS LEFT IN THE STRANGE ROOM WHICH CONTAINED all the familiar furnishings of her own room at Way's End. Somehow this seemed to make it all the stranger. One thing was a relief at any rate—the house, remote and isolated though it might be, was fitted with electric light. She had expected the dimmer kind of oil lamp, and was truly grateful.

She sat down in her own favourite chair and waited for something to happen. Uncle Henry had vanished into the blue, which was, of course, only what one might expect. He had probably already forgotten that she was here. The man would doubtless come back when he had locked the gates after William. But where was Evans—and Mrs Evans? She hadn't heard a word about their having left, and yet if either of them had been in the house when Bill came down, they would have made a point of seeing him. Mrs Evans had always had the softest of soft spots for Bill, and it just wasn't conceivable that either of them would allow *her* to arrive and be received by a stranger. Perhaps they were away on a holiday and the man in the grey coat was a stopgap. It simply wasn't conceivable that they should have left Uncle Henry after—how long was it?—twenty years.... Unless they had kicked at coming to this horrible gloomy place.... "But they wouldn't leave Uncle Henry—they wouldn't," said Meg with a quick rush of conviction. "They *wouldn't*."

The horrible desolate thought came to her that one or both of them might be dead. It was a very desolate thought.

There never had been a world without Evans and Mrs Evans in it. Right back in the very beginning of what she could remember there was Evans lifting her on to a chair with a cushion on it for dessert, peeling an orange or an apple at the sideboard and putting it solemnly before her, or fishing in the preserved ginger jar with a queer long spoon, whilst Uncle Henry sipped his port, or forgot to sip it, and looked vaguely past her at his own thoughts. And Mrs Evans, with her deep voice and her feather-light pastry—she used to let Meg roll out her own little lump of dough and make a doll's tart—only Meg's pastry always came out a funny grey colour, besides being as heavy as lead. "And you'll never make a cook, Miss Meg, not from now to doomsday."

"Not if I try *very* hard, Mrs Evans?"

"Trying's no manner of use, my dear. There's born cooks, and there's them you might teach for h'ever and h'every mite they cook 'ull lay as 'eavy on the stomach as if it was cobblestones. You're one of them, Miss Meg, and there's no getting from it. Flying in the face of providence, I call it, and a spoiling of good food, but so long as it's only dolls you're cooking for it won't 'urt 'em and no harm done."

No, it really was impossible that these two pillars of Uncle Henry's house should have removed.

The door opened and Miss Cannock came in, beaded shoes, blue dress, batik scarf, horn-rimmed spectacles, and fuzzy fringe all as unchanged since Meg had last seen them as if she had lived in a glass case during the intervening thirteen months. She shook hands in an agitated manner.

"Oh, Mrs O'Hara—I'm afraid you've been waiting! Mr Postlethwaite is so forgetful—I really did not know that you had come. If I had not met Miller, I should not have known now—and you must have been thinking it so *strange*. But you know how it is when Mr Postlethwaite is working—he becomes completely oblivious and—*immersed*. There is really no other word for it."

Meg discovered that the one thing that could make her feel worse than she had been feeling was to have Uncle Henry explained to her by his secretary—his quite new secretary. If it had been fat old Wallace now—but not this little fuss-pot of a Cannock. Out loud she said politely,

"It's quite all right. Perhaps I can go up to my room—I'd rather like to unpack."

Miss Cannock continued to fuss.

"Oh yes. Miller was taking your things up—that's how I knew you had come. Oh yes, of course."

"Where are the Evanses?" said Meg suddenly.

Miss Cannock repeated the name.

"Uncle Henry's old butler and cook," said Meg.

She was being abrupt, but she didn't feel as if she could wait and beat about the bush. She felt a desperate impatience to hear Miss Cannock say, "Oh, they're having their holiday," or, better still, "They've gone into Ledlington for the afternoon."

Miss Cannock didn't say either of these things. She produced a thick crumpled linen handkerchief and used it to chafe the end of her nose as she said in rather a flustered voice,

"Didn't Mr Postlethwaite tell you? It was most terribly inconvenient—just before the move too—most, most disturbing. But we are very fortunate in Miller and his wife—a really admirable couple."

"But, Miss Cannock—what happened—why did the Evanses leave? Was it because they wouldn't come here?"

Miss Cannock put away the handkerchief in an old-fashioned pocket let into a seam of the blue skirt.

"Well, I believe it was partly that, Mrs O'Hara. But I don't think they were well either—I know they complained of illness. And they both left together, which was very disturbing for Mr Postlethwaite—very disturbing indeed. I don't know when I have seen him so much put out. But he was able to engage the Millers at once, and they have been most satisfactory."

"Did Rose go too?" said Meg.

"Oh yes," said Miss Cannock brightly. "With her home in the village, she didn't wish to come away. Indeed I think she was engaged to Colonel Johnson's chauffeur, or thinking about it, which comes to very much the same thing." She opened the odor and led the way into the hall. "Your room is the one over this, and the furniture is what you used to have at Way's End, so I hope it will make you feel at home. Oh no—Rose wouldn't have cared to come away at all, and indeed we do very well without her. The Millers are both very active, and they manage the work between them very well.''

The hall had been dark when they emerged upon it. Still talking, Miss Cannock found a switch, when a small amber-shaded light came on at the head of the stairs. These ran up one side of the hall to meet a gallery upon which the bedrooms opened. Miss Cannock threw open the first door on the left, and they came into a bedroom of the same size and shape as the study below. The light in the ceiling showed Meg a replica of her bedroom at Way's End. With the curtains drawn it might have been the very room. Yet it was a feeling of strangeness which took hold of Meg as she looked about her and saw the bed in which she had slept until her marriage, the looking-glass which had reflected her as a bride, the curtains and the carpet which she had chosen for herself—all her own things in a place to which neither they nor she belonged. It made her feel rather giddy, and for a moment she missed what Miss Cannock was saying.

Her luggage was here, unstrapped by the efficient Miller. She noted vaguely that old Mrs Higgins' layers of newspaper must have been efficient too, since the smell of pig appeared to have been left outside with William and the barrow.

She woke up with a start to find that Miss Cannock was explaining about the meals—''So he has a tray in his study and doesn't join us.'' *He* must be Uncle Henry. But how terribly bad for him. She said this aloud,

''But, Miss Cannock, that's dreadfully bad for him! You mustn't let him do that!''

Miss Cannock fidgetted with the ends of her batik scarf.

''Oh, but I couldn't, Mrs O'Hara! I'm sure you will understand the deep reverence which I feel for his work, and I couldn't—I really *couldn't*—risk upsetting him in any way. The book is at a most critical stage.'' The handkerchief came out again, and the end of the nose was rubbed until it was quite pink.

''Do you mean to say that he has *all* his meals in his study?''

"Well, yes, Mrs O'Hara. I do hope you don't think I've been wrong, but it was so *difficult* to get him to come to meals, and he wasn't really eating enough. But I found that a nice little tray carried in and put down beside him would often tempt him when it was quite useless for me to beg him to come over from the island."

"He has his meals on the island?" said Meg. Her voice was louder than she had meant it to be.

"Oh yes, Mrs O'Hara. His study is on the island."

Meg thought of so many things to say that in the end she said nothing. What really stopped her was the sudden realization that it wasn't for her to say anything. She wasn't Uncle Henry's home niece any longer. She was just a visiting relation. Like David, she held her tongue, and, like David, it was pain and grief to her.

There was a little empty pause. Miss Cannock put away her handkerchief in a deprecating manner.

"I am afraid it will be a very *dull* visit for you, Mrs O'Hara. I am very much occupied, and Mr Postlethwaite is, if I may say so, immersed—really *immersed*. I am afraid that you will find it very dull indeed."

Meg was afraid so too. When she had been left alone to unpack, she wondered how long she would have to stay, and what on earth she was going to do with herself. She would have to go for long walks. Perhaps they would give her a key, so that she could get in and out without such a prodigious fuss. And she could read, and write letters, and mend her stockings. And she might knit herself a jumper. She hadn't had a new garment of any sort for a year. She could go into Ledlington and get the wool—there simply must be a bus into Ledlington some time in the day. It wouldn't cost much, and she could pay for it out of Bill's five pounds, which Uncle Henry must be made to pay back. He'd do it like a shot of course if she could only get hold of him in a lucid interval.

When she had unpacked, she thought she would explore so as to be able to find her way about the house, but first of all she went to the nearer of the two curtained windows and looked out. There was a blind inside the curtain. She slipped between it and the glass and waited for her eyes to get used to the darkness. It was quite dark now—the sky, veiled and heavy, the woods dense blackness, and the lake like ink. The window looked right down upon the lake. She could just see the island and the bridge which crossed to it, or rather she thought that she could see them. Yet when she strained her eyes to see more she began to doubt whether she had seen anything at all. It was as dark as that. She left the window, and the light of the room dazzled her.

She came out of her room, and considered which way she should go. Her door opened by the head of the stairs. A short length of gallery ran to the right towards the front of the house, a second crossed the back of the hall, and a third followed the opposite wall. No wonder the house looked a great barrack from the outside, with this big hall taking up so much of the inside space. It was miserably lighted—just the one small light at the head of the stairs—but she could see that doors opened upon the gallery on all three sides.

She turned to the right and came to a door which wasn't quite shut. Pushed open, it disclosed a dark passage. She went along it, feeling with her hand on the wall. Almost at once she came to a door on the left and, opening it, found the switch. It clicked, but no light came. The windows showed uncurtained and the room felt empty.

She took a few steps forward upon naked boards and retreated into the passage.

Another door on the right. This time the light went on and showed a bathroom. She went back thankfully for her towel, and washed her face and hands. The water was tepid, and she had the horrid conviction that the kitchen was about a mile away, and that the water would probably never be any hotter than this. It was a very depressing thought.

She left the bathroom light on and continued to explore the passage.

The next door showed, not a room, but an uncarpeted wooden stair going steeply down. A gleam of hope penetrated the gloom. Perhaps the kitchen was on this side of the house after all. Perhaps a hot bath was not so definitely off the map as she had feared. If Mrs Miller had a human heart under the efficiency commended by Miss Cannock, it might be possible to achieve one. She left the door ajar and went softly down to the turn of the stair and a step or two beyond it, and there stopped because she could hear voices. Perhaps it wouldn't be tactful to descend on Mrs Miller by way of the back stairs. Meg had an impulsive nature, but being married to Robin O'Hara had most painfully taught her to be afraid of acting upon her impulses. She therefore halted and was in doubt. "Better go back," said the Meg who had learnt her lesson. But before she could obey her own order a chink of light showed below her in the darkness, as if a door at the foot of the stairs had moved in a sudden draught. She could see the shape of the door, and the light beyond it—a faint, diffused light—the light perhaps of a passage dimly lit, not the light of a room. She could feel the draught blowing towards her now. The line of light narrowed and then widened again. Of course—the door at the top of the stairs was open and the draught was moving this other door.

She had just settled this in her own mind, when a man's voice said, not loud, but angrily,

"There's no sense in taking risks! You ought to have put her in one of the front rooms!"

Meg tingled from head to foot as if she had received an electric shock. It was the voice of the invaluable Miller. What an *extraordinary* thing to say!

A woman answered. If it was Mrs Miller—and it must be Mrs Miller—she spoke like an educated woman. It was not exactly a pleasant voice, but it had a certain charm, a certain attraction. It said with light sarcasm,

"Not at all. I wanted her to feel at home—with her own furniture. Old memories—childhood's days, etc."

Meg tingled again, this time with rage. If this was Mrs Miller, then Mrs Miller had a stupendous nerve.

There was no time for more than a flash of thought before the man said,

"You could have moved the furniture into one of the front rooms, couldn't you? It's asking for trouble to let her look out on the lake!"

Bewilderment succeeded anger—a cold bewilderment that was somehow touched with fear.

And then the woman laughed, a light rippling laugh which was not in the least in keeping with the back stairs, and the voice said lightly,

"What a fuss about nothing!"

"*Nothing!*" Miller was still angry.

There was another laugh.

"What does it matter when it's for such a very little time?"

The draught banged the door, and the sound gave Meg a startled impetus. She was at the top of the stair before she had formulated any definite thought of flight.

She ran back to her own room, switching out the bathroom light as she passed.

XVI

SHE WROTE TO BILL THE NEXT DAY:

"Bill darling,

This is the most mouldy show. I don't think I am going to be able to stick it for very long. You've seen the house, but you've no idea what it's like to live in. Uncle Henry met me, and I haven't seen him since. His study is over on the island. He has his meals there and everything. I think it's terribly bad for him, and the Cannock obviously hasn't the slightest control. You know what he's like when he's working, and if he isn't treated with firmness he just wanders off into a world of his own and forgets that you exist. Old Wallace used to be awfully good at rousing him—she used to insist on his going out for walks—but the Cannock just comes over helpless and wrings her hands.

I'm writing this so as to have something to do. If you write me a nice long letter I shall read it gratefully for the same reason.

"Meg."

P.S. The water is cold.

P.P.S. There is mould on my mattress, which is wringing wet.

P.P.P.S. Some time in the next twenty-four hours there'll be mould on me."

Bill got this letter at breakfast—not the day after it was written, but the day after that. He looked at the heading and the postmark, and frowned. He would like to feel that Meg's letter would reach him quicker than that.

As he turned the envelope over, something arrested his attention. It was a very little thing—a very little smear beside the flap. He slanted the envelope to get the light on it, and found the smear again, just a mere track of it on the other side of the flap. His frown deepened. Meg might have opened the envelope and then stuck it down again, or she might not. Somebody had.

After Bill had frowned at the envelope for about a minute and a half he made up his mind that Meg had written something which she had afterwards thought better of. She had therefore opened the envelope, torn up her original letter, and written another one. He wanted very badly to know what she had said in the first letter. There was no means of finding out.

He put the letter away in his wallet and went out and looked at the flat which he was taking over from the Hewletts. Jack Hewlett was just leaving the War Office and having two months' leave before rejoining his regiment in the north. Bill was therefore taking on the flat furnished for the first two months, which suited the Hewletts because they didn't want to store their furniture, and suited him because he hadn't got any. Before the two months were up he hoped that Meg would have been brought to believe that she was a widow, and that there was no reason why she should remain one. They could then buy furniture together, and he wouldn't risk putting his foot in it by getting things that she wasn't going to like. He felt sure she would like the flat, because there was a really topping view and all the rooms were light and airy. He wanted to move in as soon as possible, because he loathed living in an hotel, but he would have to fish round for a reliable couple. Mrs Hewlett gave him the address of three registry offices, and he started off with the quite irrational feeling that to engage a suitable couple was the first step towards marrying Meg.

All the offices promised him couples of unexampled integrity and efficiency. It was almost bewildering to realize that there were so many worthy people all passionately anxious to cook his dinners and serve them.

He was leaving the third office, when a man who had stood aside to let him pass looked up suddenly and exclaimed,

"Mr Bill!"

Bill received a shock of pleasant surprise.

"Good Lord—*Evans!*"

Evans took the hand which he extended and shook it respectfully.

"I beg your pardon, sir, but I was took—taken—entirely by surprise, thinking you was—you were—still abroad."

"I'm home for good," said Bill. "And what are you and Mrs Evans doing? I'd no idea you had left the Professor."

Evans' face, lofty of brow and benign of aspect, assumed an expression of settled melancholy.

"Ah, sir, and well you might say that. If anyone had told me or Mrs Evans that we should be looking for a job, and Mr Postlethwaite still above ground, well, we wouldn't have believe it, sir."

"Good Lord, Evans! *Are* you looking for a job?"

"Mrs Evans and me is—are—so obligated, sir."

"Walk along with me!" said Bill abruptly. Visions of Mrs Evans making pancakes for him and Meg—making omelettes—making those game pies which were like a beautiful dream—floated rosily into his mind. He wanted a couple—the Evanses wanted a job. Oh, frabjous day, calloo, callay! "Now tell me all about it. Why did you leave the Professor? Get it off the chest!"

Evans' melancholy became a shade more marked. Bill discerned a trace of hauteur, a trace of feelings too badly hurt to be revealed, a tinge of the "I could an' I would, but nothing will induce me too."

He patted Evans on the shoulder and said encouragingly, "You'd much better tell me."

"Mr Bill, sir," said Evans, "I couldn't have believed it—no, nor Mrs Evans neither. Twenty-five years we been with Mr Postlethwaite, and give every satisfaction."

"He didn't give you notice!"—Anyone who sacked the Evanses must be completely batty.

Evans coughed.

"I won't deny that we were took—taken—ill. And a very remarkable indisposition, if I may say so, sir. Mushrooms it were attributed to, but to ask me to believe as Mrs Evans, with her experience, could be deceived in a mushroom is just beyond the bounds of possibility. She has expressed herself very forcible on the subject, Mr Bill, and very constant. 'Snakes in the grass that wants you out of the way is one thing,' she says, 'and toadstools is another, and I know which of them I'm going to believe in,' she says. And put like that, I won't deny as—that—her words made an impression on me."

Bill turned and looked at him. It was rather a curious look.

"You mean you think someone wanted you out of the way?"

"That undoubtedly was Mrs Evans' meaning, sir." Evans' tone was one of dignified detachment.

"But good Lord—who?"

The detachment became more marked.

"That, sir, is hardly for me to say."

Bill looked at him sharply for a moment. Then he said, "Well, you were both ill. What happened after that?"

"Mr Postlethwaite, sir, who was always the soul of kindness, suggested that we should take a holiday. It was a very inconvenient time for illness to occur, being within a week of the move to Ledstow Place, and it was put to me and Mrs Evans that it would be best if the move was put through with a temporary staff while Mrs Evans and me recuperated. The indisposition was very severe, and there was no denying that we should have been more of a hindrance than a help, so we come away to my married brother in London, and when the fortnight was up and I had wrote—written—to say that being now recovered we were ready and wishful to take up our duties again, there come back a letter to say that Mr Postlethwaite was keeping the temporary staff on permanent, and enclosing a month's wages in lieu of notice.''

"A letter? From whom?''

Evans turned a mutely understanding eye upon him.

"From Mr Postlethwaite.''

"You're sure?''

"It was in his hand, Mr Bill.''

"Poor old boy—he must have gone off his head.''

"It's very kind of you to say so, sir, I'm sure. I won't say as—that—I hadn't a similar thought, but Mrs Evans, sir—''

"Yes, Evans. Go on.''

"Perhaps I'd better not, Mr Bill.''

"No, I think you'd better.''

"Well, sir, what Mrs Evans says is that Mr Postlethwaite never wrote the letter, or if he did he was drove to it. But that's a bit farfetched to my mind, and I put it down to her being upset, though I don't deny that there's those that might have worked on him for their own ends.''

"Why didn't you go to Mrs O'Hara?'' said Bill.

"Well, sir, there's no denying we were hurt—with the whole family as you might say—and by all accounts Miss Meg had troubles of her own. Then just when we were thinking what we'd better do, Lady Latimer writes and says will we go to Scotland to her mother, Mrs Campbell, and Mrs Evans says 'The further the better, William,' so we went.''

"But I thought—''

"Mrs Campbell deceased a month ago, sir. She was ninety-seven years of age. And Mrs Evans and me, not being wishful to stay in Scotland, we come to my brother again with a view to looking around.''

Bill heaved a sigh of relief. He plunged into an offer of his flat and himself with something of the trepidation which accompanies a proposal of matrimony. In some odd way the Evanses and Meg were associated in his mind. Meg might refuse him, but would she—could she refuse them?

Evans received the offer with a dignity which only thinly disguised a very real gratification. There was a touch of emotion instantly and sternly controlled. It was with an air of benign loftiness that he intimated his own favourable consideration of the offer, coupled with the necessity for talking things over with Mrs Evans.

They parted.

Bill had lunch, and after lunch went round to see Garratt.

"Has that young woman of yours seen her lawyer yet?''

Bill grinned maliciously.

"No, but I have just engaged the cook—*la cuisinière*, feminine—of her uncle—*oncle*, masculine—and the butler of her uncle—still masculine but probably batty, and I haven't the slightest idea what butler is in French. And do you know why, my friend—*ami*, masculine? . . . You don't? Then I'll tell you—*je te dirais*. It's because only England can produce an Evans.''

"Sounds more like Wales,'' said Garratt. "What are you talking about anyway?''

"*My* butler and *my* cook—once Henry Postlethwaite's butler and Henry Postlethwaite's cook, but now, owing to the Satanic activities of an—unnamed—snake in the grass, my cook and my butler. In fact, my married couple.''

"Are you drunk?'' said Garratt rudely.

"You're always asking me that. I'm only exhilarated, and if you knew all, you would be exhilarated too, because when Mrs Evans is my cook you shall come and dine with me and have the meal of your life. She always was wasted on the Professor, but how even he could have been balmy enough to let her go—''

"Have you come here to talk to me about cooks and butlers?'' said Garratt dangerously.

"Not entirely. I want to know if you've dug up anything more about the Delorne woman"—his tone was now entirely serious—"and I want to see anything you've got in the way of proof—documentary proof of O'Hara's death. You've got to give me something that will convince Meg. She won't go a step till she's sure."

Garratt fixed him with a hard stare.

"Why didn't you bring her along?"

"She's gone out of town—to her uncle's."

"Run away?"

"Run away," said Bill. Oddly enough, it had not occurred to him before, but it did now. The thrill of the chase was added to the other feelings which he had about Meg.

Garratt went over to a nest of drawers at the far side of the room.

"Damn all women!" he said, after which he jerked a drawer open and came back with a file in his hand. He threw it on the table in Bill's direction and said, "You can look at that there, but you can't take it away. We'll put everything that's necessary at the disposal of Mrs O'Hara's lawyers. The really conclusive thing is the break in the leg. We dug up the X-ray of O'Hara's break. There were some peculiar features. It's there—you can compare it with the X-ray we had done of the unnamed corpse. It's the same break—there's not the slightest doubt. Look for yourself. There's the surgeon's affidavit. It's unpleasant evidence to put before Mrs O'Hara, but if she won't take your word for it, you'll have to bring her along and let her see for herself. I want that packet, and I want it p.d.q., before the clever swab who is after it thinks out some new dodge for stopping me and getting it himself."

"What do you think is in it?" said Bill.

Garratt grimaced.

"Dunno. Perhaps t'other fellow don't either." His eyebrows went up and his scalp twitched. "Might be anything—nothing—finger-prints—complete dossiers, present whereabouts, and machinations of some of the leading shrinking violets of international crime. T'other fellow's got the jumps about it whatever it is, or he wouldn't be trying to put the wind up Mrs O'Hara or—taking pot shots at you in the dark.''

Bill looked at him steadily.

"Why at me?"

"Well," said Garratt in a drawl unnaturally removed from his ordinary staccato speech, "well, you might be considered in the light of an incentive, you know. Mrs O'Hara can't very well marry you unless she proves O'Hara's death, and if you were out of the way, they might think that she wouldn't be so keen about proving it.''

An angry colour ran up to the very roots of Bill Coverdale's hair. Garratt jerked a shoulder impatiently.

"You needn't bother to murder me— I'm not saying it. But t'other fellow may be.''

Bill mastered himself with a furious effort. It was no good raging at Garratt, it would merely gratify him. He said drily,

"I thought the official theory was that I'd invented the shot or imagined it, or that I'd done it myself, or that Meg had done it in a pair of trousers she'd been wearing under her evening dress. You'll remember that I dug in my toes about the trousers.''

"There isn't an official theory," said Garratt gloomily. "But the people who killed O'Hara certainly wouldn't stick at doing you in if they thought you were in their way. Now about this Della Delorne woman—''

"What about her?"

"Next door to nothing. She's away—it seems to be a more or less chronic state. The char-lady hasn't produced anything worth having up to date. She's been away too, visiting her sister in the country. Oh Lord—what a life!'' He grinned suddenly at Bill. "Get along out of here and bring that young woman of yours up to the scratch! I'm supposed to be doing some work.''

Bill went back to his hotel and sat down to write a difficult letter to Meg O'Hara. It was difficult because he had to convince her that Robin was dead, and to do this it was necessary to put before her with plainness the evidence which Garratt had shown him. He wrote this part of the letter two or three times, because whenever he had been really plain and convincing it sounded bald and brutal, and whenever he tried to present the evidence tactfully it didn't sound in the least convincing, and Meg had simply got to be convinced. He made a pencil draft, read it through, thought he had done it very badly, and proceeded, still in pencil, to the second part of the letter. It was even more difficult, because his thoughts were quite full of the flat, and the Evanses, and wanting to marry Meg with as little delay as possible, and it wouldn't be decent to let these things escape into a letter which contained the proofs of Robin O'Hara's death. He could, of course, tell her that he had taken the Hewletts' flat. There was nothing *ipso facto* indecent about his telling her that he had taken a flat. It looked a little bald as he added it to the pencil draft—"I have taken the Hewletts' flat." Perhaps it would be better if he didn't add anything to the first part of his letter. . . .

It would be better. But the picture of Meg in that mouldy house, getting a mouldy letter from him full of mortuary details and without so much as a friendly word at the end, was too much. He had stroked out the sentence about the flat. He now indicated that it was to be restored by making a series of dots underneath the stroke-out line. Very well, he had taken the Hewletts' flat. What about it now? Could he tell Meg how many rooms there were? Could he describe the rooms without becoming tendencious? He wrote a horrible sentence exactly like an excerpt from a house-agent's list. "There is a dining-room, a drawing-room, four bedrooms, a kitchen, and a bathroom."

He looked gloomily at this statement. It was horrible, but no one could say that it was tendencious. It was bald, blameless, and blatantly boring. If he made the flat sound boring, Meg wouldn't want to come and live in it. He broke hastily into a panegyric on the view from the drawing-room windows—tree-tops, and a bit of the river, and if you leaned out you could see the sunset and reflections in the water.

He frowned at his panegyric after he had written it, poised his pencil to cross it out, and then let it alone and went quickly on to the Evanses. The Evanses were safe ground as long as he remembered not to say anything that would look as if Meg was going to have a share in them. At this point something primitive got up and kicked. Hang it all, Meg knew he loved her. O'Hara had been a damned bad husband, and he'd been dead for a year. What was the good of all this beating about the bush?

Bill wrestled with these feelings more or less successfully, and continued his letter. He told Meg all about the Evanses, and how angry Mrs Evans had been at the suggestion that she might have cooked a toadstool by mistake. When he had finished all that, he sat considering how he should end the letter. After a bit he wrote:

> "How long are you going to stay at Ledstow? I think you ought to come back as soon as you can and see your lawyer. I should like to drive down and fetch you. Please let me.
>
> "Bill."
>
> P.S. I can come tomorrow if you wire. I think that tomorrow would be a good day, really."

He read the whole thing through, copied it out with a few verbal alterations, put it in an envelope, addressed it, and posted it in the hotel letter-box. When he had done this, he felt rather as if he had been assisting at Robin O'Hara's funeral. There was the sense of an unpleasant duty accomplished, a restrained gloom consented to, and the feeling that the blinds could now be pulled up and more cheerful things considered. He proceeded to consider them, and found them pleasant. His mind might have been less at ease if he had known that his letter would never reach Meg, and that when he posted it he had been posting a death warrant.

XVII

MEG WENT INTO LEDLINGTON NEXT DAY AND BOUGHT her wool. It wasn't a very satisfactory expedition, because Miss Cannock, kind, fussy and thick-skinned, insisted on coming too— "And your uncle would wish you to take the car, I know. He is so entirely immersed at present that I couldn't mention it, but he would, I know, be greatly distressed if you did not take the car. The buses are most inconvenient"—this Meg could well believe—"and such a horrid smell of petrol. In fact, Mrs O'Hara, it sometimes seems to me that this so-called mechanical age has some very grave disadvantages, and that life in the country must really have been pleasanter when you could drive comfortably along the lanes in a governess-cart or a pony-trap. Going into Ledlington would have been a very agreeable expedition. But I couldn't attempt to drive even a very quiet pony, with so many cars on the road, and coming round corners at the rate they do."

Meg wasn't attending to this very much. She was puzzled.

"I didn't know Uncle Henry had started a car. He always said he wouldn't have one. What has he got—and who drives it? Don't tell me *he* does!"

"Oh *no!*" Miss Cannock was quite shocked. "Oh *no,* Mrs O'Hara—of course not! But I see you are joking." She smiled, a polite little twisted smile. "But about the car— I'm afraid I'm very ignorant, but I really don't know what sort it is. He got it second-hand in a very good condition, and the colour is a pleasing shade of grey—or perhaps you would call it drab. I don't really think we could have lived here without some kind of conveyance—it's so very remote and the buses not at all convenient—in fact, I may say, most inconvenient.''

"Who drives it?" said Meg again, and not idly, because if it was the Cannock, she could drive herself, but she wouldn't get the chance of driving Meg. Life mightn't be very sweet at the moment, but it had possibilities, and anyhow she didn't want to die in a messy motor smash with a twittering female who probably didn't know a brake from an accelerator.

"Oh, the gardener," said Miss Cannock. "Such a nice man, and such an excellent driver. I am a little inclined to be nervous in a motor car, but Henderson is so very reliable that I don't feel a *twinge*, not the least twinge of anxiety, when he is driving."

Meg pricked up her ears. So there was a gardener called Henderson who drove the car. Not, oh surely not, the loutish boy who lived at the lodge. She said quickly,

"Not that boy at the lodge!"

Miss Cannock looked quite shocked again.

"Oh no—oh dear, no! I'm afraid I should be very nervous about trusting myself to John. He is a good boy, but he naturally has not his father's experience."

The family at the lodge fell into place in Meg's mind. Henderson was probably a widower, the old woman was his mother, and the loutish boy his son. Not local people, according to William. She wondered how long you had to live here before you were local. At any other time—or perhaps it would be more correct to say in any other place—she wouldn't have given the Hendersons a second thought, but at Ledstow you extracted all you possibly could from its scant and arid themes. She therefore pursued the subject.

"Have they been here long?"

"I beg your pardon, Mrs O'Hara?"

What an irritating way the Cannock had of peering through those horrible tinted glasses. She poked her head, she peered, she wore beaded slippers, and her hands were never still—"Darling Uncle Henry—how *could* you?"

"The Hendersons. They live at the lodge, don't they? William said they weren't local."

"Excellent people," said Miss Cannock. "No, not local. Mr Postlethwaite engaged them when we came here."

The excellent Henderson drove them into Ledlington in what proved to be a Bentley saloon. He certainly drove very well, but Meg did not care about his looks. She thought the whole family singularly unprepossessing. The man was powerfully built, he handled the car like an expert, and he had a manner that would have got him dismissed at sight by most private employers. His eyes were bold and his air familiar. Meg thought the Cannock even more of a fool than she had taken her for, since she praised him continually and was obviously quite unaware that his manners needed mending.

They parked the car in the Market Square and shopped. Miss Cannock had a dozen fiddley errands—a scrap of ribbon to match, a winter hat to consider, and a long list of household commissions for Mrs Miller—"And I really think I ought to have brought her with us, for it's so easy to get the wrong thing, and she's very particular. An invaluable person, Mrs O'Hara, but not very even-tempered, and I so very much dislike anything that savours of friction. But if you will give me your advice, I shall not be so afraid of going wrong. Two heads are better than one, as they say."

Meg had to abandon any hope of freeing herself. The Cannock was the worst shopper she had ever seen. Confronted with a choice of any kind, she became a prey to indecision. It was bad enough when she was buying dusters, furniture-polish, clothes-pegs, sausages, and tinned fruit, but in the hat department of Ashley's she rapidly approached complete mental disintegration. She tried on everything, and looked lingeringly at her profile in a hand mirror. Meg gazed in fascinated horror at Miss Cannock in a bright orange beret, Miss Cannock in a viridian velvet tam, Miss Cannock in a succession of fly-away shepherdess hats in a variety of unsuitable shades. In the end she came away without buying anything, extending to two exhausted ministrants a consolatory hope that she might call again next week to look through their new stock.

It was perhaps because she was rather dazed that Meg so nearly had an accident when they came out. The High Street is very narrow just above Ashley's, and the trams come round the corner and down a short incline. Miss Cannock began to cross the street at this point. Meg was beside her, certainly as far as the middle of the road, but just what happened after that she was never quite sure. It was market day and there were a great many people about. The tram came round the corner, and there was a car coming up the other way, and Miss Cannock got nervous and stopped. Then she ran back, or ran forward, or both—that was the part Meg couldn't get clear. There was a screech of brakes from the car, a warning bell from the tram, and somehow or other Meg found herself face-downwards on the track with the metal of the tram-line cold against her mouth and the most sickening sensation of terror almost stopping her heart. She didn't quite faint, but she came very near it. The next thing she knew she was being pulled up, and a woman was saying in a sobbing, gasping voice, "Right under the tram she was—right under the tram!"

It wasn't a woman who was holding her—much too large, much too strong. It was a man, and a man's voice said, "Are you hurt, miss?"

Meg opened her eyes. The tram was most terrifyingly near. The lights were on inside. They gave it the air of some fiery instrument of doom. She said to herself, "That's nonsense!" but she looked away from the tram. There was a crowd which filled the narrow street, and everyone was looking at her. "Right under the tram she was—right under the tram!" said the sobbing woman. And then the man again, close at her ear, "Are you hurt?"

Meg straightened herself up, and with the movement her head was clear again. She saw the driver of the tram, his face like a bit of wet linen, and she managed a smile and a husky sentence. "I'm all right—really." And then she was aware of Miss Cannock clutching at her arm and shaking like a person with the ague.

"Oh, Mrs O'Hara—it was all my fault! I'm so bad at

crossings, and I got nervous, and I don't know what happened. You were right under the tram!''

Meg looked over Miss Cannock's heaving shoulder and saw the head and shoulders of Henderson a couple of yards away in the crowd. She hadn't realized that he was so tall until she saw him standing like that in the crowd. He wasn't doing anything, he was just standing there and looking. He was looking at her.

All of a sudden the one thing she wanted was to get away from those staring eyes. She made a great effort and pulled herself together. When you've just made the most complete fool of yourself, you feel the need of a specially high horse to ride. Meg made her effort, and found herself in the saddle. She thanked the man who had picked her up, spoke to the driver of the tram, smiled upon the assembled crowd, and took Miss Cannock firmly by the arm.

''I'm very sorry to have given everyone such a fright. I don't know how it happened, but I'm quite all right.'' Then, to the still shaking Miss Cannock, ''We'd better go back to Ashley's, hadn't we? I want to tidy up.''

Miss Cannock twittered all the way across the road, and through the shop, and up the stairs into the ladies' room.

''So dreadful—so unnerving—so careless of me! And I have been stronger of late—it is some time since I had one of these nervous attacks—I quite lose my head, and afterwards I have no recollection—no recollection at all. Are you sure you are not injured in any way? When you fell—it was so dreadful—so nearly a terrible accident! I did not think that the tram could have stopped in time! And *what* should I have said to your uncle? *Oh, Mrs O'Hara!*''

Meg put her firmly into a chair. What a woman! What a mutt Uncle Henry was to keep her!

She went to one of the wall glasses, and saw a very pale face under a very crooked hat, with a long dirty smear across the pallor where she had felt the metal of the tramline cold and hard against her cheek. The moment came back with the added chill of realization. She had been not two inches away from the grinding death of the wheels. The room shook for a moment. It was as if a gust of terror was shaking it.

She bent down quickly, turned the cold water tap, and began to wash her face, using her handkerchief as a sponge. The cold water steadied her. She took powder and lipstick out of her bag and made herself up with care and deliberation. She wanted to postpone the moment of return to Miss Cannock. If she could have postponed it to the other side of the Greek kalends, it would have been a great relief, but she had got to drive back seven miles to Ledstow with her and be prattled to all the way.

She looked in the glass, and saw Miss Cannock at another glass, absurdly titivating. Every now and then she stopped to gasp and clutch at her side. Suddenly Meg could laugh at her, and felt better.

And then she saw the telephone-box.

She was standing at the end wash-basin. Immediately to her left an open archway led into the pleasant rest-room. Ashley's did their customers well. Serving a large country district, they catered to women who had driven long distances to shop and who were often left with an odd half hour to put in before going on to lunch or tea.

The rest-room was restfully upholstered in green. There were comfortable chairs, there were magazines and papers, and there was a telephone-box. The sight of it filled Meg with a desire to talk to someone who didn't twitter. It filled her, in fact, with a desire to talk to Bill Coverdale. It was four o'clock, and it was most unlikely that she would be able to get on to him, but she could try. It would at any rate defer the Cannock. And what a good thing the Cannock had had an urge to titivate, because otherwise she would still be sitting in a chair that faced the telephone-box—and the last thing Meg wanted was to talk to Bill under that mild inquisitive stare.

She stepped through the archway, and felt a secret pleasure in the realization that the telephone-box was quite out of range as far as the Cannock was concerned. She shut the sound-proof door and was grateful for the silence, and sorry that she had to break it by calling the exchange. Of course it was silly to think that she had the least chance of finding Bill in his hotel at this hour. She said that—just in case—

but all the time something very strong and insistent was telling her that he would be there. And with miraculous quickness there he was, speaking a half impatient "Hullo!" into the receiver at his end.

"Hullo—hullo! Who is it?"

"Me," said Meg, and had the thrill of hearing his voice change, and soften, and become the special sort of voice that was kept for her.

"Meg—is it you? I didn't know you were on the telephone."

"We're not—no such luck."

"Where are you speaking from?"

"A box—in a shop—in Ledlington."

"What a bit of luck! I'd come in for some papers, and was just going out again. Meg, how are you getting on?"

"Mouldy," said Meg. "That's why I'm ringing up—I just felt I must hear a human voice. The Cannock isn't human. I think she's a sort of sheep—she blethers. That does sound like a sheep—doesn't it? Blether, to rhyme with wether."

It was frightfully silly, but her breath kept catching in her throat and the words wobbled.

"What's the matter, Meg?"

"Nothing."

"Your voice doesn't shake like that for nothing."

"I'm all right, but I nearly came to a sticky end just now, and when I heard your voice it sort of came over me."

"Meg! What?"

"A tram," said Meg—"a beastly juggernaut of a tram . . . Bill, *don't*—I'm quite all right."

"How?"

Bill's voice had changed again. It wasn't like anything she had ever heard from him. Somehow that steadied her.

"I don't know. I suppose I tripped . . . Bill, I'm perfectly all right."

Bill Coverdale said, "Thank God!" And then, "Have you had my letter?" and Meg said, "No." And then the door of the telephone-box was opened, and there was Miss Cannock just behind her—blethering. There really was no other word for it.

"The air in these boxes—so confined, so hot! I am so afraid of your feeling faint, Mrs O'Hara—after your terrible experience!"

Meg heard this with one ear, while with the other she was aware of Bill's saying faintly but insistently, "You ought to have had it."

She took her lips from the receiver to say in a voice of cold fury, "I'm perfectly all right, Miss Cannock!" Then, into the telephone again, "There's only one post. I expect I'll get it tomorrow."

Just as she said "tomorrow" Miss Cannock gave a little gasp and clutched at her arm. Bill was saying, a horribly long way off, "You ought to have had it today." But how on earth could she talk to Bill with Miss Cannock's choking whisper close against her uncovered ear?

"I'm afraid—I feel so—I don't know—I think I'm going—to faint—" Very little satisfaction to be got out of talking to Bill with a swooning elderly spinster propped against her shoulder, and quite possibly listening in.

Meg said, "I'm sorry—I must ring off," and hung up the receiver. She was so angry that it made her feel very strong. In ordinary circumstances she might have found it difficult to transfer Miss Cannock's practically dead weight to a chair, but as it was, she hardly noticed it, being entirely taken up with combating a desire to shake her. If the Cannock felt faint, why couldn't she stay in a chair and faint there instead of staggering into a telephone-box which she quite rightly described as hot and stuffy, and fainting or trying to faint on Meg?

Meg went and fetched a glass of water with the most murderous feelings of irritation, but when she returned with it Miss Cannock was a good deal revived, and after taking two very small sips declared that she had been very foolish, but she was better now and a cup of hot tea would be much nicer than this cold water.

Over a pot of tea in the rather subfusc refreshment room she became more conversational than Meg had yet known her. She ordered scones and cakes as well as tea, and continually pressed Meg to eat.

"For after such a shock, Mrs O'Hara, you require sustenance—you really do. You have so much self-control—but it is not wise to tax yourself too far. That little round cake with the nuts is a specialty of Ashley's and I can recommend it. No sugar in your tea? Now I always think that is such a pity. Everyone cannot afford expensive pleasures, but sugar in one's tea, if you like it, is a great pleasure, and one within the reach of all."

"She must be half-witted," said Meg to herself. And then all at once she found something rather pathetic about the Cannock. If sugar in your tea had to do duty for a pleasure, her lines must indeed have been cast in stale, flat, and unprofitable regions. The stiff anger went out of her and she made polite conversation.

"It is really very pleasant here," said Miss Cannock, stirring her tea. There were two lumps of sugar in it, and the bubbles rose in little clusters. "Very pleasant indeed. And I do hope, Mrs O'Hara, that I did not interrupt you at the telephone. It was unpardonable of me—really unpardonable, but I felt suddenly very ill, and you had been so kind. I do *hope*—"

"It doesn't matter at all—I had just finished."

Miss Cannock took one of the little round cakes she had recommended. She ate in small fussy bites, using her front teeth like a rabbit and making a great many crumbs.

"You are so kind, Mrs O'Hara, but I shouldn't like Mr Postlethwaite to know that I had been so foolish. He might think I had been to blame—and indeed I feel—"

To her horror, Meg saw the little nutty cake, no longer round because of the rabbit bites, shake in the hand that clutched it. She said in a soft, distressed voice,

"Oh *please,* Miss Cannock, there's nothing to tell, but we won't tell him."

"You're so kind," said Miss Cannock. She nibbled mournfully at a nut. "I am very happy in my present post. Mr Postlethwaite is always so kind and considerate, if sometimes rather *immersed,* and I should not like him to think that my foolish nervousness—" She choked, sniffed, and producing a very large and solid linen handkerchief, dabbed at the corners of the eyes behind the tinted glasses.

Meg's soft heart was touched.

"Miss Cannock, please don't. Nothing has happened, and I shouldn't dream of saying anything to Uncle Henry. Have another cup of tea—and have three lumps."

Miss Cannock put away her handkerchief, much to Meg's relief.

They had a lingering tea. Miss Cannock had four cups, and, in all ten lumps of sugar. She told Meg the story of her life. It sounded bleak and starved beyond belief. In some water-tight compartment she must keep a brain, because she seemed always to have passed examinations with ease—she had even taken scholarships. She had no relations, and she had never made any friends. "I don't know how it was, but there never seemed to be time, if you know what I mean, Mrs O'Hara."

At long last they drove back to Ledstow Place.

XVIII

BILL COVERDALE'S ENVELOPE WAS LYING BY MEG'S plate when she came down to breakfast next morning. She and Miss Cannock had their meals in the little back room that looked out upon the lake, the vault-like dining-room on the other side of the hall being the gloomiest and least inviting of apartments.

Miss Cannock poured out the tea, and Meg read her letter. It was very short, and that was disappointing, especially after she had practically asked Bill for a long letter. And there was really nothing in it, and that was disappointing too, because from the way Bill had asked if she had had his letter she had got the idea that there was something rather special about it. Instead of which it was a short letter, and a dull letter, and rather a cold letter.

At this point Meg's colour rose, and she said to herself with as much severity as she could manage, "Be quiet! I'm ashamed of you. You don't want him to make love to you, do you?" And at that frightful moment, and under the Cannock's eye, she knew that she did.

She read the letter through again slowly:

"Dear Meg,
   I'm having a very busy time, because I have taken the Hewletts' flat and I want to get in as soon as possible. I have engaged a married couple. I hope you are getting on all right. Remember me to the Professor.

Yours
Bill."

It was a beast of a letter—a horrible, cold, detached icicle of a letter—a limp dead fish of a letter. And Bill had had the nerve to ask in the most pressing way if she had got it! For all the friendship, or comfort, or warmth it contained it might just as well have gone to the dead letter office and stayed there.

She was rather fierce with her boiled egg, cutting off the top instead of peeling it as she usually did. Miss Cannock was, fortunately, quite engrossed with an account of the marriage of two film stars.

"It seems so—so persevering," she said, with a little cough. 'They have each had four previous experiences of the most unhappy nature. One cannot approve, but it seems to me it shows—courage. Do you not think so, Mrs O'Hara?"

Meg thought it showed great courage. If Robin was dead, and she was a widow, no power on earth would make her give any other man that power to hurt which marriage gives—never, and never, and never again. And at the back of her mind a small, cold voice said, "Bill hasn't asked you to give him anything, has he?"

About this time, or perhaps a little later, Bill Coverdale opened a telegram. It was signed "Meg," and it ran:

"Your letter received. Would like to stay on here and be quiet for a little. I know you will understand. Please don't come down."

The sharpness of his disappointment actually took him aback. It wasn't reasonable to be disappointed in just this intense, undisciplined fashion. It was the most natural thing in the world that Meg, having at last received proof of Robin O'Hara's death, should want a little time to adjust herself to her freedom.

He looked at the telegram and saw that it had been sent off from Ledstow at eight-forty-five. That meant that she had got his letter by the first post and had managed to send this wire off immediately. Perhaps the village post-office had an arrangement for telephoning telegrams to Ledlington. Eighty-forty-five was pretty early to have got a telegram off in any other way.

He went on frowning at the flimsy sheet of paper. Meg had been in a great hurry to tell him that she wanted to be alone. She could hardly have got his letter before she was making arrangements to get this telegram sent off. Why, she wouldn't be out of bed at eight o'clock. Being very deeply in love, and having for the first time for at least three years begun to hope, it hurt him sharply to feel how quickly Meg had decided that he must stay away. Beneath the hurt there was something else, deep down, unformulated, a kind of dark uneasiness of which he himself was scarcely aware. If the hurt had been less sharp, this vague uneasiness would perhaps have come in for more of his attention.

He wrote to Meg before he went out, a short, careful letter, in which he tried very hard not to show that he had been hurt at all. Of course he understood, and of course he wouldn't come till she wanted him, but he didn't like to feel that she was all alone in rather a mouldy place, and she must please remember that she had only to wire at any time and he would come at once, but he didn't want to worry her, so he would wait until he heard from her. All of which gave great satisfaction to the person who had sent the telegram after reading and destroying the letter which had been intended to convince Meg of Robin's death. Meg was never to see either of the two letters, and she had certainly no idea that any telegram had been sent in her name.

When Meg had finished her breakfast, which took quite a long time because Miss Cannock kept on reading her chatty excerpts from the *Daily Mail*, she went for a walk in the dreary park. She then wound the wool which she had bought at Ashley's and began her jumper. Miss Cannock had vanished, Uncle Henry was permanently "immersed," and the house gave her the creeps. The familiar furniture made it a great deal worse. Like herself, it was in exile in a gloomy, unfamiliar place. What was the good of having enough to eat? It would be much better to be starving in London. What was the good of making a jumper? What was the good of anything? She was marooned.

Bill Coverdale, on the other hand, was extremely busy. Some of the savour had gone out of his flat-taking, but he had got to get on with it all the same, and as the day wore on, the reasonableness of Meg's attitude and the unreasonableness of his own became progressively more apparent, with the result that he cheered up a good deal and was able once more to picture Meg choosing curtains for the drawing-room. He wondered if she would like them flowery or plain. He inclined to plain himself because of framing the view. He felt quite sure that Meg was going to like the view. The Hewletts had already left, and he was moving in in two days' time. The Evanses were all fixed up, and Mrs Evans was arranging with a woman to come in and do the cleaning, so everything was well in train.

He thought he would walk back to the hotel. It was quite extraordinary what a lot of building seemed to be going on in every direction—blocks of flats springing up and altering once familiar streets. In another generation, he supposed, everyone would be living in a flat, in the towns at any rate. Quite a good plan—sensible, economical, labour-saving. He looked at all the blocks with interest, comparing the flats with his own. In the last twenty-four hours it had ceased to be the Hewletts' flat and become *his* flat. The proprietary feeling grew as he compared it with others, mostly to their disadvantage. He had taken it in a hurry, but he hadn't made any mistake. Quite definitely it was a good flat. Now this block that he was just passing—he wouldn't have liked to bring Meg here. Nothing really wrong with the locality, but not attractive—rather on the grubby side.

And then he noticed the name over the entrance—Oleander Mansions. If he hadn't been taking that special interest in flats, he wouldn't have seen it. As it was, the name did not at first mean anything to him. It wasn't until he had walked some dozen steps past it that it came back into his mind, linked with Garratt's voice, and he remembered that Oleander Mansions was where Della Delorne lived.

He turned round to have another look at the entrance, as if it would tell him something. But only Della Delorne could say whether Robin O'Hara had passed through that entrance with her on the night when Bill had seen them together—what was it—four days after Robin had disappeared. They were together in a taxi at midnight. Where were they bound for? He considered the position of the flat. They might easily have been coming here—yes, they might very easily have been coming here.

He stood there, frowning at the entrance, and became aware of a stout middle-aged woman who was descending the steps. She wore her hair in a bun, with a flat, discouraged-looking black hat affixed to it by a bright blue hat-pin. Her contours were draped in a Burberry which hitched up in front and dipped at the back. Her hands, gloveless and red, advertised her calling. She was a scrubber of steps, a charlady, a daily help. And what had Garratt said about the woman at Oleander Mansions? She'd been away—they hadn't been able to get hold of her. . . . Yes, that was it—she'd been away. Perhaps she was still away. Perhaps this was her deputy—

Perhaps it wasn't—

Bill was never quite able to decide why he should have felt such an imperative urge to settle this question. He was not very much given to acting on impulse, but he did its bidding now, and that without stopping to think. If he had stopped to think, he might well have blenched, for the lady looked as if she might be formidable. But he did not stop. He merely found himself politely lifting his hat and saying,

"I beg your pardon, but I wonder if I might speak to you for a moment?"

The woman stopped. She had a string bag in one hand and an umbrella in the other. She tipped her head back and stared at Bill in very much the same way that a cow disturbed at grass lifts its head to regard a stranger. She looked, and just as he was going to speak again she said in a deep, hoarse voice,

"I beg your pardon?"

It was like a belated echo, and the horrible part of it was that he had been on the point of repeating the words himself. He said instead,

"I'm afraid I don't know your name, but I think you are employed at Oleander Mansions, are you not?"

Her bovine expression yielded a little, and she said,

"Certinly."

It was really horribly awkward plunging into conversation with a respectable middle-aged worker who was obviously wondering what on earth he wanted with her. He thanked heaven for her middle age and her solid size. He would not at any rate be suspected of a design upon her virtue. In desperation he plunged.

"I wonder if you would mind telling me your name?"

Her stare hardened.

"Thompson," she said—"Mrs Thompson, and no call to be ashamed of it. And might I make so bold as to ask what you're wanting with me?"

It was easier now that he had her name.

"Mrs Thompson," he said, "I want very much to have a talk with you, and I quite realize that you are a busy woman and that I mustn't take up your time for nothing."

Mrs Thompson's red face flushed vigorously.

"If you're from the police, you just turn right round and go back where you come from! You did ought to be ashamed of yourself, trying to drag a respectable working-woman who has brought up half a dozen children and kept herself and them and never been mixed up with nothing—"

"I'm not from the police—really I'm not—nothing to do with them."

Mrs Thompson sniffed, the loud emphatic sniff of one who has yet to be convinced.

"Well, they've been coming round, so the lift-boy tells me. I've been away for my 'oliday, and first thing he says to me when I come in this morning, 'There's a busy been here,' he says, meaning a plain-clothes detective. And when I says 'Whatever for?' he ups and sauces me, the young limb, which if he'd been one of mine I'd have put it across him and he wouldn't have done it again in a hurry."

Bill smiled in the manner which he had always found very efficacious with his great-aunt Annabel.

"I swear I'm not a busy. I just want to ask you a few questions about a friend of mine. He's gone off without leaving an address. I thought if I might have a talk with you, and if you would accept five pounds to make up for the loss of your time—"

Her stare became extremely penetrating. He got the impression that if the mind behind it moved slowly it was nevertheless of a certain calibre.

She said, "Five pounds—" and stood there puckering up her lips and frowning. Then she said, "We can't talk here," and with that she began to walk along the pavement.

Bill moved with her.

"Nor yet walking along the road," said Mrs Thompson.

"What about a cup of tea?" said Bill.

Mrs Thompson looked sideways at him.

"You—and me?" she said. She sniffed again. This time it was a sniff of scorn.

"Why not?"

"The kind of place where I'd have a cup would 'ardly be the kind of place for you, and the kind of place where you'd 'ave a cup wouldn't 'ardly be the place for me, which I've got my pride same as other people."

It took nearly five minutes to persuade Mrs Thompson

that some kind of half-way house might be discovered. In the end she supposed that Simpson's bakery might serve their turn, and that the hour being what it was, three o'clock in the afternoon, the place was likely enough to be empty.

They sat presently in the room behind the shop, at a small table covered with green oilcloth. There were five other similar tables, but no one else was having tea. Mrs Thompson poured out two cups, asked him if he took milk and sugar, and, remarking that she liked hers strong and sweet, dropped four lumps into a dark draught of tea and proceeded to drink it in scalding sips. Bill admired her aplomb, and wished that he could emulate it. He had an uneasy feeling that he was making a complete fool of himself and paying five pounds for the privilege—five pounds and the price of this repellent tea.

"Good hot tea takes a deal of beating," said Mrs Thompson, "but it's got to be hot and it's got to be sweet, or I wouldn't give a thank you for it." She clasped both hands round her cup and sipped with audible enjoyment. "And what was it you wanted to ask me about? A friend of yours, you was saying—"

Bill leaned an elbow on the table.

"Mrs Thompson," he said, "my friend's name was O'Hara—Mr Robin O'Hara. Have you heard the name before?"

He had waited until the cup was clear of her lips. She shook her head, and sipped again. Then she put the cup down and said,

"That's Irish, isn't it?"

Bill nodded.

"I want you to go back to a year ago—October last year—October 4th last year."

"What about it?" said Mrs Thompson. She looked blankly at him.

"I think Mr O'Hara was in Oleander Mansions that night."

"What time?"

"I think he may have come there soon after midnight."

Mrs Thompson sniffed again very loudly indeed.

"And where do you suppose I'd be at that time of night, mister? When you done a hard day's work like what I do you don't go on all night long as well, thank Gawd. In my bed and asleep, that's where I am come midnight, whether it's October or January, and this year or last year. All the same—" She stopped, drained her cup, and picking up the teapot, began to pour herself another.

"Yes," said Bill.

"Nothing," said Mrs Thompson. She put four drops of milk into her tea, and four lumps of sugar.

"You were going to say something."

"Well, I'm not going to now." She lifted her cup and drank from it. "Oh lor—that's 'ot!" She rummaged in the string bag and found a handkerchief with which she wiped her face. "It's funny, so soon as I get my second cup I come over that 'ot you wouldn't believe it."

Bill might have retorted that seeing was believing. He stuck to his point instead.

"Mrs Thompson, you were going to say something. Can't you tell me what it was?"

She made an impatient movement.

" 'Twasn't nothing. But since you're so pressing, it was just that I wasn't working, not last October I wasn't—not the first ten days anyhow. I'd a bit of a naccident and I was in 'ospital, and my Beatrice she was going instead of me, to keep the place open like."

"That's your daughter?"

She nodded and sipped her tea.

"Me second. The eldest's married, and a bad 'usband she's got, but girls won't never believe that their mothers know nothing."

They seemed to have got to a dead end.

"Will you ask your daughter if she remembers anything about Mr O'Hara?"

"Well, what am I to ask—who did he come visiting? There's a matter of fifteen flats on my stair."

It had not occurred to him that there might be more than one stair. He said quickly,

"Is Miss Delorne's flat on your stair?"

Her face became heavily unintelligent. Bill recognized the withdrawal of respectability.

"Is it?" he insisted.

She said, "Yes," and shut her mouth hard.

"Is she there now? Living there, I mean."

She gave him another heavy look.

"How should I know?"

"Well, you might. Is she?"

"She's not there much. The boy says she's away."

"Mr O'Hara might have been visiting at Miss Delorne's flat," said Bill.

"*And* not the first," said Mrs Thompson with dignity.

They got no further. That she should regard Della Delorne with suspicion was a foregone conclusion, but she wouldn't talk about her. "I've my job to think of," and, "Least said, soonest mended," was as far as she would go. And upon that they parted.

Bill gave her her five pounds and a card with his address. He did not promise Beatrice another fiver, but he gave Mrs Thompson to understand that there would be a market if her daughter had anything to sell.

XIX

BILL COVERDALE WAS JUST BEGINNING TO THINK OF dressing for dinner that evening, when he was informed that a young lady had called to see him. His thoughts went rocketing to Meg with the complete lack of reason which characterizes the lover's state. She hadn't given any name. She was in the lounge. He was engaged to dine with old friends on the other side of London. If this was Meg—but how could it be Meg?—it didn't matter how short of time he ran himself.

He came into the lounge quite certain that it couldn't be Meg, but was instantly and sharply disappointed to find that he was right. The girl in the blue coat and black beret who was waiting for him did not even faintly resemble Meg. She was a pretty girl with large rolling blue eyes and yellow hair curling on her neck. Her lips were made up in a bright scarlet shade and her shoes were cheap and shabby. As Bill approached, she said in a drawling voice which would have been pretty if it had been less affected,

"Mr Coverdale? My mother said that you wanted to see me."

Bill blinked.

"Your mother?"

"Mrs Thompson," said the girl. "You were speaking to her this afternoon, and she said you would be glad if I would call."

So this was Miss Beatrice Thompson. . . . Remembering Mrs Thompson in her shapeless Burberry and still more shapeless hat, Bill admired. How did these girls manage it? Beatrice Thompson looked very much like the girls of his own set, especially at a little distance. The beret and the coat were neat and up to date, the hair of the fashionable length, the lipstick very much as worn in Mayfair. A young man who devoted as much energy and perseverance to his profession would probably rise to the top of the tree. He took off his hat to Miss Beatrice Thompson.

All this passed in a flash whilst he was shaking hands and steering her to an empty corner of the lounge. They sat in two adjacent armchairs, and Miss Beatrice opened the ball.

"My mother said—" Beneath the painstaking drawl the London accent flowed like an under-tow, sometimes weaker, sometimes stronger, but always there.

"Yes," said Bill—"I'm very grateful to you for calling. I want some information about a friend of mine, Mr Robin O'Hara. I think he may have been at Miss Delorne's flat at Oleander Mansions on the night of October 4th last year. Now Mrs Thompson tells me she was in hospital for the first ten days of October, and that you were taking her place at Oleander Mansions, so I wondered whether you could give me any information that would help me."

Beatrice rolled the blue eyes.

"Ooh!" she said. "There are fifteen flats on that stair, and people always coming and going. I couldn't say I knew any of them unless it was some of the residents. That Miss Delorne now—I'd know her again anywhere. Lovely clothes she had—and I don't know why everyone wants to think there's something wrong just because a girl makes something of herself and knows how to make herself look smart."

Bill discerned a personal grievance. He could readily imagine that Mrs Thompson might not find herself in entire agreement with her daughter about such vanities as lipstick. He said pleasantly,

"Well, it's just possible you might have noticed my friend. I've got some photographs upstairs. If you'll excuse me for a moment, I'll get them."

He came back with the photographs, to find her sitting in a carefully arranged attitude, copied probably from the latest drama she had seen. He hoped she wasn't going to be so taken up with playing her part that she wouldn't be able to attend to business.

He produced three leaves which he had detached from his photograph album and gave them to her one by one. The first was a group taken at a school dinner about two years ago. He was in it, and so was Robin O'Hara. The second displayed several snapshots taken at Way's End in the August before Meg's marriage. Robin appeared in two of them. The third was Meg's wedding group, with a line of bridesmaids, and the Professor gazing absently out of the picture, and a radiant Meg, and Robin O'Hara as a bridegroom.

Beatrice Thompson took each of the leaves, looked at it, and laid it on her knee. When she came to the wedding group, she stared at it for some time. Bill watched her, and did not know what to make of her expression. It hardened. She looked less pretty. An odd fleeting likeness to Mrs Thompson showed for a moment and was gone again. He thought she was thinking, calculating, making up her mind what she was going to say. But what she did say took him most completely by surprise. She handed him back the wedding group, pointed with an ungloved forefinger at the Professor, and said,

"I've seen that old gentleman."

"*What?*" said Bill in a tone of quite ungovernable incredulity.

"That old gentleman," said Miss Thompson, still pointing, "I've seen him." The forefinger had been roughened by work, but the nail had been clipped to a point and stained a horrible scarlet. It pointed at the Professor, and the drawling voice said with a little more drawl than before, "I can swear to him."

"Where?" said Bill. What he felt inclined to say was "Nonsense!"

"Coming out of Miss Delorne's flat nine o'clock in the morning, and I'd got my pail in the way, so I had to move it. And I took notice of him very particular, because I thought at his time of life he ought to know better, and whatever Miss Delorne wanted to take up with an old man like that—well!" She paused, rolled her eyes, retrieved the refined accent which had rather broken down, and said, "Disgusting, I call it."

Bill found himself quite unable to believe a word she was saying. But then, why was she saying it? It was quite impossible that she should have seen the Professor coming out of Della Delorne's flat at nine in the morning.

"Miss Thompson," he said, "I think you've made a mistake"—she shook her head—"but leave that on one side for a moment and tell me, are you sure you don't recognize anyone else in these photographs?"

He thought she hesitated, and he thought that it was to cover her hesitation that she said pertly,

"If you'll tell me who you want me to recognize, I might have a shot at it."

"Look here," he said, "that's no good. If you don't recognize anyone, say so. But if you do—and I think you do—why then—"

"What?" said Miss Thompson succinctly.

"I gave your mother five pounds," said Bill. "That was for taking up her time, not for what she told me, because she didn't tell me anything of the very slightest value."

"*Five pounds*—" She breathed the words in a voice that was most purely and sincerely natural—a pretty little London voice, trembling with emotion at the thought of what five pounds would buy. A string of real cultured pearls—you could get them for a guinea. . . . A real foxaline fur. . . A pair of shoes with heels like stilts . . . A bag—silk stockings. . . . Her face glowed with positive beauty as she gazed at Bill. "Coo!" she said. It was the merest involuntary breath of rapture. Then a shrewd look came into the large blue eyes. She sat up straight in her chair and prepared to drive a bargain. "You'd give me five pounds—honest?"

"Look here," said Bill, "I'll give you ten bob for your trouble in coming here, and if you can really tell me anything that will be of use to me, you shall have your fiver. But please don't make anything up, because I shall know if you do."

She threw him a sharp, good-humoured glance. He had wondered if she would take offence, but this was business, and the drawling would-be fine lady was in abeyance. This was a girl who could take hard knocks and give them.

She said, "I don't need to make things up. If I make up my mind to tell you, it'll be what happened—but I haven't made up my mind yet."

"I'll give you five minutes," said Bill, and wondered whether, after all, he was giving her time to fake a story, but he had to let the Ogilvies know that he was probably going to be late for dinner.

He got Jim Ogilvie on the telephone, and was told that they were alone and he could be as late as he liked.

He came back to Beatrice Thompson. She hadn't moved, but he thought that she had made up her mind.

"Well?" he said.

"Well, it's this way." She lifted her chin and looked at him. "Mum don't know—that's what I'm boggling at. And what I want to know is this—is all this just a private talk between you and me, or is there any likelihoods of a police-court case, and things in the papers, and no saying where it's going to stop?''

The girl had a head on her shoulders. What she had to tell was the more likely to be of value. He said honestly,

''I don't know, Miss Thompson. I've no connection with the police. Mr O'Hara disappeared a year ago, and it is quite possible that he was murdered—but please keep that to yourself.''

''Then I couldn't do it for five pounds.'' The blue eyes were as hard as marbles.

He offered her ten, and she raised him to fifteen, and then stuck out for a bonus if it should come to a case in court.

''Not that there's any harm, but Mum's old-fashioned— well, there, you've seen her for yourself. It's going to upset her because I didn't tell her at the time, but I don't want to upset her for nothing.''

Bill reflected that twenty pounds between them ought to have a soothing effect on Mrs Thompson's feelings. And then he felt rather ashamed of himself because the girl said half defiantly,

''She's been a jolly good mother to us. She's worked her fingers to the bone ever since Dad died, and it takes some doing with six, and none of them earning. You needn't think it's because I'm afraid of her, because I'm not.''

''All right,'' said Bill. ''And now let's have it, whatever it is.''

She sat forward a little with her elbows on her knees and dropped her voice to a confidential tone.

''Well, it was like this, Mr Coverdale. Mother was in hospital like she told you, and I was out of a job just then, and she asked me would I keep her place open, so I did, though I didn't like spoiling my hands—I'm a waitress by rights.''

''Yes?'' said Bill encouragingly.

''It was the fourth of October you wanted to hear about?''

''Yes.''

She gave a little laugh.

''That's an easy date for me to remember, because it's

my birthday. Well, I'd been doing Mum's job for three or four days, and I'd got friendly with a girl in one of the flats—Mabel her name was. She worked in the flat just opposite that Miss Delorne. Well, come the day before my birthday—that's October 3rd a year ago—we got talking, and I said it was my birthday next day and my friend wanted to take me out for a treat—he's a real nice boy, and he's got a good job and doing well in it. And Mabel told me her people were going away for two nights. She said, why not make up a party, her and me, and her boy friend and mine, and go to the new Palais de Danse which is just round the corner from Oleander Mansions, and me come back and sleep with her for company. She said her people had offered her to have her sister if she liked, but she said she'd rather have me, because her sister was one of those girls that can't keep their hands off another girl's boy, so she didn't want to have her butting in.''

Bill said, ''I see—''

''Mean, I call it!'' said Miss Thompson with energy. ''Mum 'd have slapped any of us, and a good job too—that sort want smacking. Well, we fixed it up, and I don't know when I enjoyed a party more. But I didn't tell Mum because of her being in hospital, and I knew she'd just lie there and worry, and make sure I was on the road to ruin—as if a girl couldn't get into trouble without ever going out of our street, if she wanted to. But it's no good arguing with Mum—it's the way she's made.''

''Well, you had your party. And then?''

''George and Ernie took us home—back to Oleander Mansions, that is—and I won't say we weren't larking about a bit down in the entrance. Mabel had got her key and she let us in, and the boys said good-night, and there was some joking and larking going on, but all very quiet so as not to disturb anyone. There's a night porter, but he don't come unless you ring for him, and there's nobody working the lift, but those that want to can work it themselves—anyhow the staff's not supposed to. So Mabel and me walked up the stairs. Her flat's on the third floor, and she'd just got the door open when I found I'd dropped my bag. 'Coo!'' I said.

'That's young Ernie and his nonsense. And I'm not going to lose that bag,' I said, 'with my new lipstick in it and all.' And Mabel, she said she wasn't going down all those stairs again, not for anybody. 'And you won't find it if you go,' she said, 'for as like as not you dropped it in the street.' Well, I knew I hadn't, so I ran down, and there it was, right by the door where Ernie had been carrying on. So I picked it up and back up the stairs with it, and when I come to the landing Mabel had gone in and left the door on the jar. I was just going to push it, when the door across the landing opened and a gentleman came out.''

She picked up the wedding group and pointed with her scarlet finger-nail at Robin O'Hara.

''That gentleman,'' she said, and sat back.

Bill's heart beat quicker.

''Sure?'' he said.

She took up the other two sheets, and pointed out Robin O'Hara in each of the photographs.

''It was that gentleman.''

''How was he dressed?'' said Bill.

Beatrice sat forward again.

''He'd taken his coat off. He'd a fancy striped shirt on, and a collar to match, and some kind of tie with a stripe in it, and dark trousers—navy blue, I think. He'd taken his waistcoat off, and he'd got his shoes in his hand putting them out. The porter does them for the gentlemen if they make an arrangement.''

''Then he'd been there before?''

''Looked like it,'' said Miss Thompson. ''And Mabel said—''

''Well?''

''I described him, and she said he passed for Miss Delorne's brother, only nobody believed it.''

''Go on,'' said Bill. ''Or is that all?''

''Not by half it isn't,'' said Miss Thompson with vigour.

''Well, what happened?''

''He pulled the door to behind him, and he put down his boots and come across very soft on his stocking feet. I'd my hand on the door and Mabel in call, so I wasn't frightened, and he didn't try to touch me. He stood a yard away and said very soft, 'Will you take a message for me? It's important.' And I said, 'What—*now?*' and he said 'Tomorrow will do.' And whilst he was saying it he was writing on a bit of paper with a pencil he'd taken out of his trouser pocket, and he put the paper in my hand with a ten-shilling note, and back across the landing and in at Miss Delorne's flat without another word.''

What an odd story. If she wasn't making it up, what had happened to the message? He said that out loud.

''What happened to the message? Did you take it?''

Miss Thompson blinked. She opened her mouth to speak and shut it again.

''Well?'' said Bill impatiently.

''Well, that's just where it's a bit awkward,'' said Miss Thompson. ''I put it in my bag and I went into the flat, and Mabel wanted to know what had kept me, so I told her, and she said she didn't believe me, teasing like. So I said, 'Seeing's believing,' and I showed her the note. Well then, she wanted to read it, and I said she shouldn't, and she said she was going to, and she made a snatch and it got torn between us. 'Now see what you've done!' I said. And she said 'Well, you can't go taking a note like that,' and before I could stop her she'd put it on the kitchen fire.''

An extraordinary sensation swept over Bill. Robin O'Hara creeping out of Della Delorne's flat and seizing a desperate eleventh hour chance of sending a message—two girls playing, and the message gone up in smoke—Robin's life gone too.... What was the message? To whom was it written? And why was it written? Yes, that above all—why was it written? Had he just learned something vital? Had he already embarked upon a hazardous course, attempted at the last moment to safeguard himself by a message to Garratt or to Meg?

He looked up, to find Beatrice Thompson's eyes fixed on him with a curious expression. He guessed at an impulse held in check by doubt or prudence. An illuminating flash passed through his mind. He leaned forward with an abrupt movement and said,

"You wouldn't let Mabel read the note, but did you read it yourself?"

A blush rose becomingly in Miss Beatrice Thompson's cheeks. She blinked again and said,

"Well, Mr Coverdale, I did."

XX

BILL WAS CONSCIOUS OF TRIUMPH, SUSPENSE, ANTICIPATION. He leaned forward and said insistently,

"You *did*. I thought so. What was in it?"

"It was only a line, Mr Coverdale." She was leaning towards him in voluble explanation. "It was only a line, and I suppose I oughtn't to have looked, but it wasn't like an ordinary note, him being a stranger and coming out of that Miss Delorne's flat like that in the middle of the night. I thought I'd just see what kind of a message it was he was asking me to take, because Mum's got a story about a girl that was given a note in the street and five shillings to take it, and the envelope came unstuck and she looked inside, and it said, 'Keep the bearer till I come,' and no name at the end, only initials. Whiteslavers, that was. So I thought I'd have a look just in case. But it was only one line, and all it said was, 'Going down to some place or other,' and initials signed to it. And I can't remember what the first one was, but there was an O, and an H after that, tight up to each other with a sort of a comma between them."

Was she making it up? No, he was sure she wasn't. But the message—he must get the message straightened out. He said,

"Please, Miss Thompson, think carefully. That message

may be most awfully important. Where did he say he was going?''

She rolled her eyes at him in a puzzled way.

"It was some place or other, Mr Coverdale."

And all at once there was a most frightful thought in his mind. "Some place or other, or some Place or other?" Which did she mean, and how was he to find out without asking a leading question? He got a piece of the hotel paper and gave it to her with a pencil out of his own pocket.

"Now, Miss Thompson, will you write that message down as nearly as possible as you saw it? Write down everything you remember seeing, even if it's only part of a word. Give me as much as you can."

She rested the paper on the wedding photograph and wrote the first few words quickly, then stopped, lifted the pencil and wrote again, leaving a gap. Then, frowning, she bent over the paper, pencil poised, and all at once with a quick movement she scribbled in the empty space.

"There!" she said and pushed the paper at him. "That's the best I can do. I can't swear to the name but it was something like that."

Bill read in a neat characterless hand, "I am going down to—" and then a gap, and then a scribble that looked like "stow." Then, most decidedly and unmistakeably, "Place," with a capital p. All his pulses jumped. "I am going down to—stow Place."

He had to put his leading question then. He couldn't keep it back.

He said, "Was it Ledstow Place?" and she blinked at him and said,

"Oh *yes*, Mr Coverdale, it was."

"Are you sure?"

She nodded and laughed.

"Oh yes. So soon as you said it I could see it just like he'd written it down."

Ledstow Place! It seemed incredible. Four days after he had disappeared Robin O'Hara had been in Oleander Mansions at Della Delorne's flat, and he had tried to send a note to say that he was going down to Ledstow Place . . . who was the note for? He asked the question with a rising excitement.

"And who was it adressed to?"

"Well, that's what I didn't see, and I was going to tell you about it. If I'd had the name and address, I'd have taken the message in the morning, as much as I could remember of it, but it was only the inside I'd looked at, and there was nothing to go by. Well, after the note got torn and Mabel had put it on the fire, which she'd no business to do, and so I told her, I began to think what I could do, because I'd got his ten-shilling note. Then it come to me p'raps I could go across to Miss Delorne's flat and just let him know I'd had an accident with his note. I told Mabel what I was going to do, and she promised to leave the door open and be just inside, but when I got half way across the landing I didn't go any further." A funny little shiver passed over her and she stopped.

"Why didn't you?" said Bill quickly.

"Well, it sounds silly, Mr Coverdale, but his shoes were gone."

"His shoes?"

She shivered again.

"I told you he was in his stocking feet with his shoes in his hand, putting them out for the porter. And then five minutes after they weren't there. It sounds awful silly, but I got a kind of a creep down my back when I saw they weren't there, and I couldn't have gone on and knocked on the door, not for anything in the world I couldn't."

Bill sat in a frowning silence. Was Robin being so watched that he had to have an excuse for opening the door of Della Delorne's flat? He had come out with the shoes in his hand, and put them down, and gone back into the flat after writing his note and giving it to Beatrice Thompson. And then, five minutes afterwards, the shoes were gone again.

That looked as if the shoes were an excuse. He was doing something he didn't want known, and if he was heard opening the door, the shoes would be a very good excuse. But he couldn't have counted on Beatrice Thompson. What was he planning to do when he came out with those shoes in his hand, very quietly and in his stocking feet? He had a slip of paper ready. And a pencil. And a ten-shilling note. All very handy. Bill thought he must have planned to put his message and the ten-shilling note through the letter-box of the opposite flat and chance Mabel's getting it to its destination—any decent girl would. If he had to write the note out there on the landing, someone must have been watching him pretty closely in the flat. The someone would be Della Delorne. That brought her into the affair of his murder with a vengeance. If she wasn't in it, if he wasn't suspecting her, he could have written his note under her eyes and walked round to the post with it. There would have been no reason why he shouldn't.

No, he had been on the track of some very dangerous people—this on Garratt's authority—and the track had led him to his death.

And this—this was the last living sight of Robin O'Hara—a figure emerging stealthily from Della Delorne's flat, sending, or trying to send, an eleventh-hour message, and then vanishing into the flat again, or so off the map and out of everybody's ken.

And that eleventh-hour message—"I am going down to Ledstow Place."

The track ended at Ledstow Place.

The violence of his mental reaction brought his head up with a jerk. It was nonsense. It was the most completely damnable nonsense. And then, sitting there in the hotel lounge with Beatrice Thompson gazing at him between interest and alarm, two things happened in his mind. They happened simultaneously but separately. It was like being aware of two quite different scenes on the same brightly lighted stage.

On the one hand he saw a window break suddenly, and on the other he saw Beatrice Thompson look at Meg's wedding group and point with a scarlet fingernail. The window was a top-storey window of the house on the island at Ledstow Place. He looked back over his shoulder in the dusk, caught a fleeting gleam of daylight on the glass, and saw it break—suddenly, inexplicably. The scarlet nail pointed at the Professor. Miss Thompson's voice said eagerly, "I've seen that old gentleman;" and then, "Coming out of Miss Delorne's flat—nine o'clock in the morning;" and then, "Disgusting, I call it."

And the track which Robin O'Hara was following had led to Ledstow Place.

It wasn't possible.

He clenched his hands and forced his voice.

"Miss Thompson—why did you say that you recognized someone else in that group you've got there?"

She rolled her eyes.

"I don't know what you mean."

"Then you've a very short memory." He leaned across and picked up the wedding group. "When I first showed you this, you said you recognized someone. Not Mr O'Hara—you didn't say anything about him to start with. I want to know why."

The eyes ceased to roll. They became shrewd and businesslike.

"Well, we hadn't fixed anything up then—had we? Of course I recognized *him* right away." She pointed at Robin in his bridegroom's array. "I recognized *him* all right, but I wasn't going to say so till we'd got the business part settled. Well, you know how it is—a girl's got to look out for herself or she'll get left."

A tremendous feeling of relief came over Bill.

"Then you didn't really see the Professor—the old gentleman—at all?"

Miss Thompson tossed her head.

"I don't tell lies, Mr Coverdale! Of course I'd seen him—like I told you. Coming out of Miss Delorne's flat he was, at nine o'clock in the morning, and looking as pleased with himself as a cat that's been at the cream, the horrid old man."

The dead weight of apprehension settled slowly down again. The Professor? Incredible. But this girl wasn't lying. She had really seen him coming out of Della Delorne's flat. . . . She couldn't have seen him. It was impossible.

"Are you sure?"

She nodded.

"He hasn't got a beard in the photograph, of course," she said.

"Then you can't be sure."

"The one I saw had a beard. And he walked sort of lame. Does this one walk lame? Because if he does, it would kind of prove it was him, wouldn't it?"

Bill took the photograph away from her and laid it down. There wasn't anything more to say. That leonine head with its shock of white hair would be easily recognized, beard or no beard. But the limp made the recognition certain. It was the Professor whom she had seen. There was only one more question to ask.

"When did you see him?"

Miss Thompson considered.

"Well, the fourth was my birthday, October the fourth, the night the other one, Mr O'Hara, gave me the note, only by the time it came to that it was well over midnight and we'd got into October the fifth, and it wasn't that day I saw the old gentleman, but it was the next, and that would make it October the sixth. And it was nine o'clock in the morning, like I told you, and he came on out and down the stairs, and that was the last I saw of him." She got up and began to button her coat. "If that's all, Mr Coverdale, I'll be getting along. It's not the Palais-de-Danse tonight, but we did think about going to the pictures, so if there isn't anything more—"

There wasn't anything more.

He paid her, shook hands, saw her out, and came back again to the place where they had talked. There wasn't anything more. The phrase summed up the feeling which was pressing in upon him and which he was resisting with an ever-weakening conviction. There wasn't anything more. He had followed the track which Robin O'Hara had followed. It led to the Professor, and to Ledstow Place, and it broke off short there. He felt as if he were standing on the edge of a cliff where the path had broken off and where one step more might take him over the edge. Robin O'Hara had gone down to Ledstow Place. Had that been the step which had taken *him* over the edge?

Meg was at Ledstow Place now.

A horrible cold fear swept over him, quite instinctive, quite unreasoning.

And then and there he remembered Meg talking to him on the telephone yesterday—"A tram—a beastly juggernaut of a tram" . . . "I nearly came to a sticky end. . . ." "I suppose I slipped. . . ." Was that to have been the step over the edge for Meg?

All at once, out of the horror and confusion which filled his mind, there emerged a clear and definite conclusion. Meg must be got away from Ledstow Place—now—at once—before anything else could happen. He hadn't the slightest idea what excuse he was going to make or how he was going to get her away. He only knew that he was going to do it.

From the telephone-box he rang up Jim Ogilvie and told him that he was called out of town. Perhaps it was a memory of Robin O'Hara that made him add, "I have to go down to Ledstow—a family emergency."

He tried for Garratt next, to be told that he was out. He didn't know whether to be glad or sorry. Garratt would have to know what the Thompson girl had said, but he had no time to waste on letting him know tonight, and no patience or temper to listen to Garratt telling him he had found another mare's nest. Yet he gave the same message to Garratt's man that he had given to Jim Ogilvie.

"Tell him I've gone down to Ledstow. Tell him I'll call him up. The address is Ledstow Place."

And with that he rang off and went out to get his car and to drive furiously through the dark upon the Ledlington road.

XXI

MEG HAD LUNCH WITH MISS CANNOCK IN THE ROOM that would have been the study if Uncle Henry hadn't had his study over on the island. This room, in which the Professor sat immersed and wrote the great work which was to bring down the high look and proud stomach of Hoppenglocker and all Hoppenglockerites, was by common consent the Study. As a result no one quite knew what to call the other room. It had, therefore, no official title, and was variously alluded to by members of the household.

Meg found herself thinking of it as the Blue Room because of her blue curtains and the delphiniums in the chintz which she had chosen for it—no, not for it, but for its furniture—in the days when she and the furniture had a home at Way's End. The chintz was getting very shabby now. Miller called it the hall room and Miss Cannock the morning room.

It was not a very comfortable place for meals. A folding table had to be brought in from the hall and cleared away again afterwards. There was nowhere to put a joint if one had to be carved, and there was nowhere to stand any extra plates or dishes except the writing-table, so that at every meal there was the feeling that the house was being turned out, and that at any moment removers might appear to pack up the furniture and take it away. As for the joint difficulty, Mrs Miller met this by the simple expedient of not cooking one, her idea of lunch for two ladies being three cutlets and a rice pudding one day, and three cutlets and a blancmange the next.

The third cutlet set up a delicate situation. Miss Cannock

in her role of hostess—and how odd to see someone else being hostess in Uncle Henry's house—was bound to offer it to Meg. Meg, hungry but polite, as became a guest, was bound to refuse. Whereupon Miss Cannock with an archly irritating laugh would daily remark, "Perhaps I had better save its life, or Mrs Miller's feelings may be hurt." The cutlets were very small, and Meg's exasperation grew. After all, Miss Cannock was indubitably the housekeeper, and could order four cutlets or even six if so disposed.

Today when offered the last cutlet, Meg thought with a sudden spurt of suspicion, "I wonder if she's starving Uncle Henry," and, nerved by this, she said, "Yes, thank you," whereupon Miss Cannock helped her, and then sat gazing mournfully at her own empty plate. Meg was hungry, but it was all she could do to finish the cutlet. Miss Cannock looked ridiculously forlorn sitting there opposite her, fidgeting with that silly long scarf which she always wore and which was continually catching in something or falling off. She got out her handkerchief and rubbed the tip of her nose with it. She patted that old-fashioned fringe of hers, she straightened her scarf, she sighed. Meg swallowed the last bit of cutlet in a hurry and said,

"I do hope it's not going to rain."

Miss Cannock sighed again.

"I am afraid it is not at all cheerful for you down here. Mr Postlethwaite is at the most critical point of his book, and I am naturally much occupied with him."

"You know," said Meg, "he ought not to shut himself up like this—it's quite terribly bad for him. He always did try to do it, but we didn't let him. I tell you what, I'll go over and see if I can't drag him out for a walk this afternoon."

The door opened and Miller came in. He removed the dish which had held the cutlets and placed a very small milk pudding in front of Miss Cannock, who seemed to be too much flustered to attend to it.

"Oh, Mrs O'Hara—indeed—I couldn't! Mr Postlethwaite can be quite severe, and his orders—his most stringent orders—are that no one should interrupt him when he is writing. Besides he locks himself in, you know, at the far end of the bridge, and though he has entrusted me with the key of the door on this side, it is on the distinct understanding that I do not let it out of my keeping." Her fluttering, fidgeting hands picked up a tablespoon and a large fork. "And now may I give you a little of this pudding?" She peered at it short-sightedly. "Rice, I believe—yes, rice. And I fear that Mrs Miller has burnt it."

Meg's back was up. If Uncle Henry was being fed on about half a cutlet and a scrape of burnt rice pudding, it was about time somebody did something about it. As a cook this Miller creature was a complete fraud. Remembering the Evanses, she boiled over.

"She's a very bad cook," she said.

Miss Cannock handed her a portion of dry pudding surrounded by black skin.

"Oh, do you think so? Mr Postlethwaite has been quite satisfied with her, I believe—but this pudding does seem—"

"Uncle Henry doesn't notice," said Meg. "But it's terribly bad for him. He'd much better get rid of these Millers and have the Evanses back. I can't think why he ever parted with them. I would never have let him if I'd been there. They looked after him so beautifully and understood all his ways, and Mrs Evans was the most melting cook." Meg stopped abruptly because Miss Cannock, abandoning her pudding, was applying her handkerchief both to her nose and to the corners of her eyes with a hand which was shaking with emotion.

"It's very hard," she said in a trembling voice. "I've done my best, and Mr Postlethwaite has been satisfied." She paused, gulped, and dabbed with increasing vigour. "It's so easy to come down and—find fault. And this isn't London, and of course you have no idea of the difficulties of catering—so far away from the shops—and fish only twice a week unless you go into Ledlington specially—and of course I was engaged—as a secretary—and had no idea that I would—be held—responsible—for the housekeeping—for which I cannot feel that I have any aptitude—and which was never mentioned by Mr Postlethwaite when—he engaged me."

Meg cursed herself for a fool. Why on earth hadn't she held her tongue? The Cannock bridling and fussing was bad enough, but the Cannock head over ears in a grievance and requiring consolation was worse—much worse. Her nose was growing steadily pinker and her sniffs more poignant. It took Meg a quarter of an hour to persuade her to stop dabbing her eyes and to eat her now horribly congealed pudding.

She escape as soon as she could to her own room. The whole question of Uncle Henry—his meals, his domestic staff, and when if ever Meg might expect him to emerge from the book sufficiently to become aware that she was a guest in his house, had been most effectually shelved. Meg felt as if she couldn't stay in the house another second. A secretary with a temper would have roused her own temper to give battle, but a weak, meek dreep of a secretary who oozed tears and went pink at the nose on the slightest provocation or without any provocation at all merely induced that frame of mind in which you hastily buy a ticket for China, or Peru, or Popocatapetl.

"What a place—what a woman—what weather!" she exclaimed to herself as she came out of the front door into a thin cold drizzle. A low mist brooded over the ground, all ready to turn into fog when the dusk came down. Now there probably wouldn't be any fog in Peru.

As she crossed the neglected gravel, she pleased herself with the fancy that an aeroplane might at any moment come swooping down out of the low grey clouds. There would be plenty of room for it to land in the park, and she would get in and fly away, and never have to eat Mrs Miller's rice pudding, or console Miss Cannock again. The pilot was a little nebulous, and the destination anywhere in the world. It was a very pleasant fancy, and it would have been even pleasanter if she had not had the feeling that she might suddenly discover the pilot was Bill Coverdale—and of course that wouldn't do at all. For one thing he had just written her a perfect beast of a letter and he certainly wouldn't want to fly away with her to the ends of the earth, and for another even if he did want to she couldn't possibly fly with him. "Oh no, no, no!" said Meg, and woke up out of her day-dream to scold herself. But of course this was just the sort of place to make you go crazy and start talking to yourself.

She had turned to the right without much thought, and was now at the point where the drive, skirting the lake, rose a little above it and then dipped again. It was from this place that Bill Coverdale, looking towards the island, had seen a window suddenly break where the house looked over the wall that guarded it. Meg stopped as Bill had done, and looked across the water as he had looked. It was a natural vantage point from which the gaunt barrack of a house, the island, and the bridge which linked them were all very clear. The wall round the island house was so high that it could only just be seen—the roof and two small windows. But one of them was broken. It was funny that Meg should have thought of that, because at once she corrected the thought and told herself that the window was open. Not broken—open. And then she had to correct herself again, because if it was a sash window, half the frame would still be filled with glass. And it couldn't be a casement, because every casement window in the world opened outwards. And if it opened outwards, where was it? No, she had to come back to her odd first impression of a window broken and the glass stripped clear of the frame so that the house now peered at her over the wall and across the water with one bright eye and one blank one. It gave her a queer sort of feeling and one she didn't much like. It was horribly bad for Uncle Henry to shut himself up in that walled-in poke of a house, with the water right up to the walls and probably everything streaming with damp. Miss Cannock didn't look as if she would ever think of having anything aired, and as for the Millers, Meg placed no dependence on them. The house was dirty and ill-kept, the meals were deplorable, and as Uncle Henry never noticed anything, the house on the island was probably even worse. She made up her mind that, tears or no tears, she must insist on seeing him. Only if Miss Cannock wouldn't give up the key, what was she going to do about it?

"What a life!" said Meg, and went on walking down towards the gates.

She thought she would go into the village to buy some stamps. She wasn't going to answer Bill's horrid icy letter today, but perhaps tomorrow she would write him a few equally chilly lines, just to show that she didn't care. The post-office was the general shop next door to the pub. Perhaps she would see William digging manure into the pub garden. What a thrilling thought! All at once she wondered whether the post-office had a telephone. Of course she hadn't the slightest intention of ringing Bill up—not today anyway—but it would be rather nice to feel that she could do it if she wanted to.

She arrived at the gates, tried them as a matter of form, and found them locked. This was only what she had expected. She would have to get one of the Hendersons to open them for her. The lodge door being unprovided with either a bell or a knocker, she was obliged to rap on it with her knuckles. It was a very hard door. The chocolate paint was peeling off, the doorstep looked as if no one had cleaned it for years, and the windows which flanked it on either side were dirty and closely curtained. Meg knocked half a dozen times and then went round to the back. There was a strong smell of dustbins and a nasty litter of old newspapers, cabbage-stalks, potato peelings, and crusts of bread.

Mentally apostrophising Mrs Henderson as an old pig, Meg picked her way to the back door and banged upon it with her clenched fist. When she had banged half a dozen times she stopped to listen, and heard a slow, dragging footstep come down the stair. Presently the door swung in a little way and Mrs Henderson looked round it with a furtive air.

Meg said "Good afternoon," and received no response, only that suspicious stare. She had a horrid undecided feeling between being angry and something else. The something else was being frightened, only she pushed it quickly into a dark cupboard and locked the door on it because it was too positively inane. How could she possibly be frightened when there wasn't anything to be frightened of?

She said quickly, "Oh, will you please unlock the gate? I'm going into the village."

Mrs Henderson went on staring at her without opening

the door any wider. She was very dirty and unkempt. After a considerable pause she said,

"I'm hard of hearing."

Meg had to come nearer, and didn't like it.

"The gates are locked. I want to go into the village."

Mrs Henderson nodded.

"They're always locked. That's orders."

"But I want to go into the village."

Mrs Henderson shook her head with its sparse untidy hair.

"I'm very hard of hearing."

Meg spoke louder, and pointed.

"I want to go out. I want you to open the gates."

Mrs Henderson shook her head again.

"Can't be done. They're to be kept locked—Mr Postle-thwaite's orders."

Meg said "Nonsense!" in a tone of brisk rage, and Mrs Henderson shut the door in her face.

She not only shut it, she shot the bolt inside. Meg heard the whingeing creak as it went home. Then she heard Mrs Henderson go upstairs again with the heel of a down-trodden slipper slapping on every step.

"*Well!*" said Meg, and boiled with righteous wrath.

There was nothing for it but to go away, and as quickly as possible Meg went. But that slammed and bolted door had changed her lukewarm feeling that she might as well go and buy some stamps in the village to a stubborn determination to get there at any cost. The cost would be to her clothes, since she would have to get over the wall, but she meant to do it, and once outside, and the stamps in her pocket, even Mrs Henderson could scarcely refuse to let her in again. Somewhere in the depths of her heart Meg was aware that a refusal wouldn't blight her very much. She would be able to bear with fortitude being locked out of Ledstow Place. But of course she wouldn't be locked out, and she hadn't even got over the wall yet. She worked her way along it on the left of the gates. There was a thick belt of shrubbery next to the drive, but between it and the wall there ran a sodden, neglected path slippery with clay and slimy with moss. There was therefore no hope of a tree with friendly branches to serve as a step-ladder. The wall was some eight feet high, built of brick with a small coping on the top, and it was in very good repair.

After about thirty yards the shrubbery stopped, and the path with it. In front of her now was the rough open park, with an occasional tree or clump of trees, and the wall running on, sheer, bare, and unclimbable. None of the trees were anywhere near it. Meg decided that her proud spirit would just have to bend to necessity, and that the stamps must wait for another day. There was, after all, no raging hurry. She hadn't meant to write to Bill till tomorrow anyhow.

She turned round and went back to the house. The drizzle was turning to rain, and there was no sense in getting wet—she hadn't enough clothes for that. She walked fast, and as she walked, she made up her mind to see Uncle Henry as soon as possible. She would have to insist on seeing him. It really wasn't Miss Cannock's place to make difficulties, and Meg was prepared to be extremely firm. Since he was at a critical point in his book, she wouldn't complain about Mrs Henderson's rudeness, but she must insist on his giving definite orders that she was to be let out whenever she chose. This sort of prison gate and eight-foot wall business was absolutely medieval. If he really wanted to be left alone with his Millers, and his Cannock, and his revoltingly rude Hendersons, he'd only got to say so, revive her suspended allowance, and press a cheque into her hand, and no one would depart more joyfully than his unwanted niece.

These meditations lasted her to the front door, which she found not quite open and not quite shut. She had given it a brisk bang when she started on her walk and it must have rebounded before the latch could click. She didn't bang it now. She wanted to get up to her room without encountering Miss Cannock, of whom she felt she had had a just sufficiency. She therefore closed the door very gently and went softly up the stairs. If the house was neglected, it was solid. Not a step creaked.

She reached her room and shut herself in.

XXII

Meg looked up from the book she was reading and glanced at her wrist-watch. If was five-and-twenty past four. She had drawn the curtains and switched on the light when she came in. Her chair was comfortable—it was her own old bedroom chair—and her book was one of those pleasant old-fashioned ones in which nothing very much happens, in a very pleasant old-fashioned way. She wondered if there was going to be any tea. She had a raging tea-urge, but one of the irritating things about life at Ledstow Place was that you never knew whether there was going to be tea or not. Some days there was, and some days there wasn't, and you never knew which it was going to be until it was half past four and the tea either arrived or didn't arrive. It was one of the things which filled Meg with a yearning to take the invaluable Millers by the scruff of their necks, knock their heads together with a good resounding bang, and give them the permanent push. It pleased her very much to dream of doing this, but it was a regretful pleasure, because she could see no immediate chance of making the dream come true.

The tea-urge grew stronger. Unwarned by her encounter with Mrs Henderson, it occurred to Meg that after all she could order tea. What was there to prevent her just going down to the blue room and ringing the bell for Miller. If she told him to bring her some tea, he could hardly refuse point blank.

But suppose he did.

It was a most frightfully daunting thought, and it ought to

have been an impossible one, but somehow it wasn't. It undermined Meg's morale a good deal. There was something about Miller and there was something about Henderson which was a warning against any assumption of authority. She would not have kept either of them in her own service for a day, but the fact that they were in Uncle Henry's service and that Uncle Henry was completely inaccessible had a very sobering effect.

She came out of her room and stood there listening. There wasn't a sound of any kind in the house. She went along the gallery and down the passage that turned out of it to the bathroom to wash her hands, and it was while she was letting the so-called hot tap run in the hope that it might, if given time, live up to its name that she had a bright idea. If she went down the back stairs as she had done on the day of her arrival she would probably be able to hear whether there was any prospect of tea or not. There is a particular kettle-cum-teapot-cum-cup-and-saucer kind of clatter which permeates any back premises when tea is being got ready. If she hung over the back stairs she would know whether to nourish hope or to abandon it.

She dried her hands on a horrid limp towel which looked and felt as if it had been hanging there for weeks, and then went to the door at the top of the crooked stair. She couldn't hear a sound, but if the door at the bottom was shut, the rattle of china and the chink of tea-spoons might very well be lost. She went down as she had done before, and wondered what she was going to say if she met Miller or Mrs Miller coming up. As a matter of fact she had never set eyes on Mrs Miller, though she supposed she had heard her voice. It seemed very difficult to think of the owner of that light laugh and that odd thrilling voice as being married to Miller.

This time the door at the bottom of the stairs was shut. Meg went right down, set her hand on the knob, and hesitated. She ought to go back. She was putting herself in an undignified position. She ought to turn right round and get off the back stairs without a moment's delay.

She stayed where she was, and without any conscious

order from her brain the hand which held the knob began to turn it. When the knob had moved a certain distance the latch became disengaged, and the door, as if by its own weight, swung slowly back until it touched her shoulder. There was a gap of two or three inches. The passage beyond was dark in the twilight, but a couple of yards away the kitchen door stood open and a bright patch striped the gloom.

In the very moment that Meg saw these things she heard Miller say in a grumbling, exasperated way,

"What's the sense of waiting about? If a thing's to be done, what I say is, 'Get on with it and get it done.'"

If this was Miller putting it across Mrs Miller because she was late with the tea, it was all very well and good. But then why have a horrid tricky feeling down the back of your spine, and why be reminded—oddly, definitely, sharply reminded—of a scene in Macbeth and of somebody saying, "When 'tis done, then 'twere well it were done quickly." But she couldn't remember who said it—was it Macbeth? —and when she tried to remember she couldn't even be sure of the words.

The voice she supposed to be Mrs Miller's was speaking now. It was nearer to her than Miller's voice had been—a voice with a thrill in it, a calmly dominant voice, a very odd voice to belong to anyone who cooked as badly as Mrs Miller did. It said,

"Who's running this show? You'll do as you're told, and when I'm ready I'll let you know!"

Miller made some kind of movement. He must have jarred the tray. There was a rattle of china. The light laugh which Meg had heard before rang out.

"As a matter of fact, I'm ready now. There—does that please you?"

If it was the tea that was ready, what was Meg waiting for? She didn't know, but she couldn't have moved to save her life.

Miller said in a changed tone, "How are you going to do it?"

"This—in the cup. Put out the cracked one so that there

won't be any mistake. The stuff's quite colourless." This was the woman again, speaking with an indifferent calm.

Meg heard her own heart beating with a strange loudness. A cracked cup—so that there should be no mistake. . . . Something colourless in it. . . . "If a thing's to be done, get on with it and get it done." . . . No, that was Miller. It was the woman who had said, "I'll let you know when I'm ready," and, "I'm ready now."

Meg still had hold of the door knob. Her straining grip pulled the door towards her, but her weight as she leaned against it kept it from moving any farther and maintained a steady gap of about two inches through which she could see the light that barred the passage and hear the voices that spoke within. And suddenly there was another voice, another woman saying querulously and with a Cockney accent,

"I don't like it, and I don't see what you wanted to have her down here for at all."

"Don't you?" The thrill in the voice was one of amusement and scorn. "You take a lot of telling, Milly. Come along now—isn't that kettle boiling?"

Through the pounding of her heart Meg heard Milly sniff and say,

"Just about."

"All right then, I'm off. Take the tea along, and if she isn't down, beat the gong."

There was a light sound as if someone had jumped down from the kitchen table. Meg had a picture of the owner of the voice sitting carelessly on the table edge giving her orders and now—yes, *now*—coming across the room, coming through the open door with the brightness of the lighted room streaming past her. Instinctively, noiselessly, and swiftly Meg pushed the door against which she was leaning. The gap through which she had been looking and listening was gone. On the other side of the panel she could hear light footsteps going away. She released the knob, controlling her hand so that the latch should engage without any sound at all. Then slowly and stiffly she turned round and went up the stairs. And along the passage. And so by the corridor to her room. It seemed to take a very long time—a very, very long time, because if she let go, if she let her panic drive her, she would begin to run and perhaps to scream. She mustn't let go.

She got to her room, locked the door, and sat down upon the edge of the bed. But as soon as she did that she felt the terror come up into her throat as if it would choke her. And she mustn't let it do that. You can't think when you're frightened, and she had got to think, and think quickly.

She went over to the washstand, tipped the contents of the jug into the basin, and plunged her face into the ice-cold water. She came up gasping, and did it again, and yet again. Then she dried her face and made herself go and look in the glass, apply powder and lipstick, and arrange her hair. Lipstick—plenty of lipstick—that was the thing. And enough rouge to prevent anyone seeing how pale she was. She hardly ever used rouge, because when she was well she had colour enough, and when she wasn't she thought it made her look worse, but she was thankful for it today.

When she had finished, she felt steady and controlled. Make-up helped, because it gave you the feeling of a part to be played. But in what a ghastly play—what a nightmare of a play!

But was it? What had frightened her? After all, what had she heard? She tried to go over it in her own mind, and found herself thinking less of the words than of the voices. There had been two women and a man in the kitchen. The man was Miller, but which of the women was Mrs Miller? She couldn't believe it was the one with the voice which at once attracted and repelled her. Voice and laugh alike belonged to another world than Miller's. They had the easy habit of command, the ring of authority, the consciousness of charm. No, it must be Milly who cooked the burnt rice puddings and the skimpy tough cutlets. If the other woman cooked at all, she would do it well. Whatever she did, it would be well done—you could hear it in her voice. But who was she—who *was* she?

The answer started out with a horrid plainness. She was someone from whom the Millers took their orders—in Uncle Henry's house, and behind Uncle Henry's back.

Right there Meg had a reaction. Her nerves were all wrong. She was behaving like a fool. After all, what had been said? What orders had been given? Never mind about the voices, get down to the words. Think—*think*. You've got to get it right. You've got to remember exactly what they said.

She put her head down in her hands and shut her eyes and thought. What was the first thing she had heard? . . . "Who's running this show? You'll do as you're told," and, "When I'm ready I'll let you know." . . . Well, there was nothing in that. But there was—there *was*. She was giving orders, and who was she to give orders to Miller? . . . Then the next thing—"As a matter of fact I'm ready now." . . . And *she* had asked Miller if it pleased him, and Miller had said, "How are you going to do it?" . . . Do what? That was what she had got to be clear about. What was it that was to be done? Because the woman had answered, "This—in the cup." . . . But what had she been holding out for them to see? . . . Meg had a picture of a hand that would match the voice—slim and delicate-fingered, with something lying on the palm, held out for the Millers to see. "*This* in the cup." The Millers had seen what it was, but Meg couldn't. She could only see her own picture of the delicate-fingered hand with something lying in the palm. And the something was to be put into the cup with a crack in it, so that there should be no mistake. The something was quite colourless. That was why Meg couldn't see it. It wouldn't show in the cracked cup. The tea and the milk would cover it and hide it, and it wouldn't show at all.

The booming note of the gong came up from the hall below. It was the same gong which had called them to many pleasant meals at Way's End. What was it calling her to now? She didn't know, but she knew that she must go and face it whatever it was. Just for a moment she wondered what would happen if she were to stay here with her door locked. She could plead a headache—sudden illness—say she was going to bed.

No, she couldn't. She couldn't wait up here and not know at what moment footsteps would come—along the passage or up the stair—Miller's footsteps—his wife's—the light footsteps she had heard come out of the kitchen and go away—lightly—down the passage. She couldn't bear that. Besides, it wouldn't help her. She mustn't let herself be isolated. She had never imagined that there would be a time when she would want to cling to the Cannock, but that was what she had come to. She needn't drink out of the cracked cup. Miller couldn't very well stop in the room to see whether she drank her tea, and she needn't drink it. And then she must put pressure on the Cannock and make her understand that she had just got to see Uncle Henry—not tomorrow, or the next day, or in the vague future, but now, at once, within the next half hour. If she could get to Uncle Henry she would be safe, and everything would be all right. She had just got to get to Uncle Henry.

XXIII

THE BLUE ROOM LOOKED COMFORTABLE, WITH THE CURTAINS drawn and the tea-table set out in front of a little crackling fire. Miss Cannock was pouring out the tea as Meg came in. There was a muffin-dish keeping warm by the hearth, and some stoney little buns with blackened currants sticking out of them on a plate belonging to Uncle Henry's mother's best tea-set. Meg wondered what she would have said to its being used every day, and used for Mrs Miller's nasty little buns.

Miss Cannock looked up with the bright smile which showed her gums.

"Ah—here you are! I've poured out your tea, because I could hear you coming downstairs, and one wants it to cool a little—doesn't one? Not to get cold, but just to cool off the least thing—don't you think so? And you *don't* take sugar, do you? I am very forgetful about things like that, I am afraid, but I always say it's better to ask, because once you've put it in you can't take it out again, can you?''

Meg said, "No, you can't," and took her cup. She sat in the little round chair she had always been so fond of and lifted the cup from the saucer as if she were looking at the china. It was one of a set which she had chosen herself—rather tall fluted cups with little bright bunches of flowers on a white ground. The cup which she held in a stiff, steady hand had a chip out of the gilded edge, and a long dark crack which ran from the chip to the base of the handle.

"It's pretty china. It's a pity it's cracked," she said.

Miss Cannock sipped her tea.

"Servants are so careless. Not the Millers—they are really most careful—but Mr Postlethwaite's china was in a terrible state when they took it over. Of course a man with his remarkable brain cannot be expected to supervise a household, and without supervision—but you are not drinking your tea, Mrs O'Hara."

"It's too hot," said Meg. She put the cup on the edge of the table and got up. "Miss Cannock, I really do want to see Uncle Henry. There's some business which I simply must discuss with him. I quite see that you don't like to take the responsibility, but I've got to see him, and I'll take care that you don't get into trouble over it. He shan't blame anyone but me."

Miss Cannock began to fuss and flutter. She was eating one of the little buns, crumbling it nervously and picking out the currants, which she arranged in a circle round her plate.

"Oh, Mrs O'Hara, I don't think—"

"It's no use," said Meg—"I've got to see him. That's what I came down here for, and I can't just go on like this day after day. He'll be months over this book, and my business won't wait."

"Oh *dear!*" said Miss Cannock. She pulled at her scarf and coughed in an embarrassed, deprecating fashion. "Oh dear, Mrs O'Hara—I'm sure I don't know what to say. Of course I see your point, but Mr Postlethwaite's orders are so stringent—so exceedingly stringent—''

Meg picked up her cup and strolled across the room to the window. She put back one of the curtains and stood there as if she were looking out, with the cup in her other hand. If the window had been open, she could have poured the tea away, but it was shut, and it was a heavy sash window, not an easily opened casement. She said aloud "I must see him," and she lifted the cup to her lips, but she did not drink from it. There was no strange smell. The tea smelled good, and she would have been very glad of a hot drink. Her mouth was parched and dry. Her throat was dry all the way down. There must be some way of getting rid of the tea. If there had been a plant in the room it would have been quite easy, but there wasn't any plant.

There was a book-case on the same side as the door. She went over to it and stood there as if she were looking at the books. She was behind Miss Cannock's back now, and from this position she spoke.

"All my old books are here. It's funny to see them." She lifted the cup to her lips again. "I don't like this tea very much. Do you? Perhaps some sugar would improve it. Shall I try a lump?"

She had gone over to the book-case with the idea of taking out some of the books as if she were going to look at them, and then pouring the tea away into the gap. The books would hide it. It would trickle down at the back of the shelves and dry up before it could do much harm. But as she stood there, a much better plan came to her. The Cannock was always pressing her to take sugar in her tea. Well, that was the way out—a really beautiful natural way, and nothing messy about it. She had hated the idea of wetting the books, and Uncle Henry would have had a fit if he had ever found out. No, this was going to be a much, much better way.

She went back to the table, dropped two lumps of sugar into her cup, stirred them well, and tasted the tea, or made believe to taste it. The warmth and the wetness just touched her lips, and at the touch she felt a shuddering revulsion. What was in it, and what would happen to her if she were to open her closed lips and drink from the cup which had been prepared for her—the cup with the crack in it?

With the shudder still in her mind, she said in a laughing, natural voice.

"Oh! It's made it worse—*much* worse! I can't think how anyone can take sugar in their tea really! It's completely repellent! There—I've wasted a perfectly good cup of tea, and I shall be in Miller's black books! Can't we pour it out of the window?"

"Oh dear!" said Miss Cannock. She dropped a bit of bun on the carpet and stooped to pick it up again. "Oh dear— what a pity! I don't like putting people out, and Miller—he seems a little upset. I suppose you couldn't—"

Meg's temper got the better of her. It set a little flare in either cheek and took her to the hearth with a whisk of her skirts.

"My dear Miss Cannock, I'm not going to drink a perfectly foul cup of tea to please Miller," she said. And then she laughed and emptied the cup into the fire. "There— he needn't know. And now we'll wash the sugar out, and perhaps the next cup will be better."

It was extraordinary how gay and confident she felt. She had outwitted the Millers, and she had thought of a really good reason for washing out the cup. She would have her tea, and then she would go straight to Uncle Henry if she had to take Miss Cannock there by main force or pick her pocket of the key to that idiotic bridge. Once they got down to brass tacks, she would be able to coerce the Cannock all right. In her present mood she felt abundantly sure of that.

"Oh dear!" said Miss Cannock again. She fussed with her scarf and watched in timid dismay while Meg washed out the cup. "There is plenty of tea left," she said. "Oh, I hope you haven't put the fire out. But of course you shall have another cup, and no sugar this time, though I prefer it myself. Now I wonder if I had better fill the teapot up the least little bit."

She did so, and managed to send her plate slipping over

the table edge on to the floor. The crumbs and the currants scattered, and Meg bent down to rescue the plate. When she stood up again Miss Cannock was pouring out her tea to an accompaniment of apology and explanation.

"So stupid of me, Mrs O'Hara—and so kind of you to trouble! I think my scarf must have caught as I leaned forward, and the plate may have been just a little too near the edge. I do hope it isn't broken. I should be so distressed if I had broken any of Mr Postlethwaite's china. I am usually most careful." She put in the milk, and paused with her hand on the sugar-tongs. "Oh dear, dear—I really can't think what is the matter with me this afternoon! I was just going to give you a lump of sugar. I am afraid I must be getting absent-minded, and that would be a most serious handicap in my profession."

She looked so exactly as if she were going to cry that Meg subdued her impatience and said all the reassuring things that she could think of. The Cannock in floods of tears would be the absolute limit at this juncture.

She took her tea and drank about half of it, standing up by the table. And then and there as she was still swallowing it and it was grateful to her parched tongue and throat, she knew that there was something in the cup. She hadn't outwitted the Millers after all. There was something in the tea, and she had drunk about half of it.

But—

But she had washed the cup—

But that meant—

She kept her face still and looked at Miss Cannock. She was nibbling at her bun. She had a faintly reassured and timidly deprecating smile on her foolish sallow face. It wasn't possible—but there was no one else. There was no one else who could have put—something—into the cup which she had washed. The Cannock could, whilst Meg stooped down to pick up the plate.

At that moment when she knew herself to be standing on the very edge of disaster, standing there and overbalancing, the fear went out of her. She came upon something which she did not know that she possessed—a hard, stubborn vein of courage which meant to go on, and to fight, and to go down fighting if it came to going down. There was no anger about it. It was cool, and tough, and strong.

She turned quite naturally from the table and knelt down before the fire. There was a black woolly hearth-rug there, and it had come to her in a flash what she could do.

"Oh, Miss Cannock," she said, "we're wasting the muffins! Won't you have one?"

"I don't think so."

Was it her imagination, or was there a veil of smoke, a veil of strange white mist, between her and the fire? Miss Cannock's voice sounded a long way off. . . .

Half—she had only had half of the tea—and she must get rid of the other half—they must think she had drunk it—she mustn't faint—or go to sleep—it would sink into the woolly hearth-rug, and no one would guess she hadn't drunk it—it might make a difference—it *might*—

She bit her lip hard on the inside. Then she lifted the cup to her lips. Her hand felt heavy. She said,

"This is a good cup of tea—"

Her voice sounded strange in her own ears. She wondered how it sounded to the woman behind her—she wondered about the woman behind her. The Cannock was behind her. Could she see what she was doing? Yes, she could see Meg's arm lifted and the cup at her lips—but she wouldn't be able to see it when it got below the level of her waist. . . .

She took the cup from her lips without drinking and lowered it. The mist was thick between her and the fire. She wanted to shut her eyes and go to sleep. She bit her lip again, but this time she could only just feel it. With a most punishing effort, and with the very last of her conscious control, she brought the cup down until it touched the rug. Then she tilted it sideways.

The tea spilled, trickling between the black woolly curls, leaving no stain. Meg remained on her knees for a moment, but she no longer knew where she was or what was happening. Fear, anxiety, and effort had all floated away from her into the mist. She did not hear Miss Cannock speak her name. She did not hear her repeat it in a loud, insistent tone. The mist blinded her eyes and stopped her ears. After a wavering moment she sank down sideways across the tilted cup.

Miss Cannock got to her feet, looked down at her with composure, and then crossed the room without hurry and rang the bell.

XXIV

MEG DID NOT KNOW HOW LONG SHE WAS UNCONSCIOUS. If she had drunk that cup of tea to the dregs as she had been meant to do, she would probably never have waked again, for unconsciousness would have held her helpless until such further steps had been taken as would have insured the deepest sleep of all. But her flash of courage and that last effort had saved her. The drug in the first cup of tea had been dissolved in water and thoroughly stirred before she came into the room. If she had drunk that cup, there would have been no awakening. But she had not drunk it. Her trick with the lumps of sugar had given her the opportunity of pouring it away and washing out the cup. And the drug in the second cup of tea was in tabloid form. There was no time to dissolve it first, and no opportunity of stirring it. Thus, since Meg did not take sugar, the liquid had never been stirred at all. She drank about half of it, standing up by the table, and she drank quickly because she was very parched and thirsty, but what she drank contained comparatively little of the drug, which was concentrated in the bottom of the cup. She had seemed to be drinking it as she knelt before the fire, but she had managed to tip it out upon the black woolly hearth-rug.

She came back to the sound of voices in the room and, more gradually, to a sense of her own whereabouts. She wasn't on the floor any more. That came to her with a sense of surprise, because she remembered kneeling in front of the fire and thinking that she must, must manage to spill the tea. The tea—there was something to the tea. . . . She drifted again into a blank state which was not quite sleep and not quite swoon. The voices came and went, just out of reach. . . . And then all at once the blankness was gone. She felt muzzy and languid, but her head was getting clearer. She wasn't on the floor, but on the couch. She looked through her lashes, and was puzzled because the wall was so close on her right and the high back of the couch so close on her left, and there was a light in the room, but she couldn't see it.

She shut her eyes again, and heard Miller say,

"What next?"

He was quite close to her, not a yard away, quite near her head. Hearing him speak like that, so horribly near, did more to rouse her than anything else could have done. Why of course, the wall was so close because they had turned the couch round, and she was lying on it quite flat with the back of it between her and the room, and that was why she couldn't see the light.

When Miller said, "What next?" a plaintive cockney voice broke in.

"I tell you I don't like it. I said all along I didn't, and I don't see any call to do it neither."

The odd thrilling voice answered her with the touch of scorn which Meg had heard in it before.

"Oh, you don't, don't you, Milly? Well then, of course there isn't any, what d'you call it, *call* to do anything. Let's all throw in our hands and stop bothering."

Milly sniffed.

"I dunno know what you mean."

"Don't you, Milly, my dear? Not very bright—are you? Perhaps you don't think it's going to matter to you personally, but don't you make any mistake, if we're for it, you're for it. If we get ours, then, my dear, you'll get yours, and I hope you'll like it." There was a note or two of musical laughter. Then the voice hardened. "You'd better get this straight, Milly. Robin O'Hara had you marked down all right in that damned packet of his—Milly Miller, alias Gertie Stevens, alias Crooked Sue."

"Ow—don't!"

The voice went on inexorably.

"I took you out of the gutter, didn't I? You'd better remember it, because that's where you'll finish up if you live to come out of prison."

"Ow—you wouldn't. *You wouldn't!*"

"Me? I shouldn't do anything. You'd do it yourself. Don't be a fool, Milly. They've got the proof of O'Hara's death, and the minute this girl knows about it we're done. You can't say I haven't fended her off, and I won't say it hasn't been quite an amusing game. I wish O'Hara could have seen me playing ghost. It would have tickled him." She laughed a little. "It was a pity he had to go. I'd liked to have worked with him, but he wouldn't come across, and the very last thing he said when he knew the game was up and he was for it, was to tell me just where we should all find ourselves when his wife and the bank manager opened this precious packet of his."

Meg lay in the shadow quite stiff, quite straight, quite flat.

Robin—the packet—Robin. . . . Robin was dead. These people had killed him. That woman who laughed had brought him to his death. Robin was dead, and the woman had tried to make her think he was alive. The marked newspaper—the letters set out on the hearth-rug—the leaf with the word pricked out on it—the card laid out at midnight in the dark flat—she could see the shining paste-board now, and a dead man's name on it. The woman had done all these things to make her believe that Robin was alive and to prevent her opening the packet. But Robin was dead. He had died bravely, doing his duty. Yes, Robin was brave—he would do that. She could think about him, brave and doing his duty. That took all the bitterness away. She could think about him like that.

Then all at once the sound of the closing door roused her. She had been drifting, and she mustn't drift. The door had shut quite sharply, almost with a bang. She wondered who had gone out of the room. And then she didn't have to wonder any more, because the woman said,

"What a damned fool Milly is! You'd better keep an eye on her."

And Miller spoke from somewhere startlingly near at hand.

"That's all right. And now what next? How long is that stuff good for?"

The stuff—that was the stuff they had put into her tea. . . . But she had only drunk half. They didn't know that. Or did they?

The woman was speaking again.

"Eight hours—ten—twelve—long enough anyhow. She had finished what was in the cup before she went off."

There was a pause. Then Miller said violently,

"Why don't you get on and get it over? Put her in the water and have done with it!"

Meg did not move, but she felt a cold inward shudder. They had drugged her, and they were going to drown her. But if she wasn't drugged, there would still be a chance of escape. She could swim. There must be a chance.

The woman laughed. The chance didn't seem worth much when Meg heard that laugh. She said with a cool whipping scorn in her voice,

"Have you got nerves aboard—like Milly?"

"No, I haven't."

"It sounds like it. Take a pull on yourself, my friend, and go on remembering that I'm running the show. I'm working to a time-table and I'm not taking any risks. She'll be out of the way by midnight, but not so very much before. The village can get to bed and go to sleep first. That boy from the inn takes his girl into the churchyard most evenings. There's no accounting for tastes—is there? Now suppose— just suppose it occurred to him to get over the wall. There's just one place where he could—I found it yesterday. There's a tombstone jammed up against the wall—well, you see? It's only a thousandth chance, but I'm not risking it.''

Miller said, ''All right.'' And then, grudgingly, ''You've got a head!''

''Thank you, Bob!'' The tone was a lightly mocking one.

''And then?'' said Miller.

''Then Henderson runs me up to town, and we put her in the river just as we did with O'Hara. There'll be nothing to show that she was drowned before she got there.''

Miller spoke again with a kind of grumbling anger.

''You keep everything mum to the last minute! What's the idea? Are you and Henderson going to light out and leave Milly and me to answer the questions that are going to be asked? Because if that's your game—''

Her laughter cut him short.

''My dear Bob, it isn't. Don't be so crass! Having disposed of the—incriminating evidence, we come straight back. Mrs O'Hara is scheduled to leave Ledlington by the eleven-fifty tomorrow. Henderson will drive her to the train. We shall stop at the village post-office and Henderson will go in and buy stamps. Everyone in the village will be prepared to swear to Mrs O'Hara having left Ledstow. They will see her luggage on the grid. They will see her hat and coat on me and she will have a cold and be blowing her nose when Henderson goes in to get the stamps. At Ledlington I shall buy a ticket for town and tip a porter to put the luggage in the van. The train is always packed on a matinée day, and no one will notice who gets out at the other end. Meanwhile I go into the ladies' room, remove her hat and coat, put on a good noticeable scarlet beret, and walk out of the station and back to the car. I keep out of sight on the floor with a rug over me coming through the village, and there we are.''

''Well, I won't say you're not clever,'' said Mr Miller with that grudging note in his voice again.

Meg's blood ran colder and colder as she listened. Not to be able to move, not to be able to do anything, just to lie here and listen while they made a plan to drown you and throw you into the river, not here but somewhere far away so that *they* would be quite safe. And then to hear them plan just how they were going to pretend that you had gone up to town by train. It was like being made to look on at your own execution. She felt her courage failing, freezing—freezing to death. She wished that she had drunk that cup to the dregs, because then she would be as good as dead already, and she wouldn't know the horrible cold touch of the water, or the hands that would put her into it and hold her down until she was drowned. Her whole body stiffened in a spasm of recoil.

And then she heard Miller say, "Mr Postlethwaite—" and at the sound of Uncle Henry's name she relaxed and listened, and began to have a little hope again.

"They'll come down and want to ask him questions when she's missing, the police will and that Coverdale. I suppose you've thought of that?"

"Oh, my dear Bob!"

"That's all very well, but what about it?"

She laughed with real amusement.

"Mr Postlethwaite has an appointment with Professor Mühlendahl in Munich. They have been corresponding about it for the last fortnight. He leaves for the continent tomorrow afternoon."

"And Milly and me? *What about us?*"

"Well, you'll be perfectly safe here."

"We're not going to *be* here," said Miller hoarsely— "not for nothing nor nobody we're not! And when I say that I mean it. What—Milly and me stay here and be badgered, and cross-examined, and dragged into an inquest as like as not, and our pictures in the papers? No, thank you! And what's more, Milly's not fit for it—she'd lose her head as like as not and give the show away, if she's pushed too far."

"Then you're all on holiday whilst Mr Postlethwaite's abroad, and the house is closed. It doesn't matter. There'll be no proof against anyone. Mr Postlethwaite will fail to keep his appointment in Munich. I owe the Paris police something, so I think he'll disappear in Paris. I'd like to score them off, and Mr Postlethwaite's disappearance will be quite a score. And now as I'm going to be up all night,

I'm going to have some sleep. Lock this door on the outside and come and have a look at her every half hour. She hasn't moved at all, has she?''

Meg heard light feet crossing the room. Someone leaned over the sofa back and looked down on her. She ought to have kept her eyes quite shut and the lashes closed, but she couldn't do it. As she lay on her back, straight and flat, she had only to lift the lids the merest fraction to be able to look up through the veiling lashes at the face that was looking down. Her courage had come back, because she had Uncle Henry to fight for as well as herself. They were planning horrible things for him as well as for her. But they weren't dead yet. Oh no, they weren't dead yet. If her lids flickered, she would betray herself. Could she look, and hold them steady? She *must*.

Someone looked down at her and laughed, an oddly ringing laugh. Meg looked through her lashes and saw Miss Cannock's bright blue dress, Miss Cannock's floating scarf, Miss Cannock's fussy fringe, Miss Cannock's face.

XXV

MEG LAY IN THE DARK, AND WAS THANKFUL FOR IT. They had put out the light, locked the door on her, and gone away. She was alone, and she could relax, move her stiff limbs, and sit up if she wanted to. She found that she didn't want to—yet. Her head swam and she felt giddy. But she mustn't give way to that. She propped herself against the end of the sofa and tried to think.

Uncle Henry was on the island, and she was here. She could get out of the window, and she could swim over to the island, but that wouldn't be any good, because she wouldn't be able to land when she got there. The wall encircled it, high, blank, and unclimbable. No, the only way to the island was by the covered bridge, and it was locked at both ends. It was locked, and Miss Cannock had the keys. Was Uncle Henry a prisoner on the island then? Yes, he was—he must be. Oh, he *was*. She ought to have suspected something when he didn't come out, and she never saw him.

Only two days ago she had been in Ledlington. She had actually rung Bill up. She had talked to him. If she had suspected something then, she could have said, "Oh, Bill, come down!" and he would have come. He *would* have come. She would have been safe. But she hadn't suspected anything, and now it was too late.

But how could she have suspected? It was so like Uncle Henry. Even at Way's End it had been the most awful business getting him to come to meals when he was working. If he had had a place like the island where he could get away from everyone and lock himself in, he might have behaved in just the way he was supposed to be behaving there.

He was a prisoner. But since when? He had met her on the evening she arrived, and she had walked up from the gates with him.

Had she?

Was it Uncle Henry who had met her?

She sat up trembling under the impact of this new idea, but with her head clear and her thoughts racing.

Was it Uncle Henry who had met her? It was dusk, but she had seen— *What* had she actually seen? An ulster, a hat, and a limp. That was what she had seen, and her mind had said *Uncle Henry*, and then, as far as the question of identity went, it had stopped functioning. Bill said the Professor had grown a beard, and she had just added the beard to her preconceived idea of Uncle Henry and taken him for granted. But she had spoken to him, and he had answered her. And anyone with the least gift for acting could mimic Henry Postlethwaite. His voice, soft and hesitating, the marked mannerisms of his speech, his way of withdrawing into an impenetrable silence, all made him the easiest man in the world to impersonate. He had hardly spoken at all on their walk to the house. She had been hurt about it at the time, but now she was sure that it was not Henry Postlethwaite who had walked beside her. She remembered how he had stalked past her into the house and vanished. And then—and then Miss Cannock had come— not at once—no, it was some time after. The woman who could play Miss Cannock so perfectly, so convincingly, without a single false note, was clever enough to play another part—any other part.

Meg let her feet down on to the floor and stood up. It was no use trying to get away yet, but the effect of the drug was wearing off. She would wait until Miller had been to have a look at her, and then as soon as he had gone again she would try and get away. She had no plan. The woman who had played Miss Cannock had her plan all cut and dried and her dreadful time-table set, but Meg hadn't any plan.

Suddenly, irrelevantly, it came to her that Miss Cannock had tried to kill her two days ago in Ledlington. She had tried to push her under the tram. Meg hadn't any doubt at all that she had tried to kill her, and she hadn't brought it off. And if she hadn't brought it off then, why should she bring it off now? This was a very heartening thought, and she made the most of it.

She moved about the room a little to get the stiffness out of her limbs, and then lay down on the couch again to wait until Miller came. Presently the clock in the hall struck eight. She hadn't known it was as late as that, and she counted the stroked with surprise. She must have been unconscious for much longer than she had thought, and that meant less time to escape, less time before that horrible time-table came into operation. She thought it must be more than half an hour since they had gone away and left her. Miller was to come back in half an hour. If only Miller would come and go away again. She began to feel the strain of waiting for him to come. Suppose he didn't come at the half hour. Suppose he didn't come at all until he came with Miss Cannock to "put her in the water." Was she to go on waiting for that? But if she didn't wait, if she got up and went to the window, then that would be the time when he would be sure to come. She would be half way across the room in the dark, or pushing back the stiff old-fashioned catch, or trying to lift the heavy sash, and the door would open and the light come on, and she would be caught. Her courage failed at the thought of it. No—whatever happened, she must stay here and wait until Miller came.

The clock had struck the quarter before she heard foot-steps in the hall, but they were not slow or heavy enough to be Miller's footsteps. They came hurrying to the door and stayed there whilst a hand fumbled at the key and at the door knob. Even after the door was open there was a dragging pause before the light went on. Meg heard a woman catch her breath, and realized with relief that it was Milly who had been sent to look at her, and that she wasn't liking the job. She came slowly and reluctantly up to the sofa and peered down at Meg. Then she went back to the door and shut it.

Meg kept her lids down and waited for what would happen next. The door had shut, but the light was on. Had Milly forgotten it, or was she still in the room? There was that catching breath again, and then Milly had crossed the room with a run and was bending down over the sofa.

"Are you awake?" she said in a shaken voice not much above a whisper. And then her hand came down on Meg's shoulder and shook it. "You'd better be. Do you hear? Come along—wake up if you're ever going to."

Meg had a moment of horrible indecision. Could she trust Milly? It might be a trap—it was her life and Uncle Henry's in the balance. . . . No, she couldn't. She made an indistin-guishable groaning sound and let herself go limp.

"If you won't, you won't," said Milly. She let go of Meg, and made that odd choking sound again, and ran out of the room, snapping out the light as she went. Then Meg heard the key turn and the footsteps go away, running, as if Milly was in haste to be gone from something which frightened her.

Well, Milly was gone, and now a horrid doubt sprang up

in Meg's mind. Had Milly come because she had been sent, or had she come on her own? Had she come instead of Miller, or was Miller still impending? She thought she would just have to take it that he had sent Milly instead of coming himself. She wondered if Milly was his wife. She was a frightfully bad cook, but she seemed to have some human feelings. Meg felt a little sorry for her—poor Crooked Sue.

She made up her mind that she would county sixty and then open the window. What she was going to do when she had it open, she did not know. They would look for her. If she couldn't find the place where she could climb the wall—and what chance would there be in the dark?—she would have to try and hide from them till daylight came, and with it the slender, solitary hope of a passing car or of someone from the village. It wasn't really a hope at all. The house was at a dead end and no cars passed it, and no one from the village would have any possible errand that would bring them within hailing distance at that hour in the morning. Well, it was no good thinking ahead. It was better to get out of the room than to wait in it until they came to truss her up and drown her. Anything would be better than that.

She felt her way across the room to the window and pushed back the catch. The sash was most stubbornly heavy to raise, and it took all her strength to lift it a couple of feet. She was still panting when she heard a sound which came near to stopping her breath altogether. Someone was coming across the hall. Miller was coming across the hall. And he was coming here—now, at once.

If she hadn't opened the window, she would just have had time to get back on to the sofa, but the window would give her away. If she dropped over the sill and ran for it, how fast could she run, and how far? Not very far, not very fast. He would catch her before she was round the corner of the house. Her heart jumped, and her head swam. She saw these alternatives in a flash, like two pictures. They didn't take any time at all—she just saw them. And then, as the key turned in the lock, she acted purely on instinct and without thinking at all. She had opened the left-hand window, but she had not drawn the curtains back. She jerked one now with all her might, and ran behind the curtains which screened the other window.

The sound of the opening door was lost in the loud knocking of her heart, but she saw the light shine blue through the stuff she had chosen long ago—before she had married Robin. It wasn't the long ago of time, but the long ago of change. There was nothing left of the things that had made her life then except chairs, and tables, and these lengths of blue stuff which she had thought so pretty when she bought them. These thoughts were in the shadows of her mind like the pattern on a dark tapestry picked out by firelight, but against this background she was sharply aware of Miller's crossing the room. At the same moment he discovered the empty couch and the open window. The startled exclamation had hardly left his lips before he vaulted the sill and disappeared into the darkness.

What should she do now? He had left the door open. Would she have time to cross the hall and hide in one of the other rooms? Would they search the house? She didn't know the answer to any of these things. She only knew that the instinct which had brought her here held her pressed into the angle between wall and window unable to move and scarcely able to breathe. He would come back. He wouldn't try and look for her alone. He would be bound to come back. She thought this when she began to think again, and close on her thought there came the sound of running feet, and Miller was scrambling back into the room. The drop was greater on the outside. He made some noise. She could hear that he was out of breath. And then he ran across the room and out of the door, leaving the light on.

There was a horrible cold interval of waiting. He would have to go and tell Miss Cannock. No, she wasn't Miss Cannock, Miss Cannock was only a part which she had played, but there was no other name to call her by. Miller would have to tell her, and she would come. But would they search the room? Or would they take it for granted that she was gone through the open window?

Meg had just to wait, her head thrown back into the angle, pressed back as far as it would go and straining, her hands on either side of her, palm outwards, pressing back too, as if she would force the wall and make it hide her. The moment was stretched intolerably by her fear—the old fear of the creature who is trapped, and waits for the trapper.

And then they came, all three of them—Miller, Miss Cannock, Milly. They came running, with a confusion of words—questions, answers, denials, protests. And then, not a yard from Meg, Miss Cannock stopped, and when she spoke the other two fell silent.

"She can't have gone far if Milly had just been in. Now, Milly—you're sure she was there?"

"I take my dying oath."

"Oh, we haven't come to that yet. Milly, if you cry, I'll slap you—I swear I will! Now, Bob, how far did you go?"

"Only to the corner of the house. It was no good going on alone, and I hadn't my torch. She might have been a yard away and I wouldn't have seen her."

"No—that's right. Go down to the lodge and get Henderson and Johnny! It's all right, you know—she can't get away. She'll probably make for the gate or try and hide in the wood. There isn't any place where she can get over the wall. There's no need for anyone to get fussed. I'll just go round the outside of the house with my torch. Milly, you stay here in case she doubles back! Now, Bob, off with you!"

They were gone. Their footsteps had died away. If only Milly had gone too. But Milly was to stay, and in the time it would take to make a circuit of the house Miss Cannock would be back, and then perhaps it would occur to her to search the room.

It was now or never. The instinct which had forbidden her to move now most insistently bade her go. Milly or no Milly, she must get out of this. It wasn't a refuge any longer, it was a trap. All at once she could move again. She looked between the curtains and saw Milly crouching on the sofa with her arms thrown out across the padded end and her head down between them. She was choking with sobs. Her shoulders heaved with them. Her body writhed.

Meg slipped off her shoes and took them in her left hand. She knew exactly what she was going to do, and she knew that she could do it. She knew it so surely that she wasn't afraid any more. She passed between the curtains and crossed the room in the most perfect silence, but even if she had tramped to the door in nail-shod boots, poor Milly's sobs would have prevented any other sound from reaching her. She cried because she would go to prison if she didn't do what she was told—and she would lose Bob—perhaps she had lost him already—and she didn't hold with murder— no, she didn't—and it was a crool shame. Whatever she did, it was going to be her fault, and as likely as not, she'd be hanged for it, when it wasn't none of her doing, and if it wasn't for Bob she'd have been picking pockets comfortable and not doing no harm to nobody. She choked and gulped, and got out a sooty handkerchief which left black smears across her face when she scrubbed her eyes with it.

Miss Cannock, swinging herself in over the window-sill with a noiseless agility which went very oddly indeed with the fussy fringe, the old-fashioned dress, the beaded shoes, switched off her torch and surveyed her with sarcasm. She had removed the tinted glasses, and her eyes behind the colourless lashes were bright, and pale, and cool. She turned without speaking, drew down the sash, and latched it. Then with a sudden decisive movement she went over to the other window and pulled the curtains back.

Meg's instinct had stood her in good stead.

XXVI

MEG WAS HALF WAY ACROSS THE HALL ON HER STOCKING feet. The thing that had told her to leave her hiding-place had brought her so far, but it didn't tell her what to do next. She went on to the foot of the stair by her own momentum, and there stayed, bewildered by the necessity for making a decision. She must hide—somewhere. . . . Where? . . . She didn't know. . . .

And then, sharp upon her hesitation, there came to her through the open door of the room from which she had fled the rattle and jangle of the curtain rings as Miss Cannock flung them back. She stopped thinking and ran up the stair as silently and swiftly as if she were moving in a dream, and then, out of sight of the hall by the door of her own room, she stopped, and thought began again.

Her own room was the first place that they would search if it came to searching the house. And the last place? Miss Cannock's room. What a perfectly *horrible* idea. She had a moment of sick physical recoil, and then, insistently, pressingly, the thought was driven home. It *was* the last place where they would look for her, the very last. And she might—yes, it was just possible she might have a chance of getting hold of the key to the bridge. It was worth any risk if there was even the slightest chance of that. But she wouldn't be taking risks—she would be avoiding them.

She passed her own door, keeping close against the wall, and so along the gallery to the other side of the hall. Miss Cannock's door faced hers, with the width of the hall between them. The door was ajar, the light burning, and the room just as it had been left when Miller came running up with the news that Meg was away.

Meg went in and looked for a hiding-place. The curtains were drawn, but she shuddered away from the thought of standing behind them with nothing but a length of chintz between her and Miss Cannock. Of all the topsy-turvy things that had happened this was the craziest, that her bones should be like water at the thought of the Cannock. It was as if a rabbit had suddenly become more sinister than a rattlesnake.

This passed in a flash. The curtains wouldn't do. There was the big old-fashioned wardrobe which had stood in the spare room at Way's End. She wouldn't dare to hide inside it, because if the Cannock was leaving here and going abroad, she would be turning out her clothes and packing them. No, she couldn't hide inside it, but if she could reach the top she could lie there very safely hidden and let the hunt go by, as she had heard it go a dozen times when they had played hide-and-seek at Way's End. There was a horned canopy, and the top was sunk a foot behind it. No one had ever thought of looking there, and she had kept it as her own special hiding-place. But she had to get up there. If she stood on the chest of drawers she could manage, but it was a tall chest, and she didn't dare move a chair to reach it. She had to use the old trick, but it brought her heart into her mouth.

You pulled out one of the drawers to make a step, and then from the top of the chest you leaned over and shut it again, and you had to be most awfully careful or the drawer squeaked. It was only the middle drawer that was any good as a step, and unless you coaxed it ever so carefully it made a noise like a skidding slate-pencil.

She got on to the chest of drawers and put her shoes out of sight on top of the wardrobe. Then she had to shut the drawer below her and keep her fingers steady against the impulse to jam it home anyhow and hide. And just as she knelt there with her hair falling forward over her face and the drawer going home by stiff, reluctant fractions of an inch, she heard the sound of voices coming nearer.

And she didn't know whether they were in the hall below, or on the stair, or in the gallery not more than a yard or two away. They came upon her ear with a terror which took away her power of judging distance. Her heart thudded, and her head swam, but her fingers went on pushing the drawer very carefully home. Then she stood up, got her knee on the lowest part of the canopy, and climbed over into the space behind it. She lay there, and heard the voices coming nearer.

Well, they could come now, because she had beaten them. The moment of sick terror was over, and she was safe. Yes, but she wanted something more than that. She wanted to be able to see. She must be able to watch the Cannock, and be ready to take a chance for the key of the bridge.

The canopy came up in the middle into two carved walnut horns and then fell away in an ornamental scrollwork. There was a very good look-out place between the horns, and another at each corner, where two smaller horns repeated the central pattern. She worked herself round until she could use either the middle peep-hole or the one on the right-hand corner without moving more than her head and neck. This would enable her to see practically everything in the room.

And the first thing she saw was Miss Cannock coming in at the door. Meg had never seen her before without her glasses, neither had she ever seen her out of the part which she had been playing. She looked now with a terrified interest, and what she saw was not Miss Cannock's dress and Miss Cannock's hair, but the pale, cold fire of anger in those unfamiliar eyes, and the air of arrogant, domineering power. She stood with her hand on the door, the light shining full in her face for a moment, and then spoke over her shoulder.

"You'll go on till you find her—you and Henderson, and Johnny! She can't get away. But I've got to have her here before midnight. I can't have my time-table upset. And warn Henderson that there's to be no rough handling!

Bruises are just what every meddlesome police surgeon's on the look-out for. That's all—get on with it!''

She shut the door, walked across to the wardrobe, and flung it open. Standing there, she was out of Meg's sight, but the room was full of her. The moment before it had been any room. Now it was this woman's room—the stage on which she walked, the scene set for her to dominate, the place from which she would marshal her forces and control events. How had it been possible for her to mask this will, this power, this force, and play with effortless skill the part of an aimless, amiable nonentity? She stepped back from the wardrobe now and came into sight again, moving towards the dressing-table which was set between the windows. She had something in either hand, and as she came into the light above the looking-glass, Meg saw what it was—a wig—two wigs—a wig in either hand, held very carefully and then set down, the one on the right-hand side of the dressing-table and the other on the left.

Meg stared through the corner peep-hole, and knew that what she had guessed about Uncle Henry had been certainly true, because the right-hand wig with its tossed leonine mane of grey hair was Uncle Henry's hair and no one else's. It was that wig, and a beard, and this woman with an ulster, and a pretended limp, and perhaps special boots to give her another inch or two of height, who had met her in the dusk and walked beside her in abstracted silence to the house.

That sank in as she stared—right in, until she was so sure of it that it seemed part of her, and she looked back at the Meg who hadn't known or guessed or suspected anything, with a kind of distant wonder, as if she had been another person.

She looked at the other wigs, the one at the woman's left hand, and immediately her own scalp began to pringle, because she knew this hair too. Oh yes, surely she knew it. It was a woman's wig, and it wasn't just carelessly plopped down like the grey one, but perched on one of those little wooden stands which people give you at Christmas, and which you are supposed to use for your hats, only you generally don't. This one was enamelled pale blue and painted with blobs of green, and pink, and orange. The wig sat on the top of it with its neat formal waves and its rows of little curls at the back—waves and curls of pale platinum-coloured hair, very fine and soft, and beautifully kept. As surely as the grey wig was Uncle Henry's hair, so surely was this the hair of Miss Della Delorne.

Something in Meg revolted and said, "No, no, *no!*" The Cannock—Della Delorne? Impossible! But it wasn't like that. It wasn't a case of the Cannock being Della Delorne. It was this woman who could play the Cannock, or Uncle Henry, or Della Delorne at will. Or any other part. Close to her now when she believed she was alone, Meg found herself convinced that what this woman willed to do she would do without fear or mercy.

She watched with a kind of terrified eagerness, because the woman was taking off her dress. No, not *her* dress—the Cannock's dress. She had dropped the scarf a while ago. Now, with the dress and the wig, she had shed the Cannock altogether. She had been doing something to her face as she stood at the glass, and when she turned round a shudder of surprise ran over Meg. She looked with all her eyes for the woman she had known, and couldn't find her. This was someone she had never seen before in her life. Instead of greying hair with an old-fashioned knot behind and a fuzzy fringe in front there was a smooth cropped head of a colour between fair and brown, and instead of Miss Cannock's sallow skin and crooked lip there was a stranger's face and a stranger's features, and they were covered with a glistening coat of grease!

The woman took a towel from the wash-stand now and began to wipe the grease away. It left the skin smooth and pale, a clear even colour. Meg stared in astonishment. The cheeks were a different shape from Miss Cannock's cheeks. The lip that had been crooked was straight and well shaped. The skin was different. Everything was different. The eyes which had been hidden behind tinted glasses now dominated the face with their cold look of efficiency and power, and the bare neck and arms were the neck and arms of a young woman, smooth and round and white. Meg had seen them before, for they belonged to Della Delorne.

As the woman stood there rubbing off the last of the grease, Meg wondered with a beating heart what part she was getting ready to play. What was the next item in her programme? Meg's evasion didn't seem to be troubling her in the least. With a calm certainty that escape from the bounds of Ledstow Place was impossible she was continuing her preparations as if nothing had happened.

When she had finished with her face, she pulled a trunk out from under the bed and threw it open. It was empty. She bent over it, and, amazingly, the bottom moved, coming away like a lifted tray and leaving behind it a space about three inches deep. Into this the woman who was no longer Miss Cannock began to pack a variety of small tubes and bottles, some odd looking objects made of rubber, a cardboard box or two, the wig which belonged to Della Delorne, and another wig which she fetched from the wardrobe. This wig had dark hair arranged in loose waves with a most attractive double row of curls across the back. Meg wondered what rôle it belonged to, what new personality it would help to substantiate. She had left Uncle Henry's wig on the dressing-table. That meant she was going to wear it now—presently, when Meg had been caught and "put in the water." It was Henry Postlethwaite who would drive up to town with the poor drowned thing to be disposed of in the river. Perhaps there would be two drowned things—perhaps the real Henry Postlethwaite was to be the other. And then this woman who would be playing the part of Henry Postlethwaite would just go quietly over to Paris and there change parts again. Henry Postlethwaite would disappear and forever. Della Delorne would disappear. The obscure Miss Cannock would vanish into her own native obscurity. And an attractive young woman in that very attractive dark wig would embark on another part in another play.

Meg looked at the woman as she went to and fro at her packing. She tried to imagine a dark pencilled line of eyebrow, and black lashes to shade those cold pale eyes, and a warm ivory complexion and scarlet lips. Who would recognize her? The indeterminate features would lend themselves to this or any other avatar. Meg wondered as she looked how many people had seen her as she was seeing her now, stripped to her own natural self.

It came to Meg that after this she would never be allowed to live. To know what she now knew *must* be fatal, because it had become a choice between this woman's death and hers. And how without a single weapon could she meet an antagonist versed in every art, every trick of her criminal game, and rendered implacable by the knowledge that her life was at stake?

Meg saw this with a clarity and a calmness that surprised herself. Instead of despair she felt an obstinate rising courage. Then all at once hope positively soared, because the woman took off the fine gold chain which the Cannock had so appropriately worn about her neck and laid it down on the dressing-table. And on the end of it, swinging and dangling from her hand as she crossed to lay it down, there was a key, and Meg guessed with a jumping heart that it was the key of the bridge.

If she could get it—if she could only get it. If the woman would only go out of the room for a moment. Meg felt as if she could dare anything, take any chance, to get the key, because it meant Uncle Henry's life. The bridge had a door at either end. If she could open those doors and leave them locked behind her, surely she and Uncle Henry together could put up some sort of a show.

But the woman gave no sign of leaving the room.

XXVII

I<small>T MUST BE GETTING ON FOR NINE O'CLOCK.</small> S<small>HE HADN'T</small> heard the clock strike since she came upstairs. If you have lived with a clock for a great many years, it is extraordinary how often you miss the strike, especially if you are thinking of something else.

Meg was getting stiff, but she didn't dare to move. The woman had replaced the false bottom, and was filling the upper part of the trunk with books and Uncle Henry's clothes. When it was full she shut down the lid and came over to the dressing-table. Meg could see her reflected in the glass. She sat down and began to rub stuff into her face from a little round china pot. It gave the skin a puckered, faded look. Then she put on a pair of grey bushy eyebrows and the beard which was such a good disguise for mouth and chin. Now she was doing things to her nose, raising the bridge with stuff that looked rather like plasticine, and then carefully, very carefully, going over it with something out of another pot until it was impossible to detect any join. When at least she pulled the wig on over her hair, Meg was so startled that she caught her breath in an almost audible gasp. Even though she knew what she knew, the likeness astounded her. Given the concomitants of dusk and a total lack of suspicion, this copy of Henry Postlethwaite would have deceived anyone as it had deceived her and Bill—for she didn't believe now that Bill had seen Uncle Henry either.

The woman passed out of sight on the other side of the wardrobe behind Meg. After some moments she came back again. She had on a man's drawers and under vest. She came to the wardrobe and stood there. Meg couldn't see her, but she knew very well that she was taking down clothes and putting them on—Uncle Henry's clothes. When she came into sight again she was fully dressed—dark trousers, waistcoat, and coat, with a white shirt showing above the waistcoat, and an old-fashioned wing collar. She had a black tie in her hand and she stood before the looking glass to tie it. That was the strangest moment of all, because over her shoulder Meg could see Henry Postlethwaite's face looking back at her out of the glass—looking back, but not seeing her—seeing only the room, the furniture, the safe solitude in which one character could be put off and another put on. And close on that there came the horrible stabbing doubt—was this false presentment all that was left of Uncle Henry? Was he dead? Had he been dead a long time? Was there anything real left at all? The thought struck her with such a sense of grief and loss that her courage drained away. Robin gone—Uncle Henry gone. Then why shouldn't Meg go too? Her whole body relaxed. She leaned her forehead against the hard, cold wood of the canopy and let the waves of loneliness and misery go over her.

And then, sharp and clear, it came to her that if she gave up now she would never see Bill again. And that mattered terribly. Even if he had stopped caring for her, even if he had written her a horrid icy letter, it mattered. She had got to fight her way through because she had got to see Bill again. Queer how the minute she began to think about Bill strength and courage came pouring back. Of course Uncle Henry was alive. He was a prisoner on the island—he must be—he was, and somehow she had got to get to him.

The false Henry Postlethwaite had finished with his tie and was putting on a pair of black laced shoes. They had, as Meg had suspected, thickened soles and rather higher heels than men usually wear. They must be padded inside, for the woman had small and pretty feet. Her hands too could never pass for Uncle Henry's hands—she would have to wear gloves. She took a pair out of the left-hand top drawer of the chest of drawers and tossed it carelessly on to the pillow of the bed. Then she took out of the wardrobe Henry Postlethwaite's ulster and Henry Postlethwaite's broad-brimmed hat.

Then she went out of the room, leaving the door open behind her and snapping off the light.

Meg shivered with excitement and strained her ears to listen. Where had she gone to, and how long would she be? She listened with all her might. Could she hear a footstep on the stairs with the width of the hall between them? Those thickened shoes would not tread so very lightly. They were a man's shoes, and heavier by the thickening than the ordinary shoe of that type. She thought that she would hear them on the stairs.

She listened, straining, because unless she did hear them she would not dare to move. And then, making all her straining needless, she heard them, carelessly loud, going down into the hall and across it to the front door. She didn't wait for anything more. Here was her chance, and she had only to take it. The key lay on the dressing-table for the taking, and she had only to put out her hand to it.

Getting down was easier than getting up had been. She was on the floor, she had the key cold in her palm, and she was out of the door almost before the impulse which brought her there had shaped itself into a conscious plan. Thought and action were so co-ordinated as to seem one.

But out in the gallery she had to stop, to listen, and to think again. She did not know this side of the house. On the opposite side a passage turned out of the gallery and ran past the bathroom and an empty bedroom to a back stair. On this side a similar passage turned off on her left. Was there a back stair over here? If there was, she had a safe path before her, because it was bound to come out quite close to the door which entered the bridge. If there wasn't a stair, she was losing time which she simply couldn't afford to lose, and she would have to take the frightful risk of going down the main stair and crossing the hall. Her recoil from this sent her running down the dark passage, and thankful for the darkness.

Yet the darkness nearly betrayed her. There *was* a stair,

but on this side it had no door at the stair head, and her foot was over the edge and her balance lost before she could save herself. A desperate snatch at the banisters served to break her fall and prevent it from being headlong, but she went sliding and bumping down until she reached the half-landing, where she picked herself up shaken, breathless, and empty-handed.

The key was gone. It must have dropped when she caught at the banisters. She had to search for it in the dark, her heart banging and her spine creeping, whilst every sense strained to catch some sound or sign of danger. She found it after what felt like a moment so endlessly prolonged as to have escaped out of time altogether into some horrible eternity. It was lying on the very edge of the landing, and when she had picked it up she had still to reach the bottom of the stair and find the door of the bridge.

The stair came into a passage, and the passage ran to left and right. The left-hand way led back into the hall, and a faint light made it visible, the walls and floor all dark and shadowy like things seen under water. To the right the twilight deepened into a black gloom. There was no window and no point of light. She felt her way along it to the end, and found three doors, one to the right, one to the left, and one straight in front of her. It would be the left-hand door that led to the bridge.

She felt for the handle and turned it, but the door wouldn't move. It was locked, and that meant that it was the bridge door for certain. She fitted the key into the lock, and then hesitated. There was an illusion of safety about this dark place, and she didn't know what might be waiting for her on the other side of the locked door. There wasn't any safety anywhere, but in this dead end she could believe for a moment that she was safe. Safe—when someone might come along the passage from the hall at any moment. She turned her head over her shoulder at the thought, and saw it take shape before her horrified eyes. Someone was coming along the passage from the hall.

She didn't wait to see who it was. The key turned, the door opened, and she was over the threshold, dragging the key from the lock, shutting the door with a desperate haste and locking it again with shaking fingers. She felt for a bolt, up as high as she could reach and down again, sliding her fingers over the smoothly painted wood. There were two bolts, one at the top and one at the bottom. She slid them home and went on shaking, but with triumph now, because she had done it—she had got away. And now she had only to find Uncle Henry.

She turned her back on the door and set out across the bridge. There were six or seven steps leading to a higher level, and then a straight way over to the island. On this higher level it was not quite dark. The bridge had glazed sides, and something which was not light and yet served to mitigate the darkness came through the glass. It is never really quite dark out of doors, and the darkness of the bridge was more like out-of-door darkness than the pitchy black of an unlighted room.

Meg went on steadily but not too fast, because there would probably be more steps at the other end. She was about half way, when she heard the door behind her tried and shaken. She wished them joy of breaking it down. It was strong, and the bolts were heavy, and long before they gave she would have the second door behind her.

She came to the steps going down to the island level, and found the door at the foot, and found it fast. Well, she had expected that, and she had the key. She felt for the lock and pushed it in. That was when the first cold misgiving touched her. The key didn't slide in. She had to push it, she had to push it hard. And when she had got it in, it stuck and wouldn't move. It would turn neither to the right nor to the left, and when she tried to pull it out of the lock it jammed. With despairing violence she shook the handle and banged upon the panels. But the only answer came from behind her. They were battering at the door through which she had come, and all at once it came to her that the bolts were poor comfort, because any door is only as strong as its hinges.

She made one last effort to withdraw the key and failed. There must be a different key to this door, though there was only one on the chain she had taken from the Cannock's table. Perhaps they kept the other key in the passage. It might be hanging on a nail, or hidden somewhere. But even if she found it she couldn't use it now. The door behind her might give way at any moment. They were using something heavy as a ram. That meant Henderson and Miller. And the woman must be there, because they wouldn't break down the door without her orders.

Meg's plan came to her in the flash which showed her the three of them behind the breaking door. She ran back up the steps and, taking off her right-hand shoe, waited for the next assault upon the door, and then broke one of the large glass panes in the side of the bridge. Then she got out of her tweed skirt and, wrapping it thickly round her hand and arm, she pushed the splinters outwards. She heard them fall into the lake. They were gone, and she must go their way if she didn't want to be trapped, because there wasn't any other way for her to take. Another blow and the door would be down.

With the noise of a rending crash in her ears she climbed through the broken window and let herself drop into the lake.

XXVIII

It was just short of nine o'clock when Bill Coverdale stopped his car at the gates of Ledstow Place. He had driven furiously, he had made record time, he had been a prey to the most horrible fears and imaginings, and now a cold reaction came upon him and he wondered what he was going to say and how he was going to explain his sudden arrival—on the top too of Meg's telegram telling him not to come, telling him she wanted to be left alone. He began to feel that he was making a most obvious and complete fool of himself. And then something in him stiffened up, because if it came to even one chance in a thousand, he was prepared to make a fool of himself and take the consequences rather than let Meg run the risk of that one chance.

He sounded his horn and waited for someone to come, but no one came. He got out of the car and tried the gates, but they were most securely locked. The lodge was just a black blur, formless and lightless. He stood there listening, and felt an oppressive silence gather about him like a fog. The horrible thought came to him that the place was empty—lights out, fires dead, and all human life withdrawn, leaving lodge and house, park and lake, to the dead stillness which seemed to brood there.

He shook himself angrily and went back to the car for a torch. He had got to get somewhere where he could see the house and dispose of the suggestion that it was deserted, and if he couldn't get in by the gates he was going to get in some other way. That locked gate had made him angry when he came down before, and it made him angrier now. Ridiculous medieval tomfoolery, and the sooner someone told the Professor so the better! If the old man wasn't balmy already, he soon would be, living like this.

He left the car where it was and prospected. The lane came to an end at the gates. There was a ditch on each side of it with, on the left, a great scrambly hedge enclosing a wood, and on the right, the churchyard wall about five feet high. The wood was no good, obviously. There was no view to be got from it, for he remembered that it continued on the other side of the wall right up to the edge of the lake, so that it would be impossible to see the house. No, he would have to get into the churchyard and see what he could see from there.

He went first to the car, chose a heavy spanner from among the tools, and put it in his pocket. He could not have explained why he did this, but it gave him the feeling of having done the right thing. Then he crossed the ditch and got over the wall. It was built very roughly of local stone, so that it was easy enough to climb, but no sooner had he followed it to the point where it became the boundary wall of Ledstow Place than it took on an extra three feet in height and became a newish brick wall, very well built and quite unclimbable. If he had hopes of the angle where it turned towards the gate and the extra height began, they were immediately dashed, because this was defended by a *chevaux-de-frise* of the most villainous double-bladed spikes. There was nothing for it but to go on following the wall and hope for a bit of luck.

It was about twenty yards farther on that he nearly trod on William and William's girl who, oblivious of cold, damp, and Mr Coverdale's torch, sat spell-bound side by side on a low table tomb with their heads on one another's shoulders and their arms doubly entertwined. They had not spoken a single word for three quarters of an hour, and they did not speak now. The light of Bill's torch flickered over them, Bill's knee took William in the small of the back, and Bill's voice said, "I beg your pardon."

There was one of those pauses. Then Miss Ellen Cade, who had been nicely brought up by the aunt who kept the post-office and village shop, lifted her head about an inch from William's shoulder and said, "Granted."

It was at this point that William began to feel annoyed. After all, it was he who had been barged into, not Ellen, and it wasn't her place to go saying "Granted" like that. He disentangled himself, got to his feet, and demanded in irritated accents, "What are you getting at?" The light of the torch shone on his very young face, his freckles, and the upstanding mat of red hair.

Then Bill Coverdale said with half a laugh, "What I want to do is to get over the wall. I've got to get up to the house, and I can't make anyone hear at the lodge. I expect you know this place like the back of your hand. Is there anywhere I can get over? And I'm most awfully sorry I tumbled over you like that, so if five bob—"

Five bob changed hands. A faint sheepish grin appeared on William's face. Ellen giggled. Bill lowered the torch and came briskly to business.

"Well, what about it? How do I get over this wall?"

William, fingering two half-crowns in his trouser pocket, found words.

"How'm I to know you ain't up to something?"

Ellen giggled again.

"I am up to something," said Bill. "I want to get over the wall. I keep telling you so."

William uttered again, conscious of Ellen, conscious that here might be the chance of a lifetime to foil a criminal and get his name into the papers.

"How do I know you're not a burglar?"

"You don't," said Bill. "But I'm not. Let's get on with this wall business—I'm in a hurry. What about the stone you were sitting on? Is that any good for a leg up?"

"There's a better one farther along, sir." Ellen Cade had been out of the conversation long enough. She didn't care about being out of things. She hoped that the torch would be turned upon her, because she'd done her hair a new way, and Aunt could say what she liked, it suited her. She slipped her hand inside William's arm and pinched it. "Come on, William, *do!* Right up by Mary and Jane Posset—that's the place."

They walked along by the wall, the three of them, on an edge of rough grass broken here and there by a green mound or a grey tilted stone, until Ellen said brightly,

"Here we are! Aunt's great-great-great aunts, Mary and Jane they were, and we've always said, William and me, it'd be as easy as easy to get over the wall from them."

Bill brought his torch to bear upon a headstone set no more than a foot away from the new red brick. It was about three feet high, and if you stood on it, the top of the wall would be well within reach. William, warming to the adventure, lent a steadying shoulder, and without more ado Bill got to the top of the wall and dropped from it into the grounds of Ledstow Place. A last faint giggle from Ellen followed him.

He had the torch in his pocket, but he didn't want to put it on. He had no wish to encounter the shambling Johnny, or a gardener—there must be a gardener. They would not be likely to be about at this hour, but it was never safe to count on people being where they were likely to be, because just when it was most inconvenient they were sure to be somewhere else.

He stood still to take stock of his surroundings. The footsteps of William and Ellen retreated. They were returning to their meditations among the tombs. It was very dark. A clump of trees and bushes screened the place where he had come over the wall, though none of them approached it to within a dozen feet. He skirted the clump, and came out upon a dim open stretch of grass, rough under foot and sloping gradually upwards. Bill followed the rise, because what he had to do was to find a point from which he could see the house. If there were lights in it, all was well—he just went boldly up to the front door, saw the Professor, saw Meg, pitched some kind of tale, and took Meg away with him. He hadn't really begun to bother about what he was going to say. He rather thought of dragging Garratt into it. Yes, that would do—Garratt, and a solicitor, and some frightfully urgent legal business which made it absolutely necessary that Meg should be on the spot bright and early in the morning. How bright and early were solicitors? He grinned a sardonic grin. It didn't matter—it would do for a tale. On the other hand, if the house was dark— His heart contracted, because that would mean—what would it mean? Something too bad to think about. And he would have landed himself behind an eight-foot wall with no friendly tomb-stone on this side of it.

He passed another clump of trees, and drew a long breath of relief. The house had come into view, a solid black cube against the soft smudged darkness of the park and the glimmer of the lake, with the fanlight over the hall door shining as yellow as a harvest moon. His forehead was suddenly wet. He got out his handkerchief and wiped it. He hadn't known how horribly afraid he was until he saw the light.

He had reached the top of the slope. He walked down it now at a good brisk pace, not caring any longer whether he was seen or heard. As he walked, he made careful plans. He would drive Meg back to town. There wouldn't be any need to hurry. And then tomorrow he would take her to see the flat. They would stand together at the window from which you could see the river. He didn't map it out any farther than that, but he felt very hopeful.

He stepped briskly off the grass on to the gravel in front of the house, and someone came running down the front steps and met him half way across the sweep. The front door stood open. He thought it was the man-servant who was running to meet him, flurried and out of breath. He stood still and let the man come to him, because an instant warning bell had started ringing in his mind.

Mr Miller came up in a fine taking. He spluttered out the name of Henderson, which was quite unknown to Bill.

"Where've you been, you lazy skulking dog? She's got away, blast her! And you're to go down to the gate and wait in the bushes in case she comes that way—and get a move on, or the boss'll want to know the reason why!" He turned to run back, not into the house this time, but round the corner. His feet left the gravel and were heard no more.

The front door stood open. The fanlight shone golden against the blackness of the house—the fanlight, and the sharp rectangle between the door-posts. Not a window on this side was lighted.

He heard someone shout in the distance.

He began to run down the drive towards the gate.

XXIX

VERY ODD DOINGS. BILL HAD SUBMITTED TO BEING Henderson and a dirty skulking dog who was at the orders of some unknown boss because when the man said "She's got away," he knew with a certainty as complete as it was irrational that this *she* was Meg. It might have been a dog, a cat, or a parrot, but he was quite sure it wasn't. He was quite sure it was Meg, in which case he was Henderson till further orders. He wondered whether he ought to have laid the other fellow out. It was a bit close to the house, and after all he didn't *know* anything. A bit awkward if he had brained the Professor's butler and then found that there was some mistake.

He stopped running at the turn before the lodge, and went softly until he came to the gates, where he left the drive and discovered, as Meg had done, that there was a path between the shrubbery and the wall. He turned off to the left and stood there a couple of yards in, waiting, and straining eyes and ears against the silent darkness. He could see nothing except the black mass of the shrubbery on his right, the black height of the wall on his left, and the skyless dark between them, and part of the drive, much darker than the sky, but nothing like so black as the bushes and the wall. He could not distinguish the lodge, though it should have been within his view. It was there though he couldn't see it. A hundred other things might be there which he could not see.

He couldn't hear anything either, except all those natural sounds of the night which at first seem veiled in silence, but gradually emerge from it until there is no silence left. A branch creaked in a stirring of the air which did not reach him. Something very small moved a dry leaf quite close to his foot. An acorn fell, striking him on the head and pattering down like a solitary hailstone.

How long was he going to wait, and what was he waiting for? Meg.

But where was she? He might wait here whilst she was in some desperate strait, but if he went looking for her in this wide, dark place, how easy to miss her, how impossible to do anything else, since she would be doing all she knew not to be found. But if she had been found already—found and taken back to the house—would they come and tell Henderson, whoever Henderson might be? It seemed reasonable to suppose that they would, unless the real Henderson had happened along—which was of course quite on the cards. . . .

Well, there was nothing for it but to wait. He remembered the wood on the other side of the drive back of the lodge. If Meg was hiding, that would be the place to make for. He wondered if he dared prospect a little, because of course she might come down to the gates in the hope of finding them open or of being able to get the key from the lodge. . . . Now that was a very bright idea. It was the world to a halfpenny that the key was hanging somewhere in that damned invisible lodge.

He crossed the drive, felt his way round to the back door, and knocked upon it. There was no answering sound from within.

Bill began to feel a most intense dislike for this place. It ought to have had a light, and smoke coming out of the chimney, and someone hopping out briskly to open those infernal gates. Hang it all, that was what a lodge was for, a kind of concrete brick and mortar welcome, but all you could get out of this one was a dark, deserted feel like a devastated area plus an amazingly powerful smell of cabbage-stalks.

He knocked again. Nobody came.

He found a window, broke it with as little noise as possible, and climbed in across an unsavoury sink. It reeked of things that a decent sink doesn't reek of. He felt his way to an open door, and thence into the very narrow passage. When he had located the back door, he decided that he must risk using his torch for a moment. The key which opened the gate would in all probability be hanging from a nail in this passage—at least in any ordinary lodge it would. Reflecting gloomily that this was about as far from being an ordinary lodge as you could get, he took out the torch, switched it on, and sent the beam travelling over the dirty walls. No sign of a nail, no sign of a key. Paper yellow with damp and curded with dirt hung loose from the decaying plaster beneath. Here and there it had peeled, and hung in tatters. He reflected that a nail would have nothing to take hold of, and that he would have to look elsewhere for the key. The kitchen was the next most likely place, and he would just have to risk someone's catching the glint of his light at the window through which he had climbed.

The room seemed to be kitchen and scullery in one. The torch showed it larger than he had supposed, with the sink up under the window and the range against the outer wall—a stupid waste of chimney heat. He turned the torch here and there, screening it behind his coat. The fires was out, or very low. The floor was greasy, and black with trampled coal. He got as far from the sink as possible, and found the opposite side of the room entirely taken up by a large kitchen dresser on which in indescribable confusion were piled dirty plates, and plates which he supposed the old woman considered clean, a much hacked leg of mutton, three cooked onions and a cold potato in a cracked vegetable dish, a jug half full of beer, part of a rabbit pie gone very high indeed, the heel of a loaf, and a pair of clod-hopping boots, presumably Johnny's. What a place! And where in all this welter was the key he was looking for? If it wasn't in the passage, it ought to be hanging from a hook on the dresser, but it wasn't. Bill had got past expecting anything in this house to be in its proper place.

He sent the beam across the chimney breast. People kept things on the ledge above the range. There was a box of matches there, and about half an inch of sooty dust. Where in the name of common sense did the disgusting old woman keep that key? It must be somewhere, unless she'd got it on her. And with that it came to him for the first time to wonder where she was.

It didn't take him more than a split second to get the answer. She was out looking for Meg. She, and Johnny, and the fellow who had run out of the house at him, and every other man jack about this infernal place—they were all out hunting for Meg. And he, as Henderson, was supposed to be on guard at the gate. That meant that they would beat the grounds and try and drive her this way. There was a lot of cover in the wood, but one or two people going through it with torches might hope to scare an already frightened girl and get her on the run. He felt a furious impatience to be there, and to know what was happening—to find Meg. But the key—if it was to be found, he must find it. Find the key, find Meg, and he had only to walk out of the gates with her and start the car.

The key might be anywhere. It might be in the old woman's pocket. It might be in Henderson's pocket, or Johnny's pocket, or anybody's pocket. . . .

He stared about him, at his wits' end, flicking the light to and fro. The kitchen table—no cloth—more dirty plates—a chair thrown down—another chair, with a soiled apron trailing over the seat, the pocket gaping, half ripped off.

Something clicked in Bill's mind. He picked the dirty rag up and shook it. There were two pockets, and only one of them was torn. Out of the other there cascaded and tumbled an incredibly filthy pack of cards, about half a packet of liquorice drops—and the key.

Bill's heart gave a bound of triumph as he picked it up. It was the key all right. There was no doubt about that. A most massive piece of ironmongery which would certainly not fit any lock in the lodge. He pocketed it, switched off his torch, and let himself out by the back door.

The first thing he did after that was to unlock the gates. If he found Meg—no, *when* he found Meg—they might have to run for it, and it might be a near thing getting away. It would be a comfortable thought to feel that the gate was open. When he had opened it, he stood there frowning in the dark. It seemed to him that the key was now a useless white elephant. The only use it could be put to was to lock the gates again, and Bill had an extremely strong and definite conviction that those gates were better open.

After some thought he went out to his car and put the key into the back of the cubby hole by the steering-wheel. If it was wanted, it could be got at here—by him. And if it wasn't wanted, it would be quite safe.

He went back into the grounds of Ledstow Place.

XXX

THE SPLASH OF MEG'S FALL WAS LOST IN THE CRASH OF the falling door. She went down into the waters of the lake and felt them close over her head. She had the illusion that it was these waters which were rushing upwards, and not she who was sinking through them. There was an ice-cold pressure at her eyes, her ears, her throat. The terror which had possessed her when she jumped from the bridge was frozen about her heart, which seemed to have stopped beating. The short time that it took her to sink and rise again appeared to her to be endlessly and dreadfully prolonged. Then, with a curious suddenness which was like the transition from a nightmare into waking consciousness, she found that her head was above water and that she was swimming. A good swimmer does certain things intuitively and without conscious volition. Meg had dived and swum since she was five years old, and even in an extremity of fear it was impossible for her to take the water awkwardly or to choke herself by getting it into her nose and throat. She had begun to strike out as she came up, from pure instinct.

She drew a long breath, and felt the nightmare fade. Her heart was beating quite normally again. All that horrible feeling of fear was gone. Her mind was calm and empty, its only conscious thought a faint surprise that the lake should be so deep. She blinked the water from her eyes and swam with long, steady strokes. She began to consider where she should land. The bank was close on her left. Should she make for it, or would it be better to strike right across the lake and get into the wood? She could hear voices behind her now on the bridge. If someone jumped in after her, she would do better to land and trust to getting away on her feet. Perhaps she would do better to land anyhow. She could reach the wood much more quickly if she ran, and she would get a good start before they came after her, because they would have to come back across the bridge and down through the house. But it would have to be now, at once.

A couple of strokes took her into her depth. She came up dripping on to mud and stones, and then with a scramble to the grass which bordered the drive. She looked over her shoulder and saw a light on the bridge and the beam of a torch darting to and fro across the dark water. She hadn't come out a moment too soon, and she hadn't a moment to waste. She picked up her wet feet and ran for it, keeping to the grass and wondering how much of a start she was going to get.

She got quite a good one, thanks to the recriminations which had been going on upon the bridge, and by the time the pursuit had been organized and Miller despatched to the lodge on a bicycle to detail the Hendersons for their share in it Meg had reached the first of the trees. She saw the bicycle lamp without seeing the bicycle or its rider, and lay flat on the grass with her face hidden until it had gone by her. Then she got up and went on again, slowly now, because there were blackberry bushes and a tangle of willow and alder and hazel growing upon rough ground which dipped suddenly into patches of bog, and deep swampy holes.

She had been lucky so far, luckier indeed than she knew, because Miller, craning out of the window she had broken, had cut his hand on a splinter of glass and let the electric torch he was holding drop, as she herself had dropped, into the lake, only unlike her it didn't come up again. He had to go and find another torch, with the result that Meg got her start.

Well, she had got it, and she had got so far. But where had she got to? A swamp in which her wet feet squelched, making noise enough to give her away the minute the pursuit drew near. Even on the grass, drenched stockings and drenched shoes had combined to produce the most horrible squeaking, squishing sound as she ran. For all she knew, the whole wood might be a bog—there might be acres of it—she had never explored in this direction. There was only one thing to be done, and she did it. The shoes and stockings must go.

She stood on each leg in turn, and left the horrid wet things to lie where they fell. It was nice to be rid of them, but she hated the squdgy feel of the slime between her toes. She could move a great deal more quietly now, and that was something. But where was she moving to? She had no answer to that. There was a bog, and an inky blackness in which she had to feel her way. Her body had begun to shake with cold, her garments dripped and clung to her like bandages. And she had no plan, and no objective. She couldn't even say, "I must go on, or they'll get me," because they were just as likely to get her if she did go on. At any moment she might hear Miller, or Henderson, or Johnny come crashing through the undergrowth. At any moment the ray of a torch might cut the darkness like a stab. Or—most horrid thought—she might at any moment, feeling before her in this black gloom, touch one of them unawares. An ice-cold finger seemed to stroke her spine at the thought of it. She tried to push the thought away. She *must* have a plan, or the fear which makes men run screaming would catch her and send her stumbling and crying into the bog, into the lake, into the very arms of her enemies.

She began to make her plan, standing still and listening for a footstep or a voice. She must get to the wall—that was the only possible thing to do. The wood ran up to the wall and on beyond it again. She must hope for a bush that would bear her weight, if for no more than a moment, in a running scramble to reach the top of the wall, or for some tree with a limb extending far enough to give some chance of a jump. It would be a desperate, dangerous chance, but there wasn't any chance in the world that Meg wouldn't have taken now. If they caught her they would put her in the water. The words jingled and rhymed in her head. They would put her in the water—perhaps here—in the dark—in one of these bog-holes. She would drown in the mud and the slime. And she wouldn't ever see Bill again. Oh no— no—not that—*please* not that! She would take any chance in the world rather than die like that in the dark. And just as her thought touched panic, she heard something move, a little to her left. The sound came to her through the fluttered beating of her heart—a splash, a muffled plop. It was the sound which her own shoes had made before she discarded them, and it pricked her with terror. It was a toss-up whether she ran or froze, but that wild beating of her heart settled it. She couldn't run, because she couldn't get her breath, and while she stood motionless, one hand to her throat, the other clutching an alder bough, she heard the sound again, farther off—and then again, farther still.

The next thing she knew, her teeth had begun to chatter so violently that she had to thrust the knuckle of her forefinger between them to prevent their making a noise like castanets, and oddly, vividly there rose before her the blue room in the days when it was her own room at Way's End, and she knitting the very first jumper she had ever made, and Bill reading "Allan Quartermaine" aloud—the fight at the kraal, and Alphonse whose teeth kept chattering, and the bit of oily rag that Allan gave him to bite on so that he wouldn't be heard and give the ambush away. She had even a sensation of an oily taste in her mouth, just as she had had it when Bill was reading. And then and there, looking back like that and seeing Bill, it came to her that she loved him with all her heart—just like that—all mixed up with Allan Quartermaine, and her first jumper, and Alphonse, and the oily rag. It wasn't romantic and it was the most romantic thing in the world. It was everyday with the light that never was on sea or land shining through—bursting through. It was the End of the Rainbow, and the Crock of Gold, and the Golden Apple, and the Story without an End. And here she was, in a black bog, drenched and muddy, trying to stop her teeth from chattering lest the sound should betray her to a particularly unpleasant death. No, she wasn't trying to stop them now—they had stopped.

She moved forward again. There was a warm feeling

instead of a cold one at her heart. It was just as if she had put out a hand to Bill in the dark and it had found him. She went forward, feeling her way. The ground rose a little and was drier. She trod on a bramble-trail and winched, pulled away from it, and found her ankle caught and flayed. When she was free again she went on. Roots—tussocks of coarse grass—a stump that grazed her shin—more brambles. And then suddenly, dreadfully, her hand reaching out before her touched flesh—the hard, firm flesh of a man's cheek. She felt the bone beneath it, the angle of the cheek-bone and jaw, and the shaved hair harsh against her palm as it slipped. Her palm slipped because she was slipping. The world was falling away from under her feet. The darkness was full of fiery sparks.

She pitched forward into Bill Coverdale's arms.

XXXI

THE ARMS CLOSED ROUND HER, BUT SHE DID NOT FEEL them. For a moment she felt nothing at all, and then waked with Bill's cheek against her own—the cheek she had touched in such an agony of terror just before she fell. She was wet, she was lost, she was being hunted to her death; the bog had her by the feet, and the darkness shut them in; but that waking moment was the happiest she had ever known. To pass from the extremity of dread to the extremity of joy, to fear the worst and to find the best, to wake from lonely grief in her lover's arms—what more poignant happiness could any woman know? The moment carried everything before it—shyness, hesitancy, doubt. She turned her lips to his and gave him kiss for kiss in an eager passion of joy.

The moment passed. She did not know how long it had lasted. It was outside time. It passed. She became aware of her body again, a drenched, trembling thing, and of Bill's lips, not on hers any longer, but at her ear with an almost soundless whisper.

"Meg—what's up?"

She had to whisper too. A word might ruin them, might ruin Bill. She said,

"They're trying to kill me."

"Why?"

"The Cannock—she *isn't*—I think Uncle Henry's a prisoner—*Bill!*"

His arms tightened about her.

"You're all wet—*Meg!*"

"I had to swim."

"It's all right—now. I've got my car. We've only got to get to the gate."

"*Only!*" Meg felt a shaky laugh rise in her throat. The gate would be watched, the gate would be locked. It wasn't any good thinking about the gate. She began to say this with her face pressed against Bill's shoulder, but all at once he stopped her. There was a sound away on their right—a splash, and a rip of cloth. There were more blackberry bushes than one, and more bog-holes.

They began to move away from the sound without a word, pushing through the undergrowth and making for the gate—making, that is, for where they supposed it to be, or where Bill supposed it to be, for Meg had stopped having any ideas on the subject. The points of the compass, the direction of the village, the position of the gate, and her own whereabouts were all gone from her, dissolved in the confusion of this darkness which had drowned everything. She followed Bill because she would have followed him anywhere. Her bare feet and legs were terribly scratched. The way seemed endless.

And then quite suddenly they were out of the wood. The wall rose up before them, solid and black, and between it and the bushes from which they had emerged there was a path. Bill took her by the arm and ran her along it. It was much less dark than it had been in the wood. If you looked up you could see the top of the wall against the sky, and the black massing of the trees. When they came to it they would be able to see the lodge, and when they came to the lodge they would be within one short dash of the gates. But they couldn't get out. The gates were locked.

The lodge loomed up. Bill's hand checked her. She trembled under it and stopped. They both stopped, listening. There was no sound at all. They crept forward until they were level with the side of the lodge, the back door behind, the front door still ahead, the gate perhaps twenty yards away, when with a sudden flash the light of a powerful torch leapt towards them from the drive and was instantly followed by a shot. And no bad shot either. The bullet passed between them. Close as they were, an inch or two higher or an inch or two lower and it would have found no room. It whistled through the gap between head and shoulder—two heads, two shoulders, as close as might be, yet leaving just that gap—and it ripped the cloth of Bill's sleeve as it went, just where armhole and shoulder-seam join. A shout followed the shot.

Bill ducked, and jumped Meg sideways. The ray followed them, and another shot—wide this time. He ran her round the corner of the lodge and in at the back door, and there drove the bolts home.

But he had broken the kitchen window. It wasn't going to take the sportsman with the revolver more than about three split seconds to find that out. The place was a trap. Upstairs would give them the best chance. The stair was bound to be steep, and with any luck it might turn. He made for it, getting out his own torch as they went. And the luck was good. There wasn't any turn, but there was something a great deal better. The stair was one of those enclosed ones common enough in old cottages. It went up between two walls and ended in a yard-square landing with a door on either side. Anyone who wanted to play rough would have to stand in that narrow space and open one of those doors, when it would be the pleasantest and easiest thing in the world to slog him over the head with a chair.

He explained all this to Meg as soon as they had shut themselves into the left-hand room. It was a bedroom, very untidy and ill-kept. The torch showed a few inches of guttered candle in a tin candlestick on the narrow ledge above the fireplace. Bill lighted it. Since it was known that they were here, they might as well see what they were doing. The candle flame, very yellow after the blue white of the electric ray, showed a sloped ceiling, a muddle of bedclothes on a pallet bed, and a battered yellow chest of drawers standing under the window with a cracked mirror hanging half out of its frame.

The opposite wall was pierced by a second door. It stood ajar. Bill took the candle and looked in. Another bedroom, overlooking the front door—the old woman's room by token of a red flannel dressing-gown hanging from a peg. He found a second candle, lighted it from the one he was carrying, and left it on the rickety chest of drawers just inside the door. Then he came back with his long, quick stride to listen at the head of the stair. There was no sound from below, no sound at all anywhere. It might have been Robinson Crusoe's house on a desert island. He looked over his shoulder at Meg.

"Get along in there and find some dry clothes. You can't stay like that!"

Meg dripped on the dirty square of carpet. She had discarded her skirt before she jumped into the lake. Her pale silk knickers were horribly smothered with mud and a greenish slime, her bare legs were scratched and bleeding, her grey woollen jumper was a sodden sponge, but her eyes glinted obstinately at Bill.

"If you think I'm going to put on any of that horrible old woman's things—"

Bill scowled ferociously.

"Don't be an absolute damned fool! You can't stay like that! Get along in there and see what you can find! And step on it, because we're going to have visitors, and you'll be happier with some clothes on!"

She stamped a bare foot and said, "I won't!" and then suddenly ran from him into the other room and banged the door.

Her flesh crawled at the thought of Mrs Henderson's clothes. But yesterday—no, the day before yesterday—she had seen a string of washing hanging out behind the lodge, and if she could find something that had just been washed—

She pulled out the drawers and looked. In the top one there was a most extraordinary collection of things—several pairs of old evening shoes; a tattered plush tablecloth which had once been blue; five or six fans—lace, silk, satin, and even paper; at least a dozen handbags; and two fur tippets in a noisome state of decay.

Meg shut the drawer with a shudder, and tried the next one, with better luck. Here were some of the clothes she had seen on the line. A voluminous flannelette night-gown came first to her hand. It was of a horrid greyish colour, but it had certainly been washed and dried again. It was quite, quite dry. Bill was right, much as she hated to admit it. It was a mug's game to stay in these sopping clothes. She peeled them off, took the next garment to rub herself dry, and pulled the night-gown over her head. If felt warm to her chilled skin.

Well, that was that. What next?

She did not feel equal to Mrs Henderson's drawers, which were made of blue and white checked stuff with very long open legs. There was a pair of these, a roll of unmade calico, and some black woollen stockings. As these also seemed to have been newly washed, she put on a pair of them.

Then she pulled out the bottom drawer. It was filled with the same heterogeneous jumble of things as the first drawer she had opened. There were boots, and table-knives, a woollen scarf, yards of frowsty black lace, a packet of candles, some gingerbread nuts, and a horribly draggled red velvet dress. But right on top of all this muddle there was an unopened brown paper parcel with the name of a Ledlington draper on the outside. Mrs Henderson had been shopping, or her so had been shopping for her, and when Meg had torn open the parcel she felt that they had shopped to some purpose, for neatly folded inside the paper was a pair of strong black stockinette knickers and a thick navy cardigan.

It took her about half a minute to step into the knickers, blessedly new and clean from the shop, and to tuck the night-gown inside them. She had to double it up from the hem and wrap it about twice round her, but that made it all the warmer, and when it was done and she had put on the blue cardigan and buttoned it up she felt grateful to Bill, and a good deal revived. She bulged—or rather Mrs Henry's night-gown bulged—but she was dry, and the feeling that she had forgotten what it was like to be warm and would probably never remember it again became less insistent.

When she opened the door Bill was still at the other one, listening. The minute she moved he spoke.

"Put out your candle and look out of the front window. No one's come into the house."

Meg looked out, waited a while, and came back.

"There's someone there—by the gate. I think it's Henderson. I think it was Henderson who fired at us."

There was a momentary pause. Then Bill said,

"How many of them are there? Do you know?"

"There are the Hendersons—the old woman, and Johnny— he's her grandson—and Henderson—he's supposed to be the chauffeur. I think they're all in it together. I don't think it's the first job they've done together. I think they're all—criminals."

"I expect they are," said Bill grimly.

Meg came across the room.

"Then inside the house there are the Millers. She used to be a pick-pocket, but she cried about their drowning me. He's—" She paused and added in a horrified whisper, "very dangerous."

"Is that all?"

"I've seen another man. I don't think I was meant to see him. I don't know his name. And then—" She broke off. "Bill—you don't know—I'm frightened. Henderson knows we're here. If he doesn't come after us it's because he's waiting for *her*. Someone's gone to fetch her—I'm sure of it—Johnny, or the old woman. *She's* running the show. They won't do anything without her."

Bill said, "Who?"

As he spoke, he put his arm round her and pulled her up to him. The movement had the same roughness which his voice had had when he told her to go and change. It was the first time Bill had ever been rough to her in his life, and all at once Meg knew why he was rough to her now. They were in a tight place, they were in a horribly tight place, and he was scared for her.

He said "*Who?*" again, and she said, pressing up to him.

"The Cannock—only she isn't really—she was just playing at being the Cannock. She can be anyone she likes. She's been Uncle Henry, and Della Delorne—"

"*What?*" And then, "Tell me—tell me quickly!"

She told him, speaking in a soft breathless whisper with his arm round her, and all the while he leaned against the door, listening to her and waiting for the first sound of a step on the closed-in stair. She left the telling about Robin O'Hara to the last. She said,

"They killed Robin—he's dead. They killed him here. They put him in the water. They were going to kill me the same way. She was going to wear my clothes, and pretend to get into a train at Ledlington so that everyone would think I had gone away, and when I was drowned they were going to drive up to town and put me in the river to make it look as if I'd killed myself." A shudder went over her. It was unbelievable and horrible, but it had very nearly happened. And what was going to happen now?

"Look here," said Bill, "we've got to try and get away before anyone else turns up. No, don't shiver and shake like that. Listen! Are you listening?"

Meg nodded against his shoulder.

"If it's only Henderson there, it'll be quite easy. The gate isn't locked—I found the key and opened it. But Henderson thinks it's locked—at least I hope he does—so I propose to make a diversion and see if I can't get him to follow me. I'll draw him away from the gate, and you must slip out, get into the car—it's about twenty yards down the road—and start the engine. Then I'll make a dash for it, and with any luck we'll get clear. If I don't come, drive into the village and raise Cain."

As he said these last words, there came a gentle knocking on the front door.

XXXII

THEY LOOKED AT EACH OTHER IN THE YELLOW CANDLE-light, drawing a little apart. Meg's hair was ruffled wildly all over her head. There was blood on her cheek, and a long green smear. Her eyes looked darkly bright. She said quickly,

"Bill, shall I go and see who it is? I can look out of the window."

"No, you stay here—I'll go. But listen, Meg—keep on listening. If there's a sound on the stair, call me."

He went through to the front room, opened the casement window gingerly, and looked out. The light of a stable-lantern set down upon the doorstep illumined the form of Henry Postlethwaite. The white hair and beard caught the light. He stood wrapped in the folds of his ulster, the broad wide-awake hat tilted off his face, gazing mildly up at the front of the house. As Bill stared at him in amazement, he leaned forward and knocked again upon the door. Then, stepping back, he looked upwards and caught sight of the open casement.

"Meg," he called—"Meg! My dear, are you there?"

Bill felt completely flabbergasted. He said in a low, astonished voice.

"Professor—is that you?"

Henry Postlethwaite stepped back, picking up the lantern and raising it above his head.

"My dear Bill! What a surprise—an exceedingly pleasant surprise! How did you come here? And is Meg with you?

We are in some concern about her. The chauffeur, foolish fellow, is unfortunately the worse for drink, and I am afraid he frightened her just now. Will you tell her I am here, and that there is no cause for alarm?''

Meg's hand fell gently on Bill's shoulder. She put her lips to his ear, whispered ''It isn't Uncle Henry—it's the Cannock—I watched her making up,'' and was gone again.

Bill followed her.

''Do you mean it isn't the Professor? Meg—are you sure?''

''Of course I'm sure! I watched her—stuff out of a bottle, and a wig, and a beard. I should think she's the cleverest actress in the world. Oh Bill—what are you going to do?''

Bill took the spanner out of his pocket and opened the door at the top of the stairs.

''I'm going to let her in,'' he said.

But when he opened the front door there was nobody there. Had some extra sense warned the woman who had stood there in Henry Postlethwaite's clothes? Or had her abnormally sharp ears caught, not the words, but the sound of Meg's whisper? She owed a good deal of her success in the life she had chosen to a lightning-quick reaction to the merest hind of danger. She had not waited for Bill to open the door. The lantern stood against the step, and somewhere beyond its circle of light a dark figure watched the house.

Bill stared at the lantern and the empty space around it, but only for the smallest measurable time. He was behind the door before he banged it to, and the bullet that was aimed at him crashed through the old wood and buried itself in the plaster of the inner wall. It missed the hand on the latch by an inch, and if he had been less quick to move, it would not have missed his heart, for the latch stood breast-high.

He shot two bolts, and met Meg at the stair foot.

''Bill—you're not hurt!''

''Not this time.''

They went upstairs again.

A voice hailed them from the back, and the horrible thing was that it was still Henry Postlethwaite's voice. Even in this tight place, there was a touch of macabre humour in the idea of the gentle, absent Professor flourishing around with a revolver and taking pot shots at them.

The voice said, "Coverdale—" and, Bill having opened the small dirty window to its fullest extend when they first came in, the name was perfectly audible.

He pushed Meg into the corner, stood well to one side of the casement himself, and said, "Well, Miss Cannock?"

"*Really,* Coverdale!"

"Come off it!" said Bill succinctly.

There was the sound of a laugh. It was Miss Della Delorne's laugh, and it made Meg's spine creep. Then Miss Cannock's earnest high-pitched voice said,

"Well, Mr Coverdale, *really!* What a way to speak to a lady! I am surprised—I really am!"

"You'll be a great deal more surprised before you're through," said Bill.

"Oh, I don't know. Do you really think so? Now I've got an idea—but perhaps I shouldn't mention it—it's only just an idea—that the—er—shoe might be on the other foot."

"Now look here," said Bill, "you can stop all this play-acting, because it doesn't cut any ice with me! Let's get down to brass tacks. I'm willing to come to terms with you, because Mrs O'Hara's had enough and I want to get her away. Your game's up."

"Oh no," said the voice from the darkness. "Oh no, Mr Coverdale."

"Oh yes, it is—and you know it. We can stick it out up here for a great deal longer than you can afford to wait. Colonel Garratt knows where I am, and if I don't ring him up within the hour, he'll get going."

"Dear me," said Miss Cannock's voice, "how very thoughtful of you! But you said something about terms—"

"Yes, I did," said Bill. "For the sake of getting Mrs O'Hara away I'll undertake that we'll hold our tongues till tomorrow morning, and you can clear out and be damned to you!"

Miss Cannock's voice sounded shocked.

"Oh, Mr *Coverdale!*" And then it ceased to be Miss Cannock's voice and took on the hard, ringing tones of Miss

Della Delorne. "Nothing doing, I'm afraid. And you can't bluff me. All that about Garratt's bluff. If you'd got anything like that fixed up, you'd see us somewhere before you gave us the chance of clearing out. And now here are *my* terms. You'll come down, Mrs O'Hara first, and I'll give you the same sort of chance you've offered me. We'll lock you up on the island, and you can stay there till Garratt fetches you."

Meg clutched at Bill's arm and put her lips to his ear to whisper breathlessly,

"No, Bill—*no!* She wouldn't dare to let us go—we know too much."

He pressed her shoulder.

"All right—leave it to me."

Then he said aloud,

"That's not good enough. We're staying here."

"Just as you like," said Miss Della Delorne.

He heard her laugh as if she were amused at something. Then she called,

"All right, Johnny, bring them along."

There was a sound of feet, a sound of voices. The handle of the back door was shaken. Della Delorne said without troubling to drop her voice,

"The window's broken—you can get in that way and open the door."

They heard him below them in the house. They heard the bolts go creaking back. Then Cannock's voice came from the dark,

"Mr Coverdale—"

"Yes?" said Bill. He was listening for a step on the stairs and didn't intend to be diverted.

"I thought you would like to know what is happening. I think you had really better reconsider your decision. At the time it was taken you had not all the—er—data before you, if I may say so, but when I tell you that Johnny has just taken three tins of petrol into the lodge, and that as soon as I give him the word he will—er—decant them, you may wish to change your mind. A match thrown in through the window would have very unhappy consequences."

"Keep on listening at that door, Meg!" said Bill. Then

he turned perforce to the window. "Talk about bluff!" he said. "Do you expect me to believe you'd risk a bonfire? Why, you'd have the whole village here before you could turn round."

The amused laugh came again.

"Oh yes, Mr Coverdale—I'd thought of that. But I'm afraid—I'm very much afraid that the village wouldn't get here in time to save you—and Mrs O'Hara. I'm really very much afraid they wouldn't. I've got an idea that the lodge will burn like tinder. I'll give you two minutes to make up your mind. Personally, I would—er—prefer being drowned to being burned if it came to a choice." There was a mocking note in the voice, which just at the end was a strange voice and not Miss Cannock's at all. "Two minutes," it said, and there was a silence.

Meg turned from the door, and Bill put his arms round her. "What are we going to do?"

"I don't know, my dear—try and make a dash for it. It's the only change. *Now*—before they're expecting it."

When he began to speak he had no plan. They couldn't stay here—they couldn't surrender. He had got no farther than that. But even as he said, "I don't know," thought and impulse rushed together into action. He had the door open and Meg half way down the stair before she realized what had happened. The faint candle-light pursued them. There was no light below. Someone loomed out of the darkness of the passage and went down with a clatter across a petrol-tin as Bill rushed him. Meg found herself jumping across the sprawled body. And then they were at the front door and the bolts had to be shot back. The top one stuck, and as Bill struggled with it, there was a sound of light running feet behind them, a small strong hand caught Meg by the shoulder, and the muzzle of a revolver was jammed hard against her spine. She made a little gasping sound as the bolt gave. The hand pulled her and she went back step by step until the width of the room was between her and the opening door. Then Della Delorne's voice spoke sharply over her shoulder.

"If you open that door, I shall shoot! I've got Mrs

O'Hara over here." The hand on Meg's shoulder shook it. "Tell him to put up his hands! If he moves, you're dead. Tell him so!"

"She's got a revolver sticking into my back," said Meg with dry lips.

"Put up your hands!" said Della Delorne. Then she called over her shoulder, "Here you, grandma—bring a light!"

It was a most horrible moment. Bill had put up his hands because he could do nothing else. He stood with his back against the door, and very faintly he could see Meg on the other side of the room. The door opened directly into the living-room. A very faint glimmer of candle-light came down the stair and through the inner door. He could just see Meg against the jamb, with the black figure behind her which was, and wasn't, Della Delorne—the Cannock—horribly garbed as Henry Postlethwaite.

A flickering candle came along the passage. The old woman carried it, holding it up above her head. It showed her white wild hair, her expression of malicious glee. It showed Meg, very white, in the dark blue cardigan and black knickers. It lit up that presentment of Henry Postlethwaite, less like him now that ulster and wideawake had been discarded. It showed the hand on Meg's shoulder, the hand on the revolver. It showed Johnny getting to his feet and coming forward.

Meg stood against the jamb. A sharp edge ran into her shoulder as she pressed against the wooden upright. She felt that, and the revolver against her spine, and the cruel grip of the hand on her other shoulder. She did feel these things, but she felt them with an effort, as if they were happening a long way off to somebody else. And the sound of the voices was far away in a fog, and the sound of Johnny groaning, and scrambling up. She gave a little choking sigh and slipped from the hand that was holding her down on to the dirty floor, and in that moment Bill got his hands on a chair and charged with it straight into the group at the door. It was a kitchen chair with a solid wooden seat and heavy splayed legs. The old woman screamed and ran back. The woman in Henry Postlethwaite's clothes fired two shots, one before the chair leg struck her, and the other from the ground to which she had been hurled. And then, sharp on that, the front door swung in and Bill went down under Henderson's weight and a cracking blow on the head. The man had jumped for him, landing with a fearful impetus. For a moment they were all on the floor together, and then Henderson was uppermost and Bill found himself held in a grip against which he could do nothing. If he struggled he would break an arm—both arms. If this was Henderson, he knew a thing or two about jujitsu.

Bill let himself go limp. He had shot his bolt, and they were in a pretty bad way. There was no point in getting his arms broken. He wondered if Garratt would really come and look for them, and how much chance he had of finding them alive. If he hadn't unbolted the front door before the woman came up, Henderson wouldn't have been able to get in, and they might have had a chance of getting away—a pretty desperate chance, but when it's a choice between a desperate chance and no chance at all you have to take what you can get and be thankful. He had these thoughts in his mind whilst Henderson knelt on the small of his back and the old woman brought a rope and they tied him up, elbows together behind his back and knees hobbled. After which Henderson jerked him to his feet—the man had the strength of a bull—and told him he could walk to the car—"And no tricks, or I'll shoot. And mind you, I'd like to shoot, so you watch your step, Mr Blooming Coverdale!"

The woman had got to her feet. She straightened the wig and beard calmly and without haste. Then she bent down and gave Meg's arm a vicious pinch. There was no response. No shudder passed over the slumped figure. There was no wincing of the flesh, no indrawn breath. She pinched again, and straightened up.

"You'll have to carry her," she said. "I don't think she's shamming, but you can tie her wrists to be on the safe side."

Bill's boiling fury must have showed in his face, for she came up to him, laughed a little, and flicked him lightly on the cheek.

"You big fool!" she said, and laughed again.

They came out of the lodge, Henderson first with Meg over his shoulder, head and hands hanging limp, face deathly pale in the candle-light. They had set the candle down on the table. It guttered in the wind of the open door, and the room they were leaving was full of shadows. Bill could just shuffle along. The old woman laughed at him and pulled mocking faces. It was a singularly ignominious approach to death.

Neither Bill nor Meg had heard the car. It was out of sight of the lodge just round the bend of the drive, with the engine ticking over but no lights showing. The most humiliating part of a humiliating experience was being hoisted and dragged into the back seat, with Meg flung down on it like a dead thing. He had a moment's horrible fear that she was dead, that one of the shots had struck her and she was dead—already. And then it came to him that he ought to be glad, because they were going to kill them anyhow, and Meg would be saved the pain and fear of dying.

The car began to back along the drive until it came to the first of the open ground, where Henderson made his turn and took them smoothly up to the house. There were six of them in the car, the woman and Henderson in front, and Miller and Johnny at the back. He didn't know where Miller had sprung from, but he was here now, and when they got out of the car and came in at the door, it was he who carried Meg, and Johnny who shoved Bill up the steps, while Henderson turned the car again and then stayed there ready at the wheel, with the engine running.

They were in the hall with its one dim light which merely served to make the gloom visible. The woman had the lead. She was still bare-headed and coatless, but Henry Postleth-waite's ulster hung over her arm and his black wideawake dangled from her left hand. In her right she held the revolver. Miller came next to her, carrying Meg, with one arm under her shoulders and the other under her knees. Bill and Johnny brought up the rear. Bill could only just hobble. At every step he was in danger of pitching forward upon his face. His arms were crossed and bound behind him, and the cruel strain disturbed his sense of balance. He felt oddly top-heavy, as if he were a mere trunk without limbs. As to his mental state, it was one of savage despair.

"Straight through the house," said the woman. She still used Miss Cannock's voice. Perhaps she had used it so long that she used it now without thought.

Bill's despair deepened. Straight through the house meant straight to the edge of the lake—at least he took it that way. It meant the end. It meant that they were to die now. He prayed that Meg wouldn't wake up. Let her sleep and not know. But a horrified flash of imagination showed her waking at the cold touch of the water—waking unprepared to an instant of panic fear—perhaps screaming. He prayed he would be dead before he heard her scream.

And then, sudden and sharp on the front door, there came a loud, insistent knocking. There was just the one instant of shock, and then the woman was giving her orders, low and steady. "Run them into the blue room! Come back at once!" And with that she was gone into the empty room on the right whose windows commanded the entrance.

Bill was propelled forward by Johnny. Miller turned once to say, "Make a sound and she's dead!" And so they came to the blue room. It was dark, but no one waited to make a light. Meg was thrown down on the floor, Bill shoved in so that he came down across her. The door was shut. The sound of running feet advertised Miller's haste to be gone. The knocking on the door persisted—a loud, continuous rat-rat-tat.

Bill had fallen with his head against Meg's shoulder, and now in the dark he felt her move. Through the sound of the knocking he heard her catch her breath and say his name in a piteous voice like a child's.

"Bill—is it you?"

"Meg! My darling! You're not hurt?"

Foolish, senseless thing to say on the edge of death, but it said itself. His heart was broken with his love for her, and her danger. He could not have said what words he used.

She gave a small bewildered sob.

"I—don't know. Where are we?"

Bill was making strenuous efforts to get up. He was on his knees as he said,

"In the blue room. Meg, get up! Can you? There's someone knocking at the front door. With any luck it's Garratt. But we ought to get out of here, because she may send someone back to finish us."

Meg's wrists were tied, but her legs were free. She got up feeling giddy and bruised. With a jerk and a struggle, Bill was on his feet.

It took them a minute to get the door open. They stumbled into the hall as a very large policeman entered it from the other side.

XXXIII

COLONEL GARRATT CAME INTO THE HALL A MINUTE LATER by way of the front door, which the large policeman had obligingly opened. He was in a very bad temper and made no attempt to conceal it. The spectacle of Bill in process of being unroped twisted his mouth into a sardonic grin. He used regrettably strong language before he noticed Meg, and then failed to apologize for it.

"Got away?" he said. "Of course they got away! It's all that damned fool Murray's fault! I never knew a Chief Constable yet—" He checked himself, glared at the large policeman, and barked, "Can't talk here! Where's a room? What's been happening? You look as if you'd been making a fool of yourself too! I suppose I'm the *deus ex machina!*"

They went into the blue room and put on the light. The sofa on which Meg had slept her drugged sleep was still pushed against the wall. Bill pulled it out, but she shuddered away from it and found a chair instead.

"Well?" said Garratt. "What's up? What have you been

doing? Murray's away chasing them—but he won't get them, the silly old fool! I denied myself the pleasures of the chase''—he smiled malevolently—"in order to find out just what kind of a fool you *had* been making of yourself.''

Bill, stretching his arms, flexing the muscles, desisted for a moment in order to grin amiably and say,

"Always the perfect little gentleman—ain't you, Garratt? The glass of fashion and the mould of form, and all that!''

"How did they get away?'' said Meg quickly.

"Yes, we'd like to know that.''

"Murray's a fool,'' said Garratt, "and I told him so. We drove up to the door—by the way, I suppose that's your car outside by the gates?''

Bill nodded.

"And you may thank me that you were able to drive in at all, because if it hadn't been for my superhuman intelligence in burgling the lodge, finding the key, and unlocking the gates, you'd be stuck outside them still—and a fat lot of use you'd have been to us there. But go on with your story. You drove up in style—and then what happened?''

Garratt scowled at him.

"One of Murray's beef-headed policemen banged on the door. No one came. He went on banging. And when plenty of time had been given for everyone to get away who wanted to, a car came out of the hinterland and biffed off into the blue at a hundred m.p.h.'' He laughed his barking laugh. "And Murray's gone chasing them in his old buzz-box!''

"Um—'' said Bill. "That would be Henderson. The car's a Bentley. He carted us up here and turned, and when he heard you coming he must have backed her up the drive out of sight. I wonder how many of them he took on board.''

Garratt made his horrible grimace.

"He seemed to have a busful. Murray's beefeaters are searching the premises. Not my job, thank heaven!''

"Is any of it?'' said Bill with atrocious ingratitude. "I won't say we weren't glad to see you, but I'd like to know how you got here, embedded, so to speak, in a solid mass of County constabulary?''

"I suppose you think you're funny!'' said Garratt.

"Oh no—it's only intelligent curiosity. Was it my message that brought you? I left one for you, but it doesn't explain the constabulary."

"Henderson explains the constabulary," said Garratt briskly.

He was warming himself at the sunk fire. He rattled a shovelful of coal down upon the embers, kicked them into a blaze, and went on speaking.

"Beastly cold room this! Damned damp here! Mrs O'Hara looks frozen. Yes, Henderson accounts for the constabulary. He's an old lag—string of aliases, string of convictions—mostly robbery with violence—and he's wanted for a job in the Midlands. One of Murray's bright lads spotted him in Ledlington the other day—made some inquiries on his own. Murray had the whole thing up before him this afternoon. Well, he was dilly-dallying over it, afraid of running his head against a stone wall—Henry Postlethwaite's household—Henry Postlethwaite's chauffeur—Henry Postlethwaite's international reputation. Murray's an old woman, you know, and he was afraid to tackle it—afraid of its being just the sort of business it's turned out to be. Well, he came up to town, dined at his club, saw me, told me all about it, and right on top of that my man rang up—said you'd been calling me, said you'd left a message to say you were off to Ledstow Place. I told Murray we'd better make a night of it, trotted him off to collect his posse, and we arrived, I gather, in the nick of time. And now I'd like to hear your end of the business."

"Tell him, Meg," said Bill.

Meg was curled up in one of the blue chairs, a boyish figure in the black stockinette knickers and navy cardigan, with the old woman's night-gown showing like a shirt in front. Her hair had dried in rumpled curls. The colour had come to her cheeks again, her dark blue eyes were brilliant. She told her story well and quickly, and when she came to the scene in Miss Cannock's room and described the astonishing changes she had witnessed from her hiding-place on the top of the wardrobe, Garratt suddenly slapped his thigh and burst out:

"Maud Millicent, or I'll eat my hat!"

Bill and Meg repeated the names—"Maud Millicent!"

Garratt slapped his thigh again and recited in jerks: "Maud Millicent Deane—daughter of the Reverend Geoffrey Arthur Deane—born Jan. 1st 1900—married 1919 John Harold Simpson bachelor, and, December 13th 1929—Simpson having gone west—Bernard James Mannister—*the* Bernard James Mannister." *

"Lord!" said Bill. "You mean she's the woman in the Denny affair?"

Garratt nodded.

"She was the Vulture's right hand while he lived—she's run the show since he died. She can act any part, write any hand, mimic any voice." He stopped, fascinated Meg by gritting his teeth audibly, and added with concentrated bitterness, "And that chump Murray's let her slip through his fingers!" He kicked at the fire, and the flame shot up. Then he swung round and snapped out, "How was she dressed?"

"As Uncle Henry," said Meg. She jumped out of her chair, ran to Garratt, and caught him by the arm. "Oh, Colonel Garratt—*Uncle Henry*—we've forgotten Uncle Henry! How *could* we? He's on the island! Oh, please come and see if he's all right!"

"*Island?* What island?"

"There's a bridge," said Meg. "It goes over to the island. This house is on the edge of the lake. It belonged to an old lady who was rather mad and thought everyone was trying to kill her, so she built another house on the island and shut herself up there. The bridge has a door at each end, and the one at this end's been broken down, but the other one's locked. Oh, do come quickly!"

Garratt scowled, walked to the door, opened it, and bellowed. When the large policeman arrived his manner was very respectful indeed.

"If you please, sir, there's nobody in the house at all except for an old woman that Hawkins has brought up from

* See *Walk with Care*.

the lodge and the cook that's crying her head off and says she don't know nothing.''

So they had jettisoned the old woman and poor Milly. Meg determined to do what she could for poor Milly who hadn't wanted her to be drowned, and had cried almost as bitterly as she was now crying for herself.

They proceeded to the bridge and passed the burst door, which hung drunkenly from one hinge, and the smashed window through which Meg had dived into the lake. The second door took some breaking down, but in the end it gave, and they came into a little dark hall on the farther side of which a line of light showed beneath a closed door.

It was Meg who ran forward and opened it. The three men came up behind her. She stood with the door in her hand and stared into the room. It was a very untidy room. The walls were entirely lined with books. The fire was out, the air was cold and damp. A brilliant globe hung from the middle of the ceiling. Beneath it at a crowded table sat Henry Postlethwaite writing busily. At Meg's exclamation, an exclamation which came very near to being a sob, he looked round for a moment, put up his hand in the familiar gesture which enjoined silence, and bent again to the foolscap page.

There was a prolonged hush. Meg's eyes were full of tears, because she really hadn't been sure that Uncle Henry was alive. She stared through her tears. Bill stared. Garratt stared. The large policeman stared. They had made enough noise to disturb the dead, but they hadn't disturbed Henry Postlethwaite. The breaking down of a door had made no more impression upon him than had the fact that the temperature of the room was rapidly approaching freezing-point. Like Gallio he cared for none of these things. On some remote intellectual plane he gave battle, he prevailed.

He wrote to the end of the page. Then he flung down his pen and turned with an air of triumph to the staring group at the door.

''That settles Hoppenglocker!'' he said.

XXXIV

THE HOUSE ON THE ISLAND GAVE UP ENOUGH EVIDENCE to consign Maude Millicent Mannister and her associates to a very long term of penal servitude, even if they escaped on the capital charge of murdering Robin O'Hara. But "first catch your thief" is a very practical proverb. They were not caught, and therefore they could neither be hanged nor imprisoned. The Bentley was discovered in a garage on the outskirts of London, but Maud Millicent, Henderson, Miller and Johnny seemed to have vanished into space. Ledstow Place had provided them with a safe retreat for a year. From the house on the island had emanated a flood of forged notes which baffled the police for months. Miller was an expert engraver, and had already served one sentence for forging and uttering. Henry Postlethwaite, who had been persuaded to the house by his secretary under pretext that it would afford him complete seclusion during the critical later stages of his book, was slow to suspect, and slower still to discover, that there was anything wrong with his household. It is difficult to say what first aroused his suspicions, but once it became evident that they had been aroused, he found himself a prisoner on the island. His precious manuscript was confiscated, and the threat held over him that it would be destroyed if he gave any trouble. Under this threat he signed cheques, signed letters typed by Maud Millicent, and was in return graciously permitted to go on with his book. On the day of Bill's visit he had seen him go down the drive. He had mislaid some important notes, and his search for them had taken him into the attic where many of his books and papers were stored. Its windows looked over the wall which surrounded the island, and across the lake. When he saw Bill going down the drive—going away, he made a bid for freedom. The window had probably never been opened since the house was built. Its bolt had rusted fast. Henry Postlethwaite took up a book and broke the glass, but before he could lean out or call the attic door flew open and the boy Johnny ran in upon him. There had been a painful and undignified scene—there had even been something of a struggle. Henry Postlethwaite refused to go into details about this. His cheeks flushed, and he assumed a vague hauteur which discouraged further questions.

He had, not unnaturally, taken a great dislike to Ledstow Place, and intended to return without delay to Way's End.

"And we shall have to let him have the Evanses," said Bill with a groan.

"I'm afraid so," said Meg. "But you know they always would have called me Miss Meg, and never really believed I was quite grown up, so perhaps it's just as well."

Garratt pulled strings. Formalities were gone through with what the official mind obviously considered indecent haste, and Robin O'Hara was pronounced legally dead.

Garratt as well as the bank manager was present when Meg opened the packet which O'Hara had deposited at the bank just before his disappearance. It contained a couple of snapshots and half a sheet of paper. One of the snapshots showed the Millers, the other Henderson standing by the car in his chauffeur's uniform. There was a note on the back of each. On the first: "Compare Rogues' Gallery Scotland Yard—Crooked Sue." On the second: "Think this is the Basher. See Rogues' Gallery."

The sheet of paper contained a very few lines of writing in the form of rough notes:

"Chauffeur's photograph—Henderson, Ledstow Place. Good references. Forged?"

"Second photograph—Millers, Ledstow Place. Man and wife."

"Cannock—secretary, Ledstow Place. Very good references from Professor Oliver Smallholm, deceased."

That was all.

Garratt put the paper down.

"The real Miss Cannock died just a month before Maud Millicent used her references to get the job of secretary to Henry Postlethwaite. By the way, I wonder what's happened to the woman she replaced—Williams—Wallace—what as her name? She left because she was ill, didn't she? So did the Evanses leave because they were ill!" He laughed his barking laugh. "I wonder if she ate toadstools too. I wonder whether the real Miss Cannock ate 'em, poor soul. Quiet, retiring woman—invaluable secretary—no friends, no money, no private life—no relation nearer than a distant cousin. Maud Millicent just slipped into her shoes and wore 'em as if they belonged to her. She's a dab at a secretary's job anyhow—that's the way she got round Mannister. I see he's begun speechifying again, the old gas-bag. I wonder what he would have said if we'd nabbed her. He likes the limelight, but he might have found it a bit too strong. Well, we shan't get her now—not until next time." He grimaced and shuffled his papers together. "That's one thing—there's always bound to be a next time, and one of these next times Maud Millicent will slip up, and when she slips we shall be waiting for her. She's got away with being Asphodel, and Geoffrey Deane, and Della Delorne, and the Cannock woman, but some day she'll go too far and she won't get away with it. Blackmail—forgery—murder—we'll get her some day, and when we do she'll have a damned heavy bill to foot."

He pushed back his chair, stood up, nodded abruptly to the manager, and went out.

Bill and Meg followed him a few minutes later. They walked silently along the grey street and did not speak. Bill was wondering about Della Delorne. Had she attracted Robin O'Hara? Had he sought her because she attracted him, or because he suspected her? Or had he begun by being attracted, and ended in suspecting? On that last night before he went down to Ledstow Place and to his death what had happened between them? Something, beyond all cavil. He had tried to send a message, and because a girl had been in a larking mood his message had gone up in smoke. What had he feared? What had he discovered? What had he written on the scrap of paper which had been burned? No one would ever know.

Meg was thinking her own thoughts—sad thoughts, hurt thoughts. Robin had been her husband. They had loved each other, and then they had stopped loving. Or perhaps he had never loved her at all. Perhaps there was no real power of loving in him—only a hot flare of passion, and then cold ash. Or perhaps not even that. Perhaps he had only wanted Uncle Henry's money. . . . She mustn't think of that. She must only think that he had died doing his duty.

They walked to the flat. A little rain began to fall. When they came into Meg's sitting-room it was so dark that Bill put the light on.

Meg went to the window and stood there looking out. The dreary houses opposite were grey against the leaden sky. She felt tired, and old, and without courage for the future. Bill oughtn't to marry someone like that. He ought to marry someone gay, and happy and full of life. A most unregenerate feeling of dislike for this imaginary female warmed her a little. She turned as Bill came up to her and put an arm about her shoulders.

"What's the matter, Meg?" And then, "Did you hate it very much, my darling?"

She nodded. Her eyes stung. Bill loved her—he did really love her. It was in his eyes when he looked at her, and in his voice when he said "My darling."

"It's all over now," he said. His arm tightened and he gave her a little shake. "When are you going to marry me?"

"Bill—I've been thinking—you oughtn't to. I feel as if—I mean—you ought to marry someone who hasn't been under a steam-roller."

"Do you feel like that?" said Bill. He put his other arm round her.

She nodded.

"Yes, I do."

"You won't when we're married." His voice was strong and confident.

"How do you know?"

Bill looked at her. It was a loving, teasing look.

"Silly muggins!" he said.

"Bill!"

"You are!" He kissed the tip of her nose. "Any special girl you'd like me to marry instead of you?"

"N-no," said Meg.

"You'd have to hustle a bit, because I'm going to get married next Monday as ever is."

"Are you?"

Meg looked up, and then looked down again. She wasn't quite sure whether she was going to laugh or cry. She felt somewhere between the two. But she wasn't cold, and sad, and grey any more. She felt warm and full of light. It wasn't just Bill's arms that were round her, it was his steady unchanging love—a love so sure of itself and so sure of her that it could laugh a little tenderly, tease a little, and hold her all the time. She knew that he would never let her go.

She said against his shoulder,

"Are you, Bill?"

And Bill said,

"*We* are."

THE END